The
QUI
GIR

DETECTIVE CARRIE FLYNN SERIES:

The
QUIET
GIRLS

J. M. HEWITT

Bookouture

Published by Bookouture in 2019

An imprint of Storyfire Ltd.
Carmelite House
50 Victoria Embankment
London EC4Y 0DZ

www.bookouture.com

ISBN: 978-1-78681-877-5
eBook ISBN: 978-1-78681-876-8

For Lou and Lisa. Two of the strongest women I know.

PROLOGUE

The man smiled. Carrie knew he was smiling even though she couldn't see the baring of teeth. It was a feeling, a knowledge. It wasn't visual. His face was a blur, non-existent. All she could see was his form, tall and strong. Stronger than her. Stronger than her sister.

Her sister.

Carrie lowered her gaze from the monster's non-face. Her sister stood by him. Her feet wheeled in the leaves under her shoes as she tried to escape him. A surge of hope inside Carrie as she silently urged her sister on.

But the little girl didn't come to Carrie. Carrie took a faltering step forward. Underneath her, the snow crunched. Carrie looked down. Snow? She blinked, confused; it was the height of summer. Her mother had made her wear sun cream.

A fresh snow shower fell; tiny icicles piercing at Carrie's skin. It bolstered her and she planted her feet firmly on the glittering, white ground. She would have to go to her sister.

She took another step forward. The man smiled again, slow and lazy. For a split second his face was visible, and she concentrated hard on his features, knowing she would need to remember him in the future.

A jagged shard of lightning, accompanied by a crash of thunder. A scream from her, or her sister? A single laugh from the man.

Then he was gone. And her sister was gone too. All that remained on the clear, white landscape was a single drop of blood, which grew and multiplied and spread.

*

The howl woke Carrie and she sat bolt upright in bed. She crawled to a kneeling position, circling atop her bed, seeking the source of the terrible, animal noise. She collapsed face down, the only sound her panting, heavy breathing.

She was the one who had screamed.

Carrie kept her eyes closed for a long minute, before turning to peer at the clock. Four a.m. From bitter experience she knew sleep was over for the night.

Sighing, Carrie dragged on her tracksuit and retrieved her blanket from the floor. Pulling it around her shoulders she padded softly out of the bedroom. In the kitchen she started the coffee machine and while it brewed she walked to the balcony doors and stared out over the Salford canal.

Nobody was around, the water was silent, black, eerie. She moved outside, gripped the railing and thought back over the dream. At the time, inside the dream, it had been terrifying, but it would soon fade to be stored away in the dark corners of her mind.

Like the detective that she was, Carrie went over each stage of the nightmare while it was still fresh in her memory. That face. *His* face, or rather, the lack of it. Always the same, unidentifiable, unknown, impossible to see. The way it was in real life.

Just as it had been on that awful, life-shattering day twenty years ago. Just the way it always would be. No hope of identifying him; no capture, arrest or justice.

Carrie banged her fist on the metal railing, not even feeling the sting. She breathed deeply, exhaled, tried to let her anger drift out over the still waters below. But her rage was fierce tonight, more so than usual.

Spinning on her feet, Carrie stormed back inside and headed for the door. Abandoning her coffee, she grabbed her running shoes and stepped out into the silent, early dawn.

1

They were there, where they'd said they would be, in front of Café Rouge. Pinpricks in the distance, but it was them all right. They were unmissable.

Eleven-year-old Melanie Wilson slowed her pace, all eagerness at meeting *them* vanishing in a second, fear in its place. Because these girls were the big-shots of the school, and she couldn't believe they'd let her, plain and nerdy Melanie Wilson, meet up with them.

She should be feeling great, but instead she felt bruised by the way her morning had started. She cringed inwardly, remembering the way she'd snapped at her dad when he'd commented on her heavy make-up. Retorting back to him that maybe *he* should show her how to put it on, seeing as he was the housewife of the home. Her face burned in shame and belated regret. She loved him more than anyone, more than even her mother and would never normally dream of talking back to him the way she had this morning. That look in his eyes. Like she'd physically hurt him. She'd made her dad sad, all because she was so nervous about this half-term meeting with the girls today.

Something like a sob hitched in her throat. She contemplated ditching Tanisha and Kelly before they saw her and returning home to her dad, getting him to take her into town for a hot chocolate like he used to.

She was twenty feet from them, unable to decide, when Tanisha looked up, clocked her and nudged Kelly. Chins up, they began to walk away. Melanie panicked, her father momentarily forgotten, and broke into a run. Why were they leaving?

'Guys, wait for me!' she called, closing the distance easily in her trainers; their heels were no match for her.

She studied their backs as she hurried towards them, Tanisha's raven-black hair, Kelly ice-blonde. Both pulled back in slick, tight ponytails. Self-consciously, Melanie tugged at her own brown, shoulder-length hair. Around the girls in front of her who strode with confidence, hands on hips, a shadow nestled against their bodies. Tanisha: a brilliant, bold blue like the sky on a really hot summer day. Kelly shimmered silver and grey, like marble.

Melanie always saw the colours in people. She had made the mistake of telling her mother once. Alice had been worried, talked about brain tumours. Harry had told Alice it was just Melanie's creative side coming out in her, the left half of her mind. Melanie preferred Harry's theory, and she stopped mentioning the colours she saw after that.

Was it just her or did they seem reluctant as they came to a stop? No matter; she forced a smile as she greeted them. The smile faltered, though, when she looked at their faces. Bare skin that glowed without a scrap of make-up. Suddenly her cheeks felt taut and heavy with the powder that caked them.

Tanisha appraised her coolly. 'Heading to a night club, sweetie?' she asked, earning a snort of laughter from Kelly.

Melanie blushed underneath the foundation. 'So, what are you up to?' she asked brightly.

Kelly shrugged, looked Melanie up and down. 'Why is your name so boring?'

Melanie looked down at her feet. *She* could talk, Kelly wasn't exactly original. She'd never say that though. And at least her own name meant something. She was named – according to her father – after one of the greatest unsung heroines in a novel; Melanie Hamilton in *Gone with the Wind.* She couldn't tell Kelly that though; no way would either of these two have even watched the film, let alone read the book.

She didn't like to think of her name anyway. Not since she'd overheard a conversation between her parents.

'My Melanie, just like the character,' Harry had said with pride. 'Well bred, educated, the moral compass of the whole story.'

Alice had frowned. 'Melanie Hamilton was downtrodden, used, cast aside. She was second best to Scarlett O'Hara, always.'

Melanie had crept away, troubled. If Scarlett was the best, why had they named her Melanie?

Melanie looked down and away over the water. Years ago, her mother had brought her here every day during the six-week holiday. A summer that seemed to stretch on forever, day after day of hot sunshine, the way it should be, her mother had said.

But they hadn't been out here enjoying the school-free season. They'd had to escape from the house because her father had been ill.

They thought she'd forgotten about *that time*. They presumed she had been too young to remember. But she recalled everything. How her mum had seemed as taut as a rubber band, likely to snap at any second. The weight loss for both of her parents. Her mum drinking. And her dad, sitting on the sofa with the curtains drawn, blocking out the lovely sun, the television blaring at first, then muted, then off, until all that was on the screen was the reflection of his thin face, the lines deep set into his skin.

Melanie shuddered.

Her dad had got better in the end, and her mum had stopped drinking so much. Everything went back to normal.

But Melanie never forgot.

'Are you coming, then?' Kelly asked, chewing and snapping gum as she walked up to her, standing closer than Melanie would have liked.

'Yes.' Melanie fell into step beside the two girls. 'What're we doing today?'

Tanisha stopped and grabbed Melanie's arm. Her fingers twisted in a painful grip through the brown leather of Melanie's jacket. 'You cannot tell anyone what we do today, right?' Tanisha's eyes, small and dark and mean, bored into Melanie's.

Melanie gulped. 'Okay,' she said cautiously.

Kelly stepped up behind her. She felt Kelly's breath on her neck, minty cool.

'You can't go squealing on us. Can we trust you, Melanie?'

Melanie nodded, her heart beating hard and fast inside her chest.

Kelly stepped away, Tanisha dropped Melanie's arm. They began to walk.

Melanie glanced behind her, towards home, where her father would put on a film and make hot chocolate. Melanie faltered. Or would he be like he was last night, sitting there, seeing her, but staring right through her?

Melanie turned back to the girls. Breaking into a jog, she hurried to catch up.

Melanie shivered as she looked at the house. At first glance it was no different from the hundreds of other terraces in the area. But the windows, covered up with thick, black material made it look unfriendly and scary.

Melanie dragged her eyes away and looked around the quiet street. They were in Eccles, a place that she usually had no reason to visit. She thought of her nice home in the new development, close to Salford Quays. This house, this street, was very different.

Tanisha and Kelly stood off to one side, whispering as they shot quick, furtive looks in her direction. Melanie folded her arms, uncomfortable, but stubborn. She had come this far, she might as well find out what was about to happen.

Moments later, Tanisha and Kelly sidled back to her.

'Do you know what they do inside there?' Kelly asked, her voice rough as grain.

Melanie considered the question as she looked back to the house. Black material, not curtains, maybe blankets or sheets covered all of the windows. Was it a squat? A drug house? Her insides quivered but she tried not to let her fear show.

She didn't want to know, but she asked anyway. 'What do they do in there?'

'Witchcraft.'

'Black magic.'

The girls answered as one. Melanie switched her gaze between them.

Witchcraft and black magic. A warm relief ran through Melanie's body. If that was what it was, there was nothing to worry about. Everyone knew things like that didn't work, didn't really exist. Science was what Harry had drummed into his daughter. Science and arts and literature, things that could be touched and seen and felt. Things that could be proven. The colours that Melanie saw crossed her mind and she frowned. That wasn't science, nor art. It was… magic. She shivered again.

'All right,' she said, 'okay.'

Tanisha blinked twice, rapidly. Kelly scowled.

They crowded her, pushing each side of her as they hustled up the alleyway that ran along the side of the house until they stood outside the back door.

'Go on, then,' whispered Kelly.

Melanie frowned, worried now. You couldn't go into other people's homes, not unless you'd rung the bell or knocked on the door and the person who lived there opened it and invited you in. Melanie didn't even know who lived in this run-down house.

'Who lives here?' she asked, softly, not taking her eyes off the missing pane of glass in the lower part of the door. It was February, and last night's frost made the black-tiled floor glitter.

'Who cares?' Tanisha snapped back. 'Nobody's home, are they?'

Kelly moved in close to Melanie. Yanking on her arm she pulled them both low into a crouch. Melanie felt her breath coming faster as she stared through the broken door into a kitchen.

'There's nobody in there, and if there is…'

Melanie snapped her eyes back to focus on Kelly. *If there is… what?*

Melanie waited. Kelly reached into the back pocket of her jeans, pulled out something concealed in a closed fist. Slowly she spread her fingers. Melanie looked at the silver piece of metal that sat on Kelly's palm. Kelly moved her thumb, slid it with precision along the shaft. With a single touch came a snap. Melanie lurched backwards as a blade shot out of its hiding place.

Melanie raised her eyes to Kelly's face. Kelly's eyes were wide, the pupils so large they almost hid the glacial-blue irises. In that moment Melanie had no doubt that Kelly would find it so easy to push the knife into some part of Melanie's body. And still her frozen expression would remain the same; knowing, fearless, unapologetic. Behind her, blocking the alleyway exit towards home and safety, Melanie heard Tanisha's heavy footfall. She couldn't go forward either, not with Kelly and her blade standing sentry. No way out. Only in.

Melanie dropped low, scurried on her hands and knees through the gap in the door. Low laughter behind her, rustling as Kelly and Tanisha followed her into the house.

Inside the house was dark, grey, shadowy. Like wintertime, thought Melanie grimly as they passed through the empty rooms. Although it was never this dark in her own home no matter what time of year it was. No matter what time of night it was, come to think of it.

Who lived here? Who lived in a house where the walls consisted of cracked and splintered wooden panels with peeling paint on the ceiling and bare patches where carpet had been pulled up and discarded in dusty, dirty corners? *A drug house*, thought Melanie. *A squat. There will be needles everywhere, spatters of infected blood from missed veins.*

The remnants of a hospital drama she'd watched with Harry last year came back to her. The devastation caused by using and injecting and snorting.

Alice had shouted at Harry for letting Melanie watch such a graphic programme that had been on after the watershed. Harry had patiently told Alice that it was a lesson Melanie needed to learn: better she see the consequences on the television than in real life. That was where Alice and Harry differed in their parental opinions. Alice wanted to shield, Harry wanted to educate.

She stared down at the tops of her boots, glad she'd worn them today, relieved that if she should accidentally stand on a discarded needle there was minimal chance of it getting through the leather and piercing her flesh. Of catching Hepatitis B and the AIDS virus. Harry's authoritative tone echoed in Melanie's head.

She took comfort from the thought that her dad was walking alongside her.

She wished more than anything she'd stayed at home with him today.

And what would Harry say? *Look around, think before you react, things aren't usually what they seem.*

Melanie closed her eyes to the sound of his reassuring voice. Opening them slowly, she looked at Tanisha and Kelly. Did they really believe this was a house where black magic was practised? Who had told them that rumour, she wondered. Or had they simply made it up to try and scare her? Did it not occur to them that it could be something far more sinister?

Tanisha's normally tanned skin was red; blotches stood out in an angry pattern on her elegant, swan-like neck. She saw Melanie looking and pulled her coat tight around her.

'What now?' Melanie's voice echoed like a gunshot around the room that was empty of furniture.

Kelly leapt across to her, clapped a hand over Melanie's mouth. 'Shut up,' she hissed as she pulled Melanie's hair.

Melanie struggled free. 'Nobody's here,' she snapped back before she could stop herself, instantly contrite; nobody spoke with an attitude to Kelly.

But even before she had finished the words a sound came from above their heads.

As if pushed apart by an invisible force the girls flew backwards to stand in three corners of the room. They looked up, the ceiling giving away nothing as to what might be up there.

A scraping, something – *someone?* – dragging along the floorboards. Another noise now from the room they were in; Tanisha, squeaking, gasping, pressing further and further back against the wall behind her. Melanie glanced through the open doorway; the square of daylight in the broken door that they had crawled through beckoned to her. She considered how long it would take to dash to it, pictured her body hurtling through it and then running, running faster and harder than she ever had before.

'Hey!' Kelly's voice, a stage whisper, resonated. Melanie looked over to her.

Kelly smiled. It sent shivers down Melanie's spine. And then Kelly moved.

Towards the hallway.

Towards the noise upstairs.

Alone now. It seemed like hours since Kelly had disappeared. The house was even darker and silent, the walls pushing in against

Melanie as she forced her feet to move down the hall. This part of the house was barren: decades' worth of layers of peeling wallpaper, cracked walls and chipped, filthy skirting boards.

Don't be a hero.

Her daddy's voice, in her head, as it so often was. But he had also taught her to help people. Tanisha was in no state to help anyone and Kelly had vanished.

Melanie had pulled and pushed Tanisha out of her corner and positioned her in a crouch by the back door through which they'd entered the house.

'If you hear anything, anything that frightens you, just run.' Melanie had pointed towards the broken panel. 'Run and get help, okay?'

'Where are you going?' Tanisha's voice wobbled and shook.

Melanie glanced at the ceiling. 'To get Kelly,' she replied grimly.

They could have both run, thought Melanie as she tiptoed through the bleak rooms. They could have got an adult and brought them back to the house to get Kelly out. But what if it had been too late? What if whatever or whoever was upstairs had hurt Kelly while they were wasting time getting help?

Or, a new thought struck Melanie, what if there was nothing and nobody upstairs after all? Melanie would have brought an adult back to a house they'd broken into. The police would be called, they would get into trouble.

She crept down the hallway in the direction that Kelly had gone, moving as silently as possible, wondering what was wrong with Kelly that she had walked willingly into a potential danger and pushed her friends in with her. *And this house…* Here, in the bowels of the place, Melanie could see barely anything, even her hand in front of her eyes.

Up the stairs, the wooden floorboards creaking horribly under her feet. Melanie cringed with each step, with each noise that announced her presence. She stopped halfway, one hand on the banister. It was rough to the touch and she peered at it to distract her from the fear that was welling up inside her. The handrail was splintered, sticky, dirty. Melanie removed her hand and rubbed it on her jeans. It left a brown stain on the denim.

Melanie glanced up. The landing seemed impossibly close, too close. Frozen halfway up the stairs she cocked her head, listened. A wheezing breath, a shadow up there.

Someone is up there! Her brain screamed at her, clipped words that spoke inside her mind faster than she could ever say them.

Kelly?

And then there she was, her ice-blonde hair swinging in her face as she appeared at the top of the stairs on her hands and knees, crawling.

Why is she crawling?

Kelly threw her head back, her hair streamed behind her, tight and taut as something, someone grabbed her and held on.

Kelly screamed.

Melanie screamed.

Downstairs, hearing but not seeing, not knowing what was happening, Tanisha screamed.

Their voices faded, leaving a few seconds of eerie silence. Kelly remained motionless. Melanie watched, darkly fascinated as Kelly's nostrils flared. Her eyes glowed iridescent in the gloom. Melanie gripped the banister again.

Who or what had hold of Kelly?

A movement up there. A leg in view now, a confusion on Melanie's senses, that the leg was uncovered, naked, all the way up to a T-shirt, black or grey or brown that fell to mid-thigh length. Melanie raised her eyes as the rest of the person revealed themselves. An arm, a hand, a face.

Melanie choked on a breath she didn't know she had been holding. Not a face; a monster, or someone terribly deformed.

The colours of this monster, dark red, edged with black. Colour combinations she'd never seen on a person before.

She didn't know she was going to move then, couldn't believe her legs as they pushed up the stairs. She reached out, someone screamed again – it might have been her – and she pummelled blindly against the bare leg while reaching out for Kelly with her left hand. Her fingers closed around material and skin. Kelly's cheap perfume filled her senses as she pulled at the girl. Something gave way, as through half-closed eyes Melanie watched with something near to joy as Kelly's hair slid like silk through the fingers that had trapped her.

Kelly fell forward, grazing her knees on the wooden stairs as she tumbled towards Melanie. Melanie stopped throwing out flurries of slaps towards the beast. She wrapped her arms around Kelly, hustling her past her and pushing her in the direction of the kitchen.

'Run,' she hissed as she shoved Kelly in the small of her back.

They plummeted together, a tangle of arms and legs and hair to land in a heap in the hallway.

Melanie pushed herself to her feet, one hand on Kelly, dragging her along the hall, not daring to look back, sure that the man, the monster, the *thing* was right behind them, would reach out and touch them, any second now…

Melanie shrieked as they burst into the kitchen, her left arm outstretched, ready to collect Tanisha and push her out of—

Her arm fell to hang loosely at her side. The kitchen was empty.

'Tanisha!' cried Melanie. 'TANISHA!'

From outside came an answering yell that rose into a scream. 'I'm out here, come on, come on!'

Melanie pushed Kelly outside first before barrelling straight after her. She saw Tanisha, at the bottom of the front garden, already scurrying away from the house.

Melanie and Kelly ran to catch her, and together they moved at speed, not stopping, not speaking until they reached the end of the road.

Slightly behind them, Melanie glanced at the back of Tanisha's and Kelly's heads. Neither spoke, neither looked at each other. Melanie stopped walking.

Neither of them turned or looked at her.

2

'You did nothing, you let it carry on. I gave you his name, where to find him, but you did nothing.'

Carrie kept her eyes on her partner as they listened. Detective Constable Paul Harper hit the pause button.

'Do you recognise her voice?' he asked, his brown-eyed gaze on Carrie.

She shook her head, lowered her eyes before looking up hopefully. 'Do you?' She frowned, her brows knitting together before meeting Paul's gaze again. 'Is it even a female?'

It was his turn to frown. 'I—I thought so,' he answered cautiously. 'Did you not?'

She shrugged, swept her hands over her eyes, felt her shoulders slouching. 'I don't know. Do you have any clue, remember any case?'

He didn't answer right away. Carrie could almost see the cogs turning inside his head as he trawled his memory, raking over all the cases they had worked together. It wasn't in Carrie's time, she was sure she'd remember instantly. Especially this, being so... close to home. But if it wasn't in her time then Paul wouldn't know; he'd joined the force three years after her.

'Take me through it again, who took this call?' he asked.

'Eddie in the control room.'

Paul twirled a finger, drawing a circle in the air. 'Play it again.'

'*You did nothing, you let it carry on. I gave you his name, where to find him, but you did nothing.*'

'Can you tell me your name?' Eddie's flat, hard voice made Carrie cringe. It was her belief that anyone taking calls should be approachable, unflappable, calm but most of all warm. Eddie, a young sergeant on secondment, was none of these things.

'No, I gave you my name before but you did nothing.'

A hint of panic as the voice pitched higher. *Female*, thought Carrie, definitely female.

'When did this happen?'

Carrie hit the pause button with such force the recorder skidded towards the back of the table, wobbling precariously on the edge. Paul shot out a hand to steady it.

'He sounds bored, Paul.' Carrie glared at him as if Eddie's shortcomings were his fault.

Paul gritted his teeth. 'Carry on,' he said, 'We'll speak to him later.'

With a lingering look that she hoped conveyed to Paul that she would speak to Eddie if he didn't, she pressed play.

'It doesn't matter.' Goosebumps bloomed on Carrie's skin as the voice of the caller turned suddenly flat. 'It doesn't matter, you just need to know that his blood will be on your hands.' A pause, a dip in the volume before the voice came back again, quiet now. 'Just like my blood was on your hands too.'

Click.

A dead line.

The tape crackled before ending. In the silence, Carrie regarded Paul. He looked off into the middle distance, giving her the chance to study him unobserved. Having worked with him for a few years now she often found she could tell what he was thinking; to her, he was an open book. Occasionally though the shutters came down, like now, and he was unreadable.

Carrie dropped her eyes. *Please don't let him dismiss this call.* She didn't know what resonated with this young, unidentified caller so strongly, but there was something in the voice, buried in the pitch and tone of distress. A plea for help. And she needed Paul's backing if she were to delve into it deeper.

This was why Carrie had joined the police. To make up for the one time she hadn't heard the cry. She planned to spend the rest of her career atoning for that one, fatal slip. A cry for help would never go unheard again. Not on her watch.

He looked back at her again, and now she knew exactly what he was thinking. He wasn't pondering the call, but Carrie's reaction to it. Where did he think it stemmed from, her past? Did he notice that it was the young ones, the hidden youth of Manchester that pricked at her?

'Rewind that, just to the last bit,' he said, suddenly.

She did as he asked, bending over the machine and resetting the audio.

As it played, she listened again, not, this time, to the young woman's voice, but to the background. There was minimal noise, all the way through the short conversation, but at the end, the line was muffled, a faint sound, a bird calling?

'There, rewind, play it again.' He had heard it too.

He held up one finger as the high-pitched noise sounded once more. 'Did you hear it?'

She blinked at him. 'Hear what?'

'Just before she says the very last words, the volume falls, like she's covered the receiver. But very faintly, there is a sound in the background. Listen again, tell me what it is.'

Eyes slightly wider now, Carrie flicked it back on. She put her hands on her knees, leaned towards the tiny speaker.

'A train!'

'What sort?' He narrowed his eyes. 'Or is it a tram? Piccadilly? Victoria?'

For a second, she was almost defeated. Her shoulders slumped only momentarily before it dawned on her. She snapped her fingers, flashed him a grin.

'That wasn't a modern train or a tram, it's a steam train!'

He nodded slowly. 'What do you think this is about, Carrie? What do you want to get from this, if you look into that phone call?'

She scrubbed her hands over her face and smoothed her hair back. 'I know it seems insignificant, but that same girl keeps calling. She's been hurt, somehow, and we didn't help her. We didn't stop whatever happened to her. She's going to take matters into her own hands soon, so it means whatever it was is still happening to her. We need to stop it.'

Paul stroked his chin with his hand, pushed himself off the desk and walked over to the window.

'She's the one threatening harm against someone, Carrie,' he said quietly. 'She's not going to be the victim here.'

'You're right, she's already the victim,' she burst out.

'All right, okay,' Paul held up a palm, a motion to placate her. 'So going by what you know, what you just listened to, how do you propose we track her down?'

Her anger gone as quickly as it came, she smiled at him, relieved.

'You think I don't know about trains, about the history of this city?' She tilted her head to one side, looking younger for a moment. 'My mum taught me all about it.' A shadow crossed her face, a look of confusion which passed as quick as it came. 'It's the East Lancashire Railway, the steam train that runs between Rawtenstall to Heywood.'

Paul nodded, intrigued. 'So what do we do now?'

Her eyes flicked from side to side, thinking, plotting, planning. 'Old files, cold cases against young females, pinpoint areas, compare them against the stations on the steam train route.' She looked up, checking he was still listening. 'She could have moved, could have travelled to make that call, but it's as good a place to start as any.'

Paul raised his eyebrows at her. 'And you thought we might have a quiet year.' He smirked, but it was friendly, a smile between comrades who were at their best when they were working side by side. 'So what are we waiting for, then?'

3

Carrie and Hattie – 1998

'Take a hat, put some cream on,' yelled Carrie's mother. As an afterthought she added, 'and take your sister.'

Carrie, one hand on the door handle, had a sudden urge to stamp her foot.

'Ma!' she cried.

Mary Flynn swept into the room, her face almost hidden by the huge pile of washing she carried in her arms. Over the top of the pile of school uniforms she glared at her eldest daughter. Carrie, knowing that look, stared down at the threadbare carpet.

'Do we have a problem?' Mary asked, one eyebrow cocked.

'No,' Carrie whispered.

Mary smiled, her eyes still on Carrie she called out for her youngest child. 'Hattie!'

Hattie barrelled into the room. Carrie groaned inwardly at the sight of her sister. Hattie was six, she wore a Muppets T-shirt, candy-striped pink and white shorts and red trainers. Carrie looked down at her fashionable cut-off jeans she'd begged her mother for and her red denim shirt with faux pearl buttons. Though Carrie was only two years older than Hattie, she felt like a grown-up. Hattie was such a baby!

But arguing with her mother wasn't an option. Mary Flynn had brought her two girls up single-handed, she worked three jobs, had never claimed any benefit, and was a force to be reckoned with. Both Hattie's and Carrie's fathers were gone, long ago. Hattie's dad was black, a fact obvious from Hattie's creamy, coffee-coloured skin. And possibly the reason why Mary Flynn cooed and clucked over Hattie so.

After realising the difference between Hattie and herself, Carrie had stared in the mirror, hating the fact her skin was nothing like her sister's. If it had been, she was sure her mother would love her more. And Hattie was dark, yet Mary still made Carrie put a high-factor sun cream on the little girl. Carrie was confused; adults were so *weird*.

'Sun cream!' snapped Mary as she pushed the laundry down into the twin-tub machine.

Carrie blinked. It was as though her mother could read her thoughts. Obediently she rubbed the cream into her bare arms as thinly as possible, moving on to do her sister's before her mother asked her. As she smoothed the lotion into her sister's skin she watched her mum heave the twin-tub over to the sink where she battled to connect the pipes to the tap. As always on wash day, she wondered why her mother still had the crusty old machine. All her friends' mums had automatic washing machines, some of them integrated into the worktops of their posh, perfect kitchens.

She never asked Mary, though. She knew the answer would be that she had to put clothes on Carrie and Hattie and there was no money left over for a luxury like an automatic washing machine.

Sometimes Carrie wondered why Mary had children at all.

'Sun hat.' Mary spoke without even turning round.

Carrie grabbed it off the side and pulled it down low over her eyes. Hattie regarded her sister warily as she sucked on her thumb.

Carrie put out her hand and Hattie slipped her sticky fingers into it.

'Come on, then,' she said. 'Bye, Mum.'

Mary raised her head, her arms deep in the bowels of the twin tub. 'Back before dark,' she said over her shoulder.

'What we gonna do today?' lisped Hattie as they walked down the road, Hattie's little legs breaking into a trot to keep up with her sister.

Carrie looked back at her. Feeling guilty, she slowed her step. Physically the two sisters couldn't be more different. Carrie was tall, skinny, her arms and legs always seemed too long for her body. Hattie still had the features of a cute child. She was squat and chubby, her cheeks round, accentuated by her sweet, gap-toothed smile.

Hattie took her thumb from her mouth. A string of saliva stretched from her lips. 'What we gonna do?' she asked again.

Gently, Carrie wiped Hattie's face with the bottom of her shirt. Hattie smiled toothily up at her. With a sudden pang of love, she grinned back at her little sister.

'I know where there's a field with horses, do you want to go see if they're there?' she asked.

Hattie jumped up and down. 'Yeah!' she cried, and, 'Thanks, Caz!'

Carrie tilted her head back and thought of the route. She'd seen them when she'd been on a school trip to the park, in the field opposite. Two of them, she recalled, one brown, one grey. Hattie would love them, she thought now, absently stroking her sister's hair. It was Mandale Park, she remembered the name. In their home town of Rochdale. She thought for a moment; the Firgrove Playing Field was a lot closer, but there were no horses there.

Carrie made a decision. Hattie deserved a treat. So did she.

She slid her hand down, wrapped it around Hattie's chubby fingers.

Now, the only way was to work out how to get there.

'Come on,' she said, suddenly feeling positive that the day might not be such a write-off after all.

4

Melanie dragged her feet, hardly able to look at Kelly and Tanisha. Neither of the girls spoke; not to her, not to each other.

What had possessed them to play such a dangerous game? What had been in that house? *That man… his face…*

Melanie's throat felt suddenly thick. She stopped, held her hand against the cold metal of a lamp post. Tanisha and Kelly walked on.

Melanie got on the bus at Milton Street. Using her school saver card she went around and around Manchester. Huddled on the back seat she found she couldn't stop shaking. In her short life, Melanie had been educated about the dangers of society by Harry. He had wanted to prepare her for the evils of the world, make sure she could take care of herself, and others.

Well, she had done that today, but to what cost?

Why had Harry never taught her how she would feel *after*?

Melanie let out a little groan. She looked at her watch. Gone six o'clock. Wiping away the condensation on the window with her sleeve Melanie peered outside. It was dark, had been for ages. It was the one stipulation Harry gave her in exchange for the freedom she was allowed. She had to be back by nightfall, no matter what time of year it was.

She abided by it always, had never let her father down.

Until today.

Melanie shivered again.

*

Alice Wilson flung her bag to the floor, whipped off her coat and strode into the living room. She blinked into the darkness. Where was everyone? Annoyance simmered; Harry had got fed up of waiting for her and had taken Melanie out for dinner.

'Shit,' she whispered, flicking the lights on as she walked into the kitchen.

She was disappointed, she had wanted to fill Harry in on the goings-on of the day. He would talk her down from her dread, reassure her that of course she wasn't messing up in her job, that she was the hardest-working lawyer he knew, that she was of enormous value to the firm.

Leaning against the worktop, she narrowed her eyes. When was the last time she had gone to him with her worries and concerns? She used to do it all the time. *Her therapist*, she called him. She eyed an unopened bottle of wine in the rack and snorted out a laugh as she grabbed it. A bottle was the remedy these days.

She poured a hefty glass.

Carrying it through to the lounge she turned the last light on.

'OH JESUS!' Her arm convulsed, red wine slopping over the edge of the glass, splattering the light switch, the wall and the floor. Alice put her hand on her neck. Her pulse thumped uncomfortably beneath her fingers.

He hadn't moved. He hadn't reacted to the light, to her yell, to the red that was staining the beige carpet at her feet. She put the glass on the table, moved over to the sofa.

'Harry?' she whispered. There was a tremor in her voice. She cleared her throat, tried again. 'Harry!'

Slowly he turned his head to look at her. His eyes were a world of pain. Alice had seen that look before.

Alice felt her underarms prickle with sudden heat.

'Where's Melanie?' she asked.

'I…I don't know.' Haltingly Harry spoke. Frowning he rubbed his arms. 'What time is it?'

'Nearly seven.' She heard the panic in her voice, felt it in her very core. 'Harry, where is she?'

He attempted to stand up but faltered. Defeated, he slumped back in the chair. 'I don't…know.'

His eyes met hers, fear in them now. He turned to face the window and with great effort he pulled back the curtains. 'It's… it's dark.'

She ran to the lobby, yanked open the front door. 'Of course it's fucking dark, Harry! It's late.' Barefoot she stumbled outside, looked up and down the empty, dark cul-de-sac. A shuffle, Harry appeared behind her, moving foggily. She spun to face him. 'Harry,' she pushed her hair out of her face, stalling. But the question was unavoidable now. 'Are you… ill again?'

He seemed to crumple a little then.

'Alice…'

She stared at him. *What?* She wanted to snap the word at him. Wanted to grab his arms and rock him back and forth until the devil that was the depression rattled and rolled out of him. Instead she gritted her teeth. 'We need to fucking find her. Can you help me do that, at least?'

His eyes shone in the moonlight with unshed tears. Her words were harsh, cruel, she knew that. *But Melanie was…*

'Melanie is everything.' Alice took three steps backwards, lifted a finger and pointed it at Harry. 'Find her. Phone her mobile, for Christ's sake.'

She didn't stop to see if he was moving. She broke into a run, the gravelly road tearing her tights as she headed for the bottom of the road. At the junction she looked left, right. Pulled her hands through her hair. 'Melanie,' she called, but her voice was cracked, broken, a whisper.

A bus rushed past, leaving her in a fug of exhaust fumes. It slowed a short way down the road, where the stop was. Through the steamed-up rear window she saw a figure moving and Alice ran towards the bus. She squinted into the night, heard her breath catch in a jagged inhalation as she spotted the brown leather jacket, the big, brown biker boots that she'd begged her mother for. *Melanie.* It was Melanie.

Alice resisted the urge to drop to her knees. Instead she stormed towards her daughter. With each step the relief faded, anger in its place.

'Jesus! Melanie!' she cried when she reached her. 'Do you know what time it is?'

'Mum.'

Was it her tone? That single word. Or the look in her eye? Alice, arm outstretched ready to grab her daughter and shake the living hell out of her instead slipped her hand into Melanie's.

'Melanie, are you okay?'

Her daughter took a breath, eyes downcast.

I can't deal with anything else, not on top of Harry. Not on top of the job I keep screwing up.

The thought was fleeting, but still Alice felt guilty. 'Nothing's wrong, is it, darling?'

Melanie looked up, Alice saw the deep breath that shuddered through her daughter.

'There was a man—' she began, stopping abruptly.

Alice stared, wide-eyed now, all thoughts of Harry and his mental state and her own career gone. Even the relief at seeing Melanie vanished.

'What man?' she asked, more sharply than she intended.

'Can we just go home?' pleaded Melanie. 'It's so cold out here, I just want to be at home, please, Mum.'

Alice shivered as she pulled Melanie close. 'Come on, your dad's waiting, he's been really worried.'

It was a lie. Harry hadn't even noticed Melanie wasn't home.

5

Harry stood at the end of the driveway, frozen. His thoughts rolled over each other, confusing him.

Was Melanie *missing*? What had happened today? He clutched at the collar of his shirt and pulled it away from his windpipe. When had he got dressed? Had he gone out today? Had he *seen* his daughter?

And he hadn't noticed that she hadn't come home.

He coughed gruffly to cover up the sob that threatened to erupt from him and hurried along the pavement.

And what had Alice just said to him? *Harry, are you ill again*? And there was something in her eyes, a plea for him to answer in the negative. To laugh, to look incredulously at her and tell her not to be ridiculous. At the end of the road he paused, rested against a lamp post. Was it too late? Could he tell her he'd been dozing, perhaps, and when she woke him so suddenly he was just confused, still half asleep?

Now Melanie was… *missing?* Shock, sudden and hot rocked through Harry's body, an awakening.

MELANIE!

He felt a cold sweat on his brow. *Melanie was missing, Melanie hadn't come home.* As if emerging from a coma, he drew in a long breath of the ice-cold air. He looked left and right, saw a bus in the distance, two people walking his way.

Alice. Alice and… Melanie!

He tried to hurry towards them, but it was as though his feet were moving through mud. He puffed and panted, reached out for her before he was even within touching distance. 'God, where were you?'

Melanie lowered her head. 'This man,' she paused, swallowed and began again. This time her words came out in a rush. 'This man grabbed Kelly, he had hold of her, he did... something, I don't know what.' Melanie began to cry.

Harry's heart began to beat at treble time. He glanced around, peering into the dusk as though the man his daughter spoke of was here.

'Inside,' he said, ushering Alice and Melanie into the house.

*

It was Melanie's dad's area of expertise, dealing with a crisis. Normally he leapt into action, always had, everything from school bullying to an attempted theft on their car one time. Tonight though, to Melanie, he seemed frozen, staring at his daughter as though she were a stranger.

Instead her mum took the lead. She sat down on the sofa, pulled Melanie close to her. Harry remained in the doorway, one hand on his chest, trying to quiet his breathing.

'What happened today?' asked Alice softly.

Tears sprang to Melanie's eyes.

'I'm sorry, Mum. We didn't mean to...' she tailed off. To what? *To break in to a stranger's house?* That was a lie, Kelly had wanted to, had *planned* to.

Premeditated. A word she had learned from her mother's own work. A word she knew the meaning of. If you planned it, it was premeditated, and because of that you could – would – be punished.

Alice took Melanie's hand and whispered, 'What did he do to you?'

Melanie closed her eyes. Behind her lids she saw. The naked leg. The grubby T-shirt. The horrible, deformed face.

'Melanie!' Alice hissed her name. Harry leapt forward, placed a calming hand on her mum's shoulder.

'Let her talk,' he murmured.

'Nothing, not to me.' To say the words was a struggle. She looked at them both, standing together, her dad's hand around her mother now.

'I don't know if he did anything to Kelly; we heard her scream, I made her leave,' Melanie finished and raised her eyes to meet her mum's again. 'I made both of them leave.'

'Did you see him? Did he say anything to you?'

Melanie shook her head. 'He came around the corner upstairs, he was… undressed, I think. He didn't have any trousers on. He had a hold of Kelly's hair, I think he was angry because we were in his house.' Melanie felt tears rising and she chewed on her lip to stop them escaping. 'He had something wrong with his face, like he was burned, or something.'

'Jesus Christ,' Harry said, his voice loud in Melanie's ear. She flinched.

'What were you doing in the house?' Alice asked, high pitched, eyes round and disbelieving.

'It was a dare.' Melanie felt tears coming again, couldn't stand to look at her dad, knowing he'd taught her better than that. But she was relieved when her dad pulled her close to him. She felt his hands run the length of her ponytail. Closing her eyes she saw the man, Kelly's long hair in his grip. She snapped her eyes open, pulled out of her dad's reach.

'Stay in tomorrow, or call Chloe, maybe.' Alice rose and turned to the window, straightened the curtains, her motions calm and soothing. 'I don't want you hanging around with those other girls.'

'So, I'm not in trouble, for… going into his house?'

Alice covered the floor space in two strides. She pulled Melanie close, jostled Harry out of the way, smothered her hair in kisses. 'Jesus, no, baby. Just… just don't ever go there again.'

Melanie breathed a sigh of relief, turned her face to her dad, waiting for him to join in their embrace. Instead, Harry stayed standing, his arms wrapped around himself, his eyes wide with horror.

*

The digital clock mocked Harry with its numbers. It was 3.08 a.m. A noise; a half-moan. Harry closed his eyes against the darkness, his heart beating treble time until he realised the sound had come from him. From deep inside.

He thought back to what had happened earlier, to Melanie's revelation. It made him feel sick all over again.

A little angry, too. For this was his issue, the whole damn, rotten root of his depression: the fear that something was going to happen to the most important person in his life. Today it had.

The discussion in hushed voices after Melanie had gone to bed; him wanting to call the police, get this poisonous, perverted person put behind bars. Alice, the voice of rationality, had gone into work mode and looked at it from all angles.

'They broke into this man's house, from the sounds of it he was sleeping. What if nothing actually happened? What if he was just angry, frightened even, at finding people in his home?' she had reasoned.

In a flash of unheard-of anger Harry banged his fist on the coffee table. 'They're little girls, Alice,' he'd shouted.

Alice pinched her lips, shook her head slowly. 'They *broke in*, Harry.'

Round and round they went, Harry going so far as to pick up the cordless phone and dial 999. Gently, Alice had taken it from him. She made her disagreement plain, for maybe the first time in their marriage.

'If I'm right, if we tell the police about this and it turns out Kelly bloody Prout was dramatising the whole thing, then our daughter could be in trouble for breaking and entering.'

She had changed the subject then, scrutinised him, her eyes narrow slits that made it seem she was looking right inside him. 'I'm making a doctor's appointment for you.'

Uneasy, Harry had nodded, left the subject of Melanie's near-abduction alone. For now.

Alice didn't stir when he scrambled from the bed and crept into the bathroom. The florescent light hummed a low thrum as Harry made his way to the cabinet next to the bath. For a moment he gazed at his reflection in the mirrored doors.

Who was this man? Harry didn't recognise him. Could find no familiarity in the jaw that sagged and the eyes that stared back at him, dark and filled with pain. A man who'd had no idea his daughter hadn't come home. That was what frightened him the most; that he'd had no idea that his daughter had been at risk. Regardless of what Alice thought, *there had been danger*.

He lowered his eyes as he opened the cabinet, only lifting them when he was sure there was no chance of looking at himself again.

He spider-walked his fingers through the shelves, feeling blindly for a box of medication, nothing in particular, just anything that would either help him sleep or deaden the dread that had curled in a vice-like grip around his chest.

Harry pulled out three boxes and squinted at them. Codeine – could work – hay fever remedies and, oh yes… bingo! Zopiclone, sleeping tablets from when Alice went through a bout of insomnia. How long ago was that now? Harry peered at the label; 2012. Seven years ago. And still they had not passed the expiration date.

Harry popped two from the blister and swallowed them dry.

Sleep was all he needed. Sleep was the healer of all ills, this he firmly believed. It was what his mother used to say.

His mother.

A fresh wave of misery smothered him.

Forty years she'd been gone, along with his father. Quietly Harry closed the cabinet door and forced himself to look in the mirror.

He couldn't live like this. Melanie shouldn't have to live like this. Things had to change; his depression, the state of the world they inhabited, the dangers and the destruction.

Something must change, thought Harry desperately. *Only what? How can I mend this? How can I keep my daughter safe?*

Back in the bedroom, the clock ticked on.

6

Carrie scooped another file off the ever-growing pile of old, cold cases and opened it up. The details inside, like all the others she'd looked at, sickened her.

There had been another call from the mystery victim.

The victim.

It was how Carrie was thinking of her. Paul preferred to call her the perpetrator.

'She obviously has reason to threaten him,' she'd snapped to Paul the second time the call came.

'But it's not how the law works, is it?' Paul had replied gently.

And the case, not that it even was a case yet, but whatever it was kept Carrie awake at night. Something in the girl's voice, some hurt, buried deep for maybe a long time but which was now bubbling to the surface. This girl, the caller, knew that what had happened to her was wrong. She was taking steps to fix it, to stop it. Carrie had longed to be able to do that for herself. She still craved the knowledge, rather than the blank space that filled her head and her memories.

'I will find you, and I will find him,' Carrie whispered to herself.

'Carrie?'

Carrie looked up to see Paul standing in the doorway. Long and lean, he seemed to fill the space, a thought she often had about him, though he never seemed overpowering or threatening. She blushed, wondering if he'd heard her talking to herself.

'I've got an interview, thought you might want to sit in.'

She stood up, bundled the files together and locked them in the cabinet behind her. 'What's it about?' she asked as they left the office and walked down the corridor.

'A mother's here with her daughter. Mum is Mrs Prout,' he glanced at his notebook, 'Victoria Prout. Daughter is Kelly Prout.' He twisted his lips as he glanced sideways on at Carrie. 'The daughter says she's been sexually assaulted.'

Carrie glared at him. 'Why do I get the impression you don't believe her?'

Paul shook his head. 'It's not so much the girl, as her mother.'

Carrie took a deep breath to steady herself. 'Let's do this,' she said.

The girl was a mess. Paul sat across the table from her, trying not to stare but finding it hard not to. He could tell by the styling and the clothes and the make-up this wasn't the way she usually presented herself.

He dragged his gaze away from the girl's tear-stained and mascara-soaked face and looked down at his notepad.

'Can you tell us what happened, Kelly?' he asked, as gently as he could manage.

The girl stared down at her lap, her chest heaving as the occasional sob erupted from her.

'I'll tell you what happened.' The mother leaned across the table, raised a finger.

Carrie found herself mesmerised by the perfectly manicured red nail that pointed at her.

'She was dragged into a house, off the street, pulled upstairs and assaulted!' With each syllable of the last word Victoria Prout thumped the table.

She sat up straight, resisted the urge to look at Paul. *Dragged off the street?*

'All right, we're going to take some details from you, Kelly,' Paul said pointedly at the young girl. He flicked a look at Victoria. 'Is that okay with you, if we talk to your daughter, if we take a statement from her?'

Victoria Prout barked out a laugh. 'Why the hell would we be here if she wasn't going to give a statement?' She threw a disbelieving look at Carrie, hoping to get her onside against him, no doubt. Carrie bristled.

'Mrs Prout, do you want to get a coffee, maybe, and we'll chat to Kelly.' Carrie made to stand.

Victoria Prout glared. 'I'm not leaving my girl.'

'Okay, but we will need Kelly to tell us what happened. Sometimes it can be easier for the person giving the statement if their loved ones are not in the room.' Carrie nodded at Kelly with a smile. 'Right, Kelly?'

Kelly shrugged. Victoria folded her arms. Paul sighed and tried to cover it with a cough.

'All right, I'm going to record this, Kelly, okay?'

The girl didn't acknowledge him.

Paul flicked on the tape.

'I don't want to do this!' Kelly shrieked suddenly, pushed against the table as she stood up. A crash as her chair toppled to the floor.

'Kelly!' At Mrs Prout's yell, Kelly froze.

Paul watched, disturbed, as Kelly crumpled momentarily before rising up to her full height.

'I won't say it again,' she hissed. 'I won't go through it again.' She swiped at her face, mascara smudging across her cheeks. 'You can't make me, I know my rights.' She moved over to stand by the door, pressed her back against it. 'I can't even remember where it was, I'll never be able to find the house again, anyway.'

With that, she fumbled behind her: against the shouts of her mother and Paul's pleas she found the door knob, opened it, slipped through and was gone. The only sound her heels smacking against the floor as she fled down the hall.

Carrie caught up with Kelly outside. The girl fumbled around in her bag, casting hasty glances behind her. Carrie approached quietly and as casually as she could muster. Inside the reception she saw Paul, talking with Mrs Prout. She stared hard at Paul, hoping he would keep the mother inside. He nodded, once, and she smiled. Their working relationship was among the best she'd had. The best relationships – work or personal – were always great when no words were needed.

'Kelly,' she said now as she reached the girl.

The girl jumped, shoved the packet of cigarettes back in her handbag. Carrie's eyes widened.

'How old are you, Kelly?' she asked.

The girl raised her chin defiantly. 'Twelve in a few weeks.'

Carrie let the cigarettes go. Underage smoking wasn't the point here. An alleged abduction was far more important. But before she could think how to phrase her question, Kelly spoke again.

'I don't remember the house, the road, the man. I don't remember anything.'

Something shifted inside Carrie. For a moment she felt light-headed. Her body and mind separated; suddenly she was eight years old again. Seeing a bench a few yards away she stumbled over to it and sat down. Out of the corner of her eye she saw Kelly drifting over to her. Carrie's own childish voice echoed in her mind.

I don't remember. I can't remember. It's all a blank.

The faces of those tasked with interviewing her. Their pinched faces, their eyes thin as they glared at her. Their barely concealed frustration at her inability to tell them what had happened.

'You okay?' the young girl asked gruffly.

'Yeah, sorry.' Carrie cleared her throat, embarrassed.

'It was in Eccles, the house,' Kelly blurted suddenly.

Carrie looked up at her, trying to ignore the headache which sent zig-zagging lights across her vision.

'Probably near Milton Street, I remember walking past the sign for Milton Street when we left.'

Carrie squeezed the sides of her face, trying to keep up, trying to focus. 'When "we" left?' she asked. 'You were with friends?'

Kelly's mouth closed, the shutters came down over her eyes. 'I don't remember anything else,' she said firmly. Kelly's hard stare went to the door of the police station. 'There's my mum,' she said.

'Wait,' called Carrie, but Kelly had gone.

7

Melanie heard the front door close and she walked over to the window. Her mum and dad were making their way across the icy pavement to Alice's car. Alice steered her father to the passenger side and helped him in the car. Melanie's breath caught in her throat as she stared at her dad. He seemed a hundred years old and it hurt.

You did this.

The voice in her head that she'd been denying was suddenly impossible to ignore. It was true, she knew it. Melanie had turned her father into this shrivelled, sad husk of a man. A man so unhappy that her mum was now taking him to see the doctor.

That day, the day of the visit to the house of horrors, Melanie had spoken to him nastily, in a way she never had before. She had sneered at him, jeered at him, told him he was doing women's work, mocked him for washing up by hand and not using the dishwasher. Perhaps what had happened in the house was her punishment for speaking to her dad in that way. Perhaps she deserved the fear she had felt, the horror that stayed with her, sitting in the pit of her belly every single day. Since Harry had found out, he'd barely spoken to her, nor to her mum. Despite what Alice said, that she wasn't in trouble, Melanie knew her dad was angry with her. *She had let him down.*

She covered her mouth with her hand and ducked behind the curtain as he glanced up from the car. From behind the drapes she watched his pale face, his dark eyes, his sad, sad mouth.

You did this.

Unable to watch anymore, Melanie ran to her bed and threw herself down. Putting her face in her pillow she cried as if her heart would break.

*

For the rest of the week Alice watched Harry like a hawk, not going to work, not even calling them, but chickening out and sending an email to the partners instead. The surveillance of her husband was more exhausting than spending a full day at the office.

Doctor Patel had been brisk but kind, his tone and manner suggesting that he saw this a hundred times a week. *Clinical depression*, he had announced, very common. It should have been comforting to know they were not alone. But Alice took no solace in that fact.

The doctor explained it away as a chemical imbalance, but Alice was never convinced by that. What if she, Alice, were to suffer from this 'chemical imbalance'? She would have to push it to one side and get on with things, she wouldn't have time to waste with appointments, time off work and medication. But even as she checked herself with the reminder that this wasn't how depression worked, she still felt a needle of annoyance.

The doctor had prescribed Fluoxetine, and Alice had made Harry take the first pill as soon as they got home. Now, it was a waiting game.

When Alice woke on the sixth day the house was silent. Eerily quiet, like a house of the dead. She glanced at the clock and her heart rate sped up. Ten a.m.! Throwing back the quilt, she ran downstairs to find the kitchen empty.

Where was everyone? She peered outside, noting that she didn't have to draw the curtains. They were already open. As she looked out into the street, she saw the rows of cars and instantly she was

calmed. It was Saturday. She wasn't late for work. And then she
remembered; she hadn't been there all week anyway.

Harry had probably taken Melanie out for breakfast. She
hoped so, hoped that Melanie wasn't out with those girls she'd
been hanging around with lately. They were trouble, a fact proven
by last week's events. She shivered, thinking again of *what could
have happened.* The long discussion with Harry about not calling
the police for fear it would be Melanie who got into trouble, and
not the guy who had grabbed her friend.

But what of that man? What if he hadn't just been a disgruntled
home owner? What if he really was a… a paedophile?

She shuddered. Knotting the belt of her dressing gown around
her she moved into the kitchen. The coffee was on, freshly brewed,
a clean mug waiting beside it.

Harry.

It was something he'd always done in the early days on a
weekend when Melanie was tiny. Saturday lie-ins were a luxury
after being up before dawn five days in a row. Harry would get up
when Melanie woke, and it was too early for Alice to have coffee
in bed. Instead Harry would set up the machine in the kitchen,
leave a mug on the side for Alice and take Melanie out. The
aroma of the freshly ground beans would rouse Alice eventually
and she would make her way downstairs, grateful that she could
dive straight in to her morning caffeine fix.

Now, as she poured, it seemed unfamiliar, so long it had been
since he'd done this tiny thing for her. Like the once-nightly
conversations they'd had about their retirement plan, it was yet
another activity that had fallen by the wayside. And as Alice
sipped the strong, black brew she resolved there and then to try
and get things back to how they'd once been.

Maybe, she thought, they could have a holiday. The three of
them, somewhere hot while it was still cold here. And for the
first time in a long time Alice felt hopeful.

8

Melanie left the house on her own for the first time since the terrifying trip to Eccles.

She took a tram this time, and she didn't tell Tanisha or Kelly where she was going. She didn't tell either of her parents. Alice was too busy, having stayed at home all week; her work stuff spread out over the dining room table, huffing and puffing and occasionally swearing over how far behind she'd got. Her mum had still been in bed when Melanie left the house. Her dad had also gone out and for that Melanie was relieved. Hopefully it meant he was feeling happier.

And now here she was, on the corner of the road where the house was which had scared her more than anything ever had before.

The third house down, wedged between two better-looking homes. For a while, as she loitered, Melanie looked at the houses on either side. *Who lived here? Did they know what went on in their neighbour's home? Did they care?* Or, another awful thought – *did they join in?*

It was something she hadn't considered before, and Melanie pulled her phone out of her pocket and stabbed at Kelly's number.

'Melanie?' Kelly answered, and her voice was nothing like it usually was. She sounded fearful, just the way she had when they left the house that Melanie now stood in front of.

'Kelly, how many men were in that house?' Melanie demanded.

'What?' Kelly's voice was a whine. 'Why?'

'I just want to know.' Across the road, on a little green area, three children played without a chaperone. Melanie felt suddenly furious. These kids were tiny; what if they were lured into the house of horrors? 'What did he do to you?' Her voice faded to a whisper before she found her strength again in her tone. You tell me now, Kelly Prout, or I'll—'

'You'll what?' Kelly's tone was back to normal, sneering and hard as nails.

'I'll tell the police everything.' Melanie felt the heat of rage in her face. 'I'll tell them you lied, that you were not snatched off the street, that you broke into the—'

'All right, shut up,' Kelly hissed. 'I don't know how many men were in there, it was too dark, I didn't see any *fucking*-thing.'

Melanie swallowed as the curtains in the front window swished. She turned her back on the house, as though that man, that creature, was watching, lip-reading.

'What did he do to you, before I came up the stairs?' she whispered.

Silence.

Melanie looked at her phone. Kelly had hung up.

The curtain moved again. Melanie closed her eyes and rubbed her balled fists hard against them.

A naked leg.

The filthy material of a shirt.

A terrifying face.

She backed away. Before she reached the corner, she was running hard for home.

*

Alice had just showered and dressed and was on her second coffee when the doorbell rang. Thinking Harry and Melanie hadn't taken their keys she hurried to open it, eager to try out her vacation proposal on Harry.

When she opened the door, she didn't even recognise the woman on her step.

'Alice, Melanie's mum, right?'

The voice however, she identified that in an instant. Victoria Prout, Kelly's mother. The two women had never met; Harry was the one who had stood all those years at the school gates, and he'd regaled Alice with funny descriptions and impersonations of the other mothers. She recalled his 'Prout pout' as he'd called it, and stifled a smile.

'Hi, yes, I'm Melanie's mum.' Alice shook Victoria's hand. 'Victoria, isn't it? Is everything okay?'

'Not really.' Victoria narrowed her eyes.

Like mother, like daughter, thought Alice now, as she stepped backend gestured for Victoria to come in. *Hard, brittle and mean.*

'Kelly's in a right state with this abduction stuff. What did the police say to you?'

Alice's heart began to pound as she closed the door. *Abduction?* 'I haven't heard from the police, I assumed… I mean, I don't think I'll hear from them now.' Alice swallowed; it sounded loud in the room. 'What did they say to you?'

'The police are shit,' replied Victoria loudly. 'Kelly refuses to say where this happened and they don't seem to think it's important to find out. What did they say to you when you reported it? Did they not even take a statement?'

Alice ignored the last part of Victoria's question. 'Maybe it didn't happen quite the way Kelly thought,' she said, cautiously.

Victoria tilted her head to once side. Hand on hip, she glared at Alice. 'Are you saying my Kelly is a liar?'

At Victoria's tone Alice straightened her spine. 'Oh, God no,' she laughed, trying to lighten the atmosphere. 'It's just when I spoke to Melanie she didn't know what had happened, and Kelly didn't tell her.' When Victoria said nothing, just continued staring Alice shrugged. 'So, I'm not so sure how I could help, you or the police.'

Victoria shook her head very slowly and then, she broke out into a laugh. It wasn't humorous, it was like her smile; blunted, cold.

'You didn't report it, did you?' she asked, disbelief heavy in her tone. 'Does it not keep you up at night, thinking what could have happened to them in there?'

No! What keeps me up at night is worrying about my husband and his breakdown, and the work I'm missing trying to get him better, and the way I keep fucking up in my job.

'It doesn't matter, like I said, the police are shit.' Victoria's eyes grew smaller and smaller as she chose her next words. 'Some of the other parents are going to the house.' A tiny smile before she carried on. 'Are you in?'

'I thought you didn't know what house it was.' It was all Alice could think of to say.

'We don't, yet.' That cold smirk again. 'But we will. Kelly will give up any information to get her iPhone back.'

Oh Jesus. Alice rested against the windowsill and passed a hand across her eyes. 'Victoria,' she said. 'I... my husband has been ill, I can't have him—'

'But Melanie was there, this man dragged her into his house, don't you care?'

'Jesus, Victoria, nobody was dragged into that fucking house, they broke in. Or, more to the point, your daughter masterminded the whole bloody thing. We're lucky the police are not busting down our doors to give a warning to our kids!'

Underneath her full make-up Victoria paled. Alice groaned inwardly, regretting her outburst. That wasn't the way you dealt with people like Victoria Prout.

'You don't know what you're talking about, is that what your precious daughter told you to save her own skin?' Victoria moved to the door and wrenched it open. 'I can tell you have more important things on your mind than your kid's own welfare. If you change your mind, you know where to find me.'

An hour later, the shrill ring of her phone startled Alice. She bolted upright, snatched it up and answered the call, noting even as she did so it was from a number she didn't recognise.

'Hello?'

'Alice, its Victoria Prout.'

Alice closed her eyes. How did Victoria get her number? She exhaled a breath of fury. *Harry.* How many times had she asked him not to give her number out to the parents at the school gate? 'Victoria, hello.'

'I just wanted to keep you in the loop, we've found out the address of the house where Kelly, Tanisha and Melanie were attacked. We're going round there tonight, are you in?'

Alice covered her eyes with her hand. 'Jesus, Victoria, shouldn't you tell the police?'

'Tried that, I told you they weren't interested. I just need to know if you're in or out. Listen, it's Irwell Road, number three. We'll meet outside at seven o'clock.' With that, Victoria hung up.

Alice, still with her head in her hands, let her mobile fall to the table.

With that awful woman off the line, Alice thought about Victoria's call. Irwell Road, she knew that: it was over in Eccles, on an estate that neither she nor Harry would ever consider raising their child on. And what did Victoria mean when she said 'we're meeting there'. Who was 'we'? Tanisha's parents? A whole group of school mums and dads that she'd roped in, perhaps.

Alice shuddered. She needed to get out of the house. Perhaps this was Harry's problem; too little to do equated to too much time to think. Grabbing her keys, she pulled on her coat.

*

At half past six, once all the shops had shut and after driving around aimlessly, Alice fully intended to return home. Instead, she found herself at the top of Irwell Road. She sat in the car, engine idling, the windscreen steaming up until she had to crack open the windows to clear it.

Did she want to drive down to the bottom of the road when the clock hit seven? And what would she do when she got there, or, more to the point, what would she see?

Alice leaned her head back and closed her eyes. Burning torches, women shouting, men hitting. Alice allowed herself a little smile. They were British; they didn't do things like that.

Or did they, when it came to their children?

What if it had been Melanie, the one who actually came into contact with this monster, how would she feel then? A part of her didn't need to think about it. She would want to kill him. But she was a lawyer, she believed in punishment and rehabilitation. Legal consequences. And just what had Melanie seen? A dirty, downtrodden house, a man with a disfigured face, and who hadn't been wearing any trousers. A man who had grabbed Kelly. A man who had done… *what?*

Alice pressed a hand to her lips. Horrid, awful things for young girls to experience. But could it be this man, whoever he was, was simply infuriated that his home had been broken into? Could he have been upstairs, sleeping, practically naked when he was bothered by pranksters?

Alice came to a decision. Victoria didn't know her car; Harry almost always had walked to and from the school run. The windows were steamed up, concealing her in case Victoria should be there. Putting the car into gear she drove slowly down to the end of the road.

*

There were more of them than she'd expected. A mob, she thought, as she watched the dozen or so people circulate at the front of the house.

And there was Victoria, arms waving, pointing at the house. No, Alice saw now, not just at the house, at the face scarcely concealed in the front window. And Victoria was at the window now, using her palms to bang on the glass. The face backed away, the window now empty.

Tearing her eyes away from Victoria, Alice looked at the rest of the group. They milled around, seemingly uncertain, throwing hasty glances over their shoulders at the road and the houses next door. With the heater on, the misted windows began to defrost, leaving Alice visible should Victoria turn around. Alice put her head down and drove away.

9

Carrie and Hattie – 1998

They walked out of the residential area where they lived and headed along the Ashworth Road. After half a mile Hattie began to whine.

Carrie ignored her.

'Caz, my legs ache.'

Carrie walked faster.

'Caz!' A hitch in her childish voice, loud sniffing.

'I know, I'm sorry, Hat.' Carrie slowed to a stop. Maybe this was a silly idea; the park was further than she remembered. She sat down on the grass verge to think.

'Ice-cream?' asked Hattie, hopefully.

Carrie looked away. 'Don't have no money,' she replied glumly.

Hattie fell silent and Carrie lay back in the grass. Even if she did have money, they were out of town now, heading into the green spaces where there would be no ice-cream vendors. She shivered as the sun went behind a cloud. The day was suddenly cooler, and she struggled to her feet. They could easily walk it if the sun wasn't beating down on them.

'Come on, up,' said Carrie, pushing herself upright and crouching down. Her sister rarely got treats, neither of them did. Money was scarce and Mary worked all hours. Hattie deserved to see the horses and Carrie would give her a piggy-back if that was what it took. 'Hop on,' she said, grinning over her shoulder at her sister as Hattie clambered on her back.

Half an hour later they didn't seem to be any closer. Carrie staggered to a stop and lowered Hattie to the ground. It was much further than she remembered, Mandale Park. Which was strange because when she'd gone with the school it seemed to take no time at all. But then she remembered – they had been on a coach that time. Carrie had really enjoyed that day. Just like Hattie would enjoy the horses today. If they ever got there, that was.

'We'll be there soon, at the park. It's a massive park, Hat, with slides and swings and this rope thing that you can play on, then we'll see the horses. You'd like that, wouldn't you?'

Hattie shrugged and dragged her feet. Carrie felt a surge of anger, but it was directed towards her mother. Why couldn't her mum be like other mums, and take her daughters to the park, preferably in a car? It wasn't fair she had to take care of her little sister, if her mum came along then Carrie wouldn't be responsible for Hattie, and *both* girls would be able to have fun.

And the anger helped, Carrie realised as she marched up the umpteenth hill. But Hattie wasn't angry, Hattie was tired, and Hattie was drained.

Carrie stopped and looked around. They were far off the beaten track now, far from home, far from people who knew them who might stop in their cars and give them a lift home. Carrie felt the stirrings of panic.

'Hey, girls, you okay there?'

Carrie snatched up Hattie's hand and averted her eyes. *Just drive on by*, she thought.

But the car engine thrummed as the vehicle stood still beside them, idling until the driver turned the engine off.

'Where are you girls going?'

Carrie chanced a look across at him. The fear vanished.

'Mr Lacey!'

'Young Carrie.' Her school caretaker slung one arm over the driver's door and smiled, showing gaps and yellowing, tombstone teeth. He looked down at Hattie who was hiding behind Carrie. 'Who's this, then?'

'My little sister. I'm taking her to Mandale Park, but I didn't realise just how far it was to walk.'

Mr Lacey smiled even wider. Twisting in his seat he banged his fist on the rear passenger door. 'Hop in, I'm going that way.'

Carrie hesitated. *Stranger Danger.* The words drummed into her at home and school flooded her mind, making it hard to think. But Mr Lacey wasn't a stranger, was he? He was the caretaker at her school, everyone knew him, even her own mother would greet him if they passed in the street or happened to be in the same shop.

Hattie pulled on her hand. Carrie looked down at her.

'My feet hurt,' she whispered.

Carrie looked back at Mr Lacey. He raised his eyebrows, nodded and thumped the car again.

Taking a deep breath, Carrie herded Hattie towards the car.

10

'I think it's about time we thought about a change of scenery.'

Harry made the announcement over dinner. Alice and Melanie paused, forks halfway to their mouths, and exchanged a glance.

Alice regarded Harry carefully. He had spoken no more about Melanie and the horrible situation that Victoria Prout had drawn them all into. Or was this his way of dealing with it, to get them away from Salford and the dangers Harry saw? But if it meant a holiday, a fortnight on a sandy beach… She'd had the same idea herself. It would be good for all of them.

'Well, yes, that would be wonderful.' Alice's face stretched in a smile. It felt unnatural, and only served to remind her how much she used to smile with Harry, and how long it had been since she had done so.

'Where, Dad?' Melanie asked. 'Where are we going to go, and when?'

Harry chased the last of his casserole around his plate with a thick chunk of buttered bread. Alice was pleased to see his empty plate. Along with the pleasure was the all-too-familiar guilt that she hadn't noticed how much his appetite had decreased since the depression had come back. She put her fork down and gripped his hand, hoping to convey in that little touch without words just how much she loved him, and how happy she was that he was coming back to them. He looked down at her hand on his in surprise before blowing her a kiss. Alice erupted into a giggle in response.

'Dad, where are we going?' Melanie asked again, impatient now, no time for her parents' silliness.

'Somewhere quiet,' he replied, shoving the last of the bread in his mouth, 'a place where it's just us, a deserted island.' He looked at them, expectancy clear on his face.

Alice's heart sank. When she went away, she enjoyed company, the buzz of crowded streets, nightlife, heaving markets and busy restaurants, the holidaymakers that Harry got friendly with. Singapore was a dream yet to be realised that they had discussed many times over the years. She pondered on this now: Harry's latest idea for a deserted island holiday. Barring his depression, he was an incredibly outgoing and social man; without fail he would find someone at a bar to chat with through to the early hours. People were drawn to him, and Harry had all the time in the world for socialising. It was why he was so good at the school gates, she thought now, suppressing a smile.

But what harm could a quiet holiday do?

'Somewhere hot,' she instructed, gazing out at the lawn still laden with frost.

Harry began to collect the plates. 'I've actually been looking at the Hebrides,' he said as he carried the dinner things over to the kitchen worktop.

'Scotland?' Alice wrinkled her nose in distaste. She had been thinking Thailand, the hundreds of islands like where they filmed *The Beach* with Leonardo. Minimal clothes, fresh fish, warm seas, white sand.

'The Outer Hebrides,' said Harry as though Alice hadn't spoken.

'There are hundreds of islands in the Outer Hebrides,' piped up Melanie, adding, 'and thirty-six inhabited ones in the Inner Hebrides.'

Alice blinked at her daughter. Harry planted a kiss on Melanie's head as he walked past.

'That's my girl,' he said softly.

'It'll be cold,' said Alice.

But Harry and Melanie had moved onto the sofa to pore over maps of the Hebrides that Harry had produced on the iPad. They didn't answer her.

Harry stayed up long after Alice and Melanie went to bed. He smiled as he put the iPad on the table where Alice's work papers had been hours earlier. For a moment he stared blankly into space, wondering if he should feel guilty. Alice had misunderstood the logistics of his desert island idea. He snorted a little laugh, she had reacted just how he had expected her to. You didn't spend all these years married to one woman without knowing exactly how she thought.

He hadn't corrected her misconception, either. Let her think it was a holiday, for now. He knew her well enough to know she was just so happy that he was 'on the road to recovery', as she put it, that she would do anything to keep him that way.

As if hearing his thoughts, an alarm on his digital watch beeped, a reminder to take his pill. Letting the iPad screen fade to black, he swallowed the Fluoxetine. He stared outside into the darkness and thought about his girl, his daughter, his Melanie, the most important thing in the world, trapped in a stranger's home with a potential paedophile. That was what they were saying. *Paedophile*. Victoria Prout and her clan of justice-seeking vigilantes. And Alice didn't even want to call the police.

He shuddered, and it wracked his entire body.

The trouble with Alice was she dealt with criminals all day, every day. She had become hardened to the evil people in the world. To her, this man who'd cornered their daughter was simply another man. A bad man, yes, but not so bad that she felt the need to *act* like Harry did.

Alice was immune. But Harry refused to accept that this was the way his child had to live. When he had found out about Melanie's near miss, something sparked inside him. After the initial numbness of deadened horror had worn off it had been like an electric shock, fizzing through his veins. Senses previously dulled by the depression and the pills he took for it had come alive and the whole world was in Technicolor.

The spark had turned to rage, primal with a need to protect. The depression had dulled now, no longer the thing that blanketed him. No, at the forefront of his mind now was a plan.

Pushing the bottle aside, Harry grabbed his mobile and tapped out a quick text. He switched the phone off, sure that come tomorrow morning there would be a reply.

*

Alice was running late the next morning. She dashed around, trying to put into some sort of order the brief she'd been working on last night. Finally, she gave up, shoving it all in her briefcase and hoping the court hearing wasn't scheduled first thing.

I should know what time it is, she thought. *There was once a time when I didn't even need to write this shit down.*

As she pushed her feet into her shoes, she saw Harry dusting the fireplace. She stopped, one shoe on, the other dangling uselessly from her fingers.

'Shit, what time it is?' she asked. 'I must be really fucking late if you're up and cleaning already.'

'Morning, lovely!' he said, waving with his feather duster. 'You're not late, I'm just very early today. But,' he gave a furtive glance around, 'language, darling, please?'

She raised her eyes to the ceiling. 'Whatever. Anyway, thank God I'm not late. I have to go, though.' She waggled her fingers in his direction, wedged the remaining shoe on and hurried to the door.

'Alice?' Harry called.

Trying to restrain the sigh that threatened, she clung onto the doorframe and poked her head back into the room. 'What?'

'I've invited the Hadleys over for dinner tonight.'

Alice frowned. 'Who?'

'The Hadleys, Liz and Gabe and the twins. Their kids are a few years above Melanie in school.'

Alice took a deep breath. 'Right. Um, why?'

'Because it's been ages since we hosted a dinner party, and I thought it would be nice to be a little more social.' Harry raised his eyebrows. 'That okay with you?'

Alice bit back a sharp retort. It was fine for Harry to be social, he had the next ten hours to prepare for a dinner party, put something in the slow cooker, start on the red wine early. While she had to go to work and to court and try to do a job that once upon a time was as easy as breathing but which now took every ounce of energy she had not to screw up.

'Fine. See you tonight,' she said crisply. She slammed the door behind her and rushed to her car before she was tempted to go back inside and tell Harry everything she'd been thinking.

She had to be in court at 3 p.m. The relief was palpable and she spent the morning happily putting the papers she'd attempted to look over last night into order. With each sheet she read through carefully until she was confident she knew this case inside out. Granted, it was an easy one, but she felt a sense of accomplishment that had been missing for a while.

Later, she gave her colleague, Maxine a smug wave as she exited the building and made her way to the court house.

Judge Rackshaw peered down at her. His stare of disapproval was ten times worse than the looks Maxine had given her lately.

'So you're not ready to proceed, Ms Wilson?' he asked.

It was the second time he had said that. Alice clenched her fists and spoke through gritted teeth. 'No, Your Honour. As I explained I understood today to be the preliminary hearing, not to actually start this trial.'

Judge Rackshaw exchanged a look with his clerk. He inserted his pencil underneath the lining of his wig and scratched at his scalp. Alice groped for something to say, anything to make it better.

There was nothing. And this had been Alice's last chance.

She hurried from the court, threw the case load on the passenger seat and slumped behind the wheel.

Last chance. Last Chance. *Last chance.* The thought echoed in her head and as the light faded to the darkness of evening Alice put her head in her hands.

*

'Darling, where have you been? We're just about to start, couldn't keep it warm any longer without spoiling it.'

As Alice kicked off her shoes and opened the door to the living area it was all she could do not to groan.

Harry's bloody dinner party. She'd clean forgotten in the mess that was her working day, and here they all were. The Hadleys and their brood; a family she didn't know anything about, couldn't remember ever meeting and she had no idea why Harry felt it necessary to invite them to her home. Why not their actual friends, rather than people who were practically strangers?

She glanced at her slippers, big, fluffy black and white checked ones which she sometimes spent minutes of each day at work dreaming about getting home and slipping off the uncomfortable heels and putting on. A quick look at the woman who must be Liz Hadley told Alice she wasn't wearing slippers, or trainers or even pumps. So, she pushed her sore feet back into her heels before walking into the room.

'I'm sorry, horrid day at work,' she said, unable to stop herself shooting a pointed look in Harry's direction.

Why did he have to do this tonight, with less than twelve hours' notice? Why not a Friday or a Saturday when they could crack open all the wine and not have to worry about it being a school night?

'Hi, I don't think we've met, I'm Gabe, this is Liz.' The man stood up, stuck out a hand.

Alice appraised him, quite liking what she saw.

'Hi Gabe, Liz,' she raised her hand in a wave to the quiet, mousy-looking woman and averted her eyes to take in the two youngsters sat between Harry and Liz.

'Kids?' Gabe prompted gently.

'Hi, thanks for having us over,' said the girl.

Melanie leapt up from her chair and took her mother's briefcase from her. 'Sit down, Mum, we're all starving.'

'Thanks, honey,' Alice said distractedly as she took the empty chair opposite the children.

Children? Not quite, she thought as she looked them over. They were far older than Melanie, though hadn't Harry said they were only a couple of years above her in school? Both of them were tall, she could tell by the way their shoulders slumped over in their chairs. And both of them were…

She frowned as she discreetly looked at them. There was nothing remarkable about them, with their light brown hair, grey eyes and pale, pale skin. But they were mesmerising.

Yes, Alice decided. *That was it*, there was something about them that was simply special.

The boy caught her staring. 'I'm Lenon,' he said. 'Willow,' he added, nodding towards his sister.

'You're twins!' Alice exclaimed.

'I told you that,' said Harry.

Lenon and Willow offered her a tight smile. Alice looked down at her place mat, unsure how she had ended up feeling chastised. It was like being in court all over again.

'Harry tells us you're a lawyer,' said Gabe as he reached for the bottle of white and poured her a hefty glass.

Alice smiled, though it felt more like a grimace. White wine wasn't what she needed tonight; she had to face Maxine and possibly the partners tomorrow, a hangover was the last thing she should be risking.

'Hmm, yes,' she said. 'And what do you do?' It was an effort, this being nice after a shit day, but Harry had obviously gone through a lot of trouble, she noted, as he placed steaming plates and bowls on the table with a hearty 'Dig in'.

'Carpenter, general handyman,' replied Gabe. 'Harry, this looks fantastic!'

Alice had to admit it certainly did. Indian dishes came out of the kitchen, one after the other, and Alice smiled at Harry fondly. When he put his mind to something, he could really pull it off. And she had to admit, it was so good to see him back on form. *A relief.* One less thing she had to worry about.

'Ah, a trade for life,' commented Alice to Gabe. She waved the serving spoon at the youngsters around the table. 'To learn a trade is one of the wisest decisions you can make. If you have a skill you'll never be unemployed.'

'Dad hasn't got a trade,' remarked Melanie, earning what might have been a snigger from Lenon.

Alice was momentarily shocked into silence. It wasn't the sort of comment Melanie would normally make. She looked up and over at Harry, but he seemed blissfully unaware. Surprisingly it was Gabe who came to Harry's defence.

'Ah, but your father put this delicious meal together, there are some restaurants that couldn't put on a spread as good as this.'

Alice smiled gratefully at him. Silence fell upon the table as everyone served up their plates.

*

Harry had indeed heard the comment that his daughter made. It stung a little, but he let it go. In fact, it was the perfect opener for his proposal. He cleared his throat.

'Your mother is right,' he said to Melanie. 'A trade is important, and it's kind of why I invited Gabe and his family here tonight.'

He had their attention now, he saw, as one by one they stopped eating to look inquisitively at him. All except Liz, he noticed, who carried on forking tiny, bird-sized bites of food into her mouth.

'What do you mean, Harry?' Gabe asked. 'You need some work doing?' He glanced around the room as though mentally pricing up such a job.

'Oh, no.' Harry leaned forward. 'Alice and I are considering a move to a desert island, somewhere we can build our own community. We'd like you and your family to be a part of it.'

A stunned silence. Only the sound of Liz's cutlery scraping against her plate.

'Harry, you're inviting Gabe and Liz on our holiday?' Alice's voice was high-pitched with astonishment.

He took a deep breath, reached over and patted Alice's hand. 'Sweetheart, you misunderstood me, it's not a holiday we're going on. I want us to move to a place where there are no other people, no society, no community. Just us, a select few others, and we'll build our own colony.'

Alice barked out a laugh. 'That's crazy,' she said.

'Hey, I think the man's serious,' said Gabe. He leaned across the table to look Harry dead in the eye. 'Are you serious?'

'Deadly.' Harry met Gabe's stare.

Gabe fell back in his seat. The twins, like their mother, remained motionless, detached. Melanie seemed confused. Harry chanced a look at his wife's face. She appeared furious. Her lips moved, but nothing was coming out.

Yet.

Luckily, Gabe saved him from the explosion. 'Where are you thinking, mate?'

Harry studied his expression. He looked mildly interested, mildly amused. Harry decided to press on. 'Originally I was thinking of the Outer Hebrides, there are lots of little islands just waiting to be inhabited.'

'Over a hundred,' Melanie piped up.

'But,' Harry held up one finger, 'but I thought perhaps somewhere closer to the city, at least to start with.' He leaned forward, laid his eyes on each of them in turn, lingering on his wife's livid stare only briefly. 'Did you know we have an island right here, alongside Manchester?'

Gabe frowned. 'We do?' he asked. 'Where?'

Harry reached under his plate, unfolded a piece of A3 paper, gestured to the diagram he had highlighted. 'Pomona Island, a narrow strip of land wedged in the River Irwell.'

Gabe took the paper, flicked his eyes over it. 'For real?' he asked. 'What's on this island?'

Harry nodded, sat back and folded his arms. 'Nothing,' replied Harry. 'Well, that's not true. Nobody is on it, but it's got rather an exciting history. It was once docklands, it was once home to a botanical garden. It had a palace once, too. It's been industrial, it's been beautiful.'

'Okay, enough.' Alice wiped her mouth with her napkin. 'Let's not be silly, Harry.'

He smiled at her. Silly. Was he being silly? Didn't she know him well enough by now to know he *always* put his plans into action?

But she did, and that was why she was nervous, he realised. He narrowed his eyes as he watched her, wondering if she was remembering the times before when he'd gone so far down the road of a plan before she found out, and by then it was too late to back out.

Their wedding was one. They hadn't discussed marriage, or even an engagement, but Harry had known that Alice was the woman he wanted to spend the rest of his life with. They'd not yet had Melanie, and Alice was far too busy concentrating on her degree to even discuss a wedding. So, Harry had gone ahead and organised it.

By the time he'd picked her up on the pretext of taking her to breakfast, with a white, silk dress in a carrier bag on the back seat of the car and pulled up outside the registry office, she could hardly say no, could she?

And that was what Harry had been afraid of, he admitted to himself some time later. That if he asked, if he did it all tradition-ally down on one knee, that she might say no.

And there was no response now, from anyone around the table. But Harry had sowed the seed, which was all he had intended for tonight anyway.

'Think about it,' he said, smiling at his guests. 'Gabe, you can keep that. I've got another copy.' He turned to Alice. 'Sweetheart, can you pass me another samosa, please.'

11

'I told you about him, his name, where to find him. You did nothing.'

'Please,' Carrie begged. 'Let me help you. Tell me now, I'm listening. I want to help you.'

But the caller fell silent. Carrie cast a desperate look at Paul, who was listening in. He spun his finger in her direction, a silent command. *Keep her talking.*

'At least tell me your name. I'm Carrie. Have we spoken before?'

'He won't stop, you know. And neither will I.'

A click. A dead line. Carrie replaced the receiver softly.

'She wants help, she needs it. She's asking for help, for God's sake, Paul.' She moved over to him. 'Did you trace it?'

He shook his head, his jaw tight with tension.

'She'll call again.' Carrie nodded, certain of it. 'I just need to build up a trust with her before she does something stupid.'

Paul nodded. 'You'll get there,' he said kindly. 'But right now we have someone else to see.' He passed her a note, hastily scrawled, from the reception desk. 'Interview room four.'

Carrie looked down at the name in front of her, and then back up at the man who sat opposite. She shook her head slightly, her hair flicking against her shoulders, ridding her mind of the young female mystery caller in order to give all her attention to this man.

'Ganju?' she asked. 'That's your name?'

He nodded. 'Yes, ma'am, Ganju Bandari,' he replied, his voice a murmur, his eyes respectfully lowered.

'Where are you from, Ganju?' she asked, intrigued, unable to place his soft accent.

'Nepal, ma'am. That's where I was when all this happened. It wasn't me, I wasn't there, no matter what these people are saying.'

Carrie tilted her head; the words that fell from Ganju's mouth were far further in the conversation than they were at. She held up a hand.

'Slow down, tell me why you're here.'

Ganju folded his hands in his lap and looked at a spot behind Carrie on the wall. 'I come back from work in Nepal, with my brother, we live together, you see.'

'Where?' asked Carrie. 'Can I take your address?'

'Number three, Irwell Road.'

She motioned for him to continue.

'And on the nights just gone, people come to my door. They shout at me, eggs cracked on my windows. They threaten me. They tell me I…' he tailed off, lowered his eyes and his voice. 'They say I touch this child, this girl, that I take her from the street and force her into my home.' Ganju's voice broke like the eggshells on his windowpanes. 'I would *never*, ma'am, never do such a thing.'

A memory, sharp as a knife, punctured Carrie's preoccupation with this fascinating, gentle man. She leaned forward. 'Do you have a name, any names of the people who threatened you?'

He shook his head, gazing at her with doleful eyes.

She looked back down at her pad. 'Irwell Road, is that in Eccles?'

Ganju nodded.

'Near Milton Street,' Carrie clarified. She tapped her pen against her teeth thoughtfully. 'When did this alleged incident happen, did they say?'

Ganju shrugged. 'I've been away, my brother and myself, we are guides on Everest. Here, in Manchester, we bought this house together, it was in bad shape, semi-derelict, so we get this man to do it up while we are away so we can move in upon our return. February is the month that is busiest for booking, then we go back in May for the actual climb. We visit in February to confirm our upcoming work and also to visit our mother and celebrate *Maha Shivaratri*, our holy night.'

'An Everest guide?' Carrie said. 'That must be exciting, how many times have you been up there?'

'Nine,' he said, a smile breaking out on his face now he was speaking about something he was obviously comfortable with. 'My brother, six.'

'Wow.' Carrie, happy to have got him talking, continued with the matter at hand. 'Then you were not even in the country when this was alleged to have happened. Did you tell the people who came to see you that?'

Ganju shook his head. 'They would not let me speak. And I have to keep my brother inside.' Ganju lowered his eyes again. A flush stained his throat. 'My brother can be hot-headed.'

'I assume you can verify that you were in fact abroad? Visa, passport stamps, documentation?'

Ganju nodded, his sad brown eyes regarding her warily.

'All right, you write down all your contact details here, and we'll be in touch with you. Okay, Ganju?'

He accepted the form she gave him with a grateful smile. Carrie excused herself and went in search of Paul.

She had a feeling she knew exactly who was behind the threat on Ganju's home.

'Paul.'

He looked up as she came in. 'You spoke to the Sherpa?'

She was surprised. 'Yes, how did you… never mind. Paul, you know it's that Prout woman, don't you?'

He nodded. 'I gathered. She seems like the sort to take matters into her own hands. So, we'll speak to her and at least now we have an address of where this assault happened.'

'But Ganju was out of the country, the house was empty.'

Paul leaned back in his chair. 'A break-in? A house sitter?'

He watched with concern as the blood drained from her face.

'I… I didn't ask. Shit, Paul. My mind was… elsewhere. I'll go back and speak to him.' But instead she pulled out a chair and flopped into it. 'It's that girl, that caller, it got me all—' she broke off, shook her head. 'Doesn't matter.'

Paul studied her. Carrie knew what he was thinking; her mind was never elsewhere but on the job.

'You mean the anonymous caller, the young girl?' Paul got up and took a stack of filing to his cabinet. 'What is it about her that speaks to you?'

He turned his back to her, busied himself with the files. For a long moment she considered not answering, but then she spoke softly.

'I don't know. It makes me think of something I can't quite remember.'

'Another old case?'

'No. Something… I don't even know. That other girl, Kelly, she said some things when I spoke to her outside that made me feel strange.'

Paul shoved some files into the drawer. Slamming it closed, he opened the next one down and slipped a single sheet in. 'Strange, how?'

But he'd lost her. The clang of the filing cabinet pulled her back from a memory she couldn't even remember. She stood up, the chair legs shrieking on the tiled floor.

'I need to catch Ganju before he leaves.'

12

Alice flicked between the two websites on her screen, studiously ignoring Maxine who hadn't said two words to her since she'd got in.

She minimised the sites on her PC so they sat side by side. One of them, side effects of Fluoxetine. The other, Pomona Island. Two seemingly different things that to her, were inextricably linked.

Harry's latest plan. She shook her head as she recalled his flights of fancy of the night before, the bewildered expression on the Hadleys' faces, the almighty row they'd had once their guests had left.

'What the fuck are you thinking?' she'd shouted. And it wasn't just the stupid prank he'd pulled about moving to a deserted island, it was all the frustrations of the recent weeks, the courtroom cock up, the work errors, Harry's depression, Victoria bloody Prout and Melanie's near miss.

'I just want to raise our daughter somewhere that's not riddled with drugs and murders and *paedophiles*.' Harry had emphasised the last word. 'Is that so unreasonable?'

She hadn't answered him. Instead she had gone to bed. In the spare room.

But she hadn't slept. She had gone over and over Harry's stupid dinner party in her head. And what on earth had possessed him to get Gabe Hadley on board? Was it simply because he was a skilled manual worker? And if so, what the hell did that say about the island Harry had in mind for them to all live on? Were there

even houses on it, or did Harry expect them to reside in yurts
or tepees?

Not that it mattered, it was a stupid idea and one that
wouldn't happen. And it wasn't even the island living plan that
was the main issue. It was Harry and the fact that he'd gone
behind her back.

Again.

Despite herself she scrolled through the details on the Manchester history website. It differed somewhat to the information
he had tried to tell them about last night. He had spoken of a
fantasy land, utopia, a perfect, residential Eden. The website
images showed graffitied concrete walls, wire fences, open,
stagnant rivers surrounded by open water.

Alice shuddered.

Harry wanted to live here, on this once beautiful but now
barren, industrialised land? She went back to the Fluoxetine
site, seeking evidence that over-exuberance and crazy plots were
a common side effect. There had to be a link. Or did there? Was
this just the old Harry coming back to her, the one who excited
and frustrated her in equal measure?

'Alice, a word?'

She looked up to see one of the partners, Simon, in the
doorway. Alice glanced at Maxine, but the other woman refused
to meet her eye.

Alice stood up, smoothed down her skirt and strode confidently
into his office. Her assurance faded as she saw Adrian, leaning
on Simon's desk, arms folded, his usually friendly face closed off
and serious.

'Hey, what's going on?' She offered a smile, but the two faces
were stone cold serious.

'You've had a little trouble, lately, Alice,' Adrian said. 'How's
it all going?'

Alice resisted the urge to turn around and glare at Maxine through the window. Instead she managed to put a puzzled frown on her face as she addressed the two men.

'Trouble?' she said. 'I'm not sure I understand. There was a misunderstanding in the court a couple—'

'Frequently late, preparing for a case that wasn't due and failing to have everything ready for one in court that very day. Leaving early, unable to be productive when you are here.' Adrian pursed his lips and studied her. 'It's unlike you, Alice. Come on, what's troubling you? Is the workload getting too much for you to handle?'

It was like a knife between her ribs. For over ten years she had given her all to this firm, and as soon as she needed a little leeway they were all over her like a pack of hyenas. She opened her mouth to speak, but it seemed they hadn't finished, as Simon stepped forward.

A strange, fuzzy feeling came over her as she watched him speaking. He was talking, she could see his lips moving, but only a few words reached her.

Reputation. Errors. Mistakes. Time off.

'I quit,' she blurted.

And as soon as she said the words, she relaxed for what felt like the first time in months. Tension drained out of her shoulders and it was all she could do not to sigh out loud. She nodded, a real smile breaking through now.

She drove on autopilot, cold to her very core even though the heating was turned up high.

She was unemployed. She had never, ever been out of work before. And it wasn't a matter of income. The awfulness of Harry and her having both lost their parents in childhood had meant two large trust funds. The house was purchased with money left to Harry twenty-five years ago and her own trust fund had barely been touched. Mentally she went over their financial reserves. A few hundred grand saved already, possibly slightly more with Harry's, all in a pot for their early retirement to sunnier climates. A quarter of a million was their target. But that had been based on her working until she was fifty, another ten years away.

Alice pulled the car over on Broadway. Thawing slightly, she pulled a piece of paper and pen out of her briefcase and scrawled on it. Figures swam in front of her eyes as she added up the sums. They could live comfortably without her working for a good couple of years and not have to touch the retirement pot. She put the pen on the dashboard and sat back, gazing thoughtfully out of the window. It wouldn't come to that, she could walk into another job tomorrow. But what about references, would Adrian and Simon oblige? Probably not, she thought. A wave of shame; they'd not tried to change her mind. They had actually been glad to see her go.

Alice gripped the steering wheel. Well they could go to hell. She would take some time, enjoy Melanie's transition from middle to high school like a normal parent. Harry had had all the joy of raising a child for eleven years; now she could join in.

Alice put the car into gear and drove the rest of the way home feeling more than a little lost.

*

Harry chewed the ragged skin around his fingers as he handed the documents back. A clap on the back, a handshake with the man whose name he couldn't remember. Not that it mattered, he was cutting ties and the most burdensome one had just been signed away.

Harry smiled as he showed the man out of the door. His happiness dimmed somewhat as Alice's car turned into the cul-de-sac, screeching to a stop in the driveway.

'What're you doing home so early, love?' he called as she dragged her coat and briefcase out of the car and stumbled up to the house.

'Long story,' she said, thrusting her coat at him as she turned to watch the man drive away. 'Who was that?'

'Long story,' he said ironically as he ushered her inside. 'You go first.'

He watched her as she headed for the fridge and pulled out a bottle of white wine. He raised his eyebrows: wine before noon, it really must be big news. A thought struck him, what if she'd got a promotion? That wouldn't do at all, it would ruin all his plans.

As Alice poured out wine, he pulled out a stool opposite her.

Draining the glass, she slammed it down on the counter and dragged the back of her hand across her mouth. 'I quit,' she said hoarsely.

Harry's heart hammered against his breastbone. Two words he never, ever expected to come out of Alice's mouth.

'Oh!' Leaping off his stool he rushed around the breakfast bar to grab her by the elbows. 'Alice, this is amazing, wonderful, and it couldn't be better timing! But why, what made you jack it all in?'

She wrestled free from his grasp. 'I had enough, Harry. It was time.' She nodded as though confirming this to herself. 'I want a break.'

Harry snatched up the bottle. 'Give me that,' he said as he made to pour one out for himself.

She lurched forward, covering his glass with her hand. 'Harry, you're not supposed to drink on your medication… hold on, what did you mean when you said it couldn't be better timing?'

Gently he moved her hand aside and poured himself a decent measure. Holding his glass aloft he took a deep breath.

'I just sold the house to a quick sale company. Alice, we're moving to Pomona!'

*

Melanie scuffed her feet on the walk home from school and considered how her day had gone. Badly, she decided. And it would only get worse come September. High school students were ruthless and Melanie could barely stand the way she had become an outcast now, in middle school.

It was Kelly and Tanisha, she thought now as she walked home on her own. Somehow they'd found the need to save face from their illicit breaking-in to the house of horrors and they had turned it around on *her*. And it was infuriating, the other students sniggering behind their hands in her direction. When she'd got changed after PE she'd found a Post-it note stuck to her coat. *Melanie the paedo-lover*, it said. And yet she'd been the one to save them in the house. Tanisha had been a crying, shaking wreck in the corner of the kitchen and Kelly had been trapped upstairs with the man with the face.

She stopped walking, considered actually telling everyone what really had happened. She could embellish even, tell all the other kids that Tanisha had wet herself and Kelly had been so scared she threw up.

But those two were the leaders of the whole year at school. All the kids looked to them. Nobody would be on Melanie's side and Melanie had to remember she was moving up to high school with them all. The whole plan of hanging out with Tanisha and Kelly was so that she would be protected come September, and not labelled as she was now: a geek.

As she turned into the cul-de-sac where she lived, she pulled up again. Her mother's car was home. Melanie glanced at her watch. Not even half past three. Unheard of. Another thought struck her; *what if Dad was bad again?* Anxiously she chewed on the end of her scarf. He'd been so much better lately, since her mother had made him go to the doctor and he'd got those new pills. He'd been better than better, he'd been the Harry of her childhood, up at dawn, fussing over her, finding fun things to do, crazy ideas and in and out of the house all day. Melanie wiped her eyes which were suddenly watering. She couldn't stand it if he were back to his old, tired, miserable self again. Not now; after all, with school the way it was, home was all she had.

Melanie broke into a run. It took four tries to insert her key into the lock, and pulling off her coat and leaving it on the floor behind her she paused, fingers clenched around the handle that would open the door to the living area. It was silent inside, no television or radio on, no shadows moving around. Taking a deep breath, she pushed the handle down and crept into the room.

Her mother and father were at the dining-room table, facing each other, an almost empty wine bottle between them.

'Hi,' she said, hesitantly, eyeing the bottle. She hated it when they got all drunk and silly in the daytime.

'Go to your room, Melanie.' Her mother's voice was tight, clipped and controlled. Alice spoke without even looking at her.

'What's going on?' Melanie aimed this at her dad.

'Room, Melanie.' Alice flicked a glance her way. 'Now.'

Harry shook his head. 'She's as much a part of this as you and me. She should stay.'

'There's nothing to be a part of!' Alice shouted, making both Harry and Melanie jump.

Melanie bolted for the stairs.

'Melanie!' Harry called.

'Leave her!' roared Alice.

Melanie slammed her bedroom door. Sinking onto her bed, she wrapped her arms around herself.

*

In the reflection of the French doors, Harry's heart leapt at the sight of Alice as she stood up from the table, tall and thin and beautiful. In the glass he saw his own reflection. He ignored his drawn face, his heavyset frame, his thinning hair. Not for the first time, he wondered how he'd got Alice. They were the most mismatched couple he knew. It was a fact he tried very hard not to dwell on.

'How can you even sell this house?' she asked quietly. 'It's in both of our names.'

'It's not sold yet. But the guy reckons it can go through in as little as a week. You'll need to be on board, you'll need to sign the paperwork too,' he replied. A beat, then, 'I'm hoping you will, Alice. I hope you can see how good this is for all of us.'

He turned as she approached.

'I have some points I need clarified,' she said. She gripped the counter behind her and he saw the breath that she drew in. 'If we're going to do this.'

He covered the space between them, pulled her into his arms. He stroked her hair and covered it in kisses as she squirmed against him. With a palm flat on his chest she pushed him away.

'Points, Harry. That I need you to agree to if we're going to do this.'

He nodded eagerly. 'Anything.'

'This is a trial. We will live on Pomona for three months then we revaluate. If at any point before the three months is up, I want to leave then I'm leaving, and I'll take Melanie with me. I want half the funds of the sale of this house transferred into my bank account. Half the profit was mine, because we're married, Harry, and I made this place a home just as much as you.'

'I'm closing my bank account,' Harry interjected. 'I'm putting all the money in a trust for Melanie when she's twenty-one.'

Alice blinked at him. Her mouth worked uselessly for a few moments before she sank into a chair. 'Harry, don't you understand that we are married, that everything you've done, are things we should talk about?'

'Don't debase this by talking about money, Alice,' he said quietly. 'We're losing all that, shedding it. Where we're going, we won't need money.'

He thought he saw her shudder and he pulled up a chair next to her and rubbed her arm.

'When?' she asked, 'when are we going, and please tell me that weird family aren't coming with us.'

'They're not weird,' Harry protested. 'Gabe has a lot of skills that we're going to need, and his wife worked at a doctor's surgery so she knows first aid. Why do you think I selected them, Alice?' He breathed in deeply. 'But I don't think they're coming, anyway. Too much to organise.'

'Jesus.' Alice rubbed her forehead. 'It's going to take months to set this up, you do know that, don't you?'

It was Harry's turn to stare at her. 'We leave in a week.'

13

'Ma, I bought you some of those jelly sweets you like.' Carrie placed the box of Berry Fruits on her mother's table before leaning over to kiss Mary's cheek.

Mary didn't react. Mary hadn't reacted to anything for twenty years. The unit where she had lived for more than a decade tried, as well they should for the price Carrie paid on a monthly basis. Art therapy, music, hypnotherapy, hydrotherapy, cognitive behavioural therapy and counselling. None of them had worked, and part of Carrie knew that her mother would remain in this almost vegetative, non-responsive state for the rest of her natural life. The other part of her, the fighter, tried every new thing she heard of.

At least she was out of bed today and in her chair. It wasn't much, but for Carrie it was a comfort. The days Carrie visited and her mother hadn't got out of bed brought back all the terrible memories of the days after Hattie had gone. Everyone drifted away and Carrie had dropped through the system, a forgotten child who did her very best to take care of her bedridden mother. A kitchen fire, the result of Carrie cooking beans for her dinner, had brought her back to the attention of the authorities.

Carrie had wept with relief when they took her mother away.

She picked up the box of sweets, rattled them gently near her mother's face. 'Shall I open them, Ma?'

Silence. Shutters down across Mary's eyes.

Carrie peeled off the wrapping, opened the box and selected a red one. A memory from childhood, Mary taking all the red and black sweets, Carrie and Hattie grumbling at being left with the boring orange and green ones.

'Open,' Carrie said.

Mary's lips remained still, slack. Carrie pressed the sweet against them until Mary opened her mouth slightly. Chewed slowly. Eyes still as blank as the night sky that hung over the canals outside.

Carrie stood up, made her way around her mother's room. Checked the cupboards for supplies, ensuring Mary had clean night clothes, that the wash cloths smelled fresh and not stale like they had the other week. The flowers that Carrie had put on the windowsill four days ago were fine. She would bring new ones next time.

Carrie stared out of the window. She would cry when she left tonight. Sometimes she didn't. Sometimes she was angry that Mary, who made such a big deal of naming her daughters after strong, influential women, had sunk like a stone when the going got tough.

You gave up, Ma, she said to herself. *I never did. One day I'll find something out, I'll bring him to justice. I'll never give up.*

She would never say these words to her mother. But she said them to herself every day.

Peeling a single, brown leaf off the bouquet, Carrie slipped it in her pocket and walked back over to her mother. She stared down at Mary, at the wizened, shrivelled woman who had once seemed so large and scary.

'Maybe I should say those things to you, Ma, huh?' Softly she stroked Mary's cheek. 'Maybe I'd get a reaction from you if I said her name.'

She dropped her hand, walked briskly to the door. 'I'll see you next week, Ma,' she said.

*

Outside, she checked her phone as she wiped her damp cheeks with a gloved hand. Missed calls from Paul.

She rang him back.

'Carrie, that Ganju came back. Remembered he had a decorator in while he was away.' Paul spoke fast, no time for niceties or greetings.

'Excellent. I'll stop by his house, I want to take a look at it anyway,' said Carrie. A beat, then, 'Are you still at work?'

'Of course,' Paul laughed wryly. 'You don't have to stop in now, it's late.'

'It's fine, I was just leaving the gym.' The lie came easily, years of practice. 'I'll catch up with you tomorrow. Goodnight, Paul.'

Carrie parked, unnoticed by the cluster of people who gathered on the path outside Ganju's house. She spotted Victoria Prout immediately, the ringleader, stalking around her group, polished red nails pointing, high-pitched voice screeching.

Carrie groaned as she heaved herself out of her car.

'Mrs Prout,' she said, pointedly as she crossed the road.

One of the other women blinked at Carrie. The group of people hesitantly parted as Carrie strode up to Victoria.

'What are you doing?' she asked Victoria in a low voice.

'Fucking getting justice for our daughters, and who the hell are you, a paedo sympathiser?' A short woman with unkempt hair bounced up to Carrie.

Carrie smiled tightly as she reached into her pocket and flashed her ID at the newcomer. 'I'm DS Carrie Flynn.' She swept her eyes up and down the woman as she pulled out her notebook. 'And you are?'

It had the desired effect. All of the group flicked their hoods up and slowly vanished into the night until Victoria stood on her own. Carrie turned to Ganju's house and took in the paint, the eggs, the flour. Car engine oil and… a tin of fuel. She turned sharply to Victoria.

'Who is responsible for that?' she asked icily, pointing at the tin.

Even in the darkness she saw Victoria colour. Shame, or embarrassment at being caught?

'This is why we're here, on the streets, this is our job.' Carrie stood face to face with Victoria. 'Come on, you're smarter than this.'

For a moment Victoria's mouth worked, her eyes narrowed and Carrie watched as her fists clenched. Suddenly, the woman took a step backwards.

Carrie nodded. 'Look, these guys,' she gestured towards the house, 'they were not even in the country when this happened. You need to leave this to us, we will get to the bottom of it.' Carrie reached out a hand, laid it on the other woman's arm. 'Go home,' she said softly.

When she had been swallowed up by the night, Carrie walked up to Ganju's door, stepping carefully to avoid the mess that had been made of the driveway. He opened it before she even raised her hand to knock, his eyes wide and fearful, darting left, right and behind her.

'Come in,' he muttered, barely allowing her time to step inside before he slammed the door closed behind her.

'I can't find his card, that decorator, I can't find his business card.' Ganju's words came out in a rush.

'How did you pay him?' Carrie asked. 'Bank transfer, cheque?'

His face fell. 'Cash,' he replied.

Carrie suppressed a sigh. It would be cash. 'His name, just his first name? Did he work in a team, were there more than one of them, can you remember which area of Manchester he worked out of?'

He looked faintly scared by the questions she fired at him with a bullet-like velocity. Carrie stepped back, surveyed him. Here was a man who led ordinary people up and down the tallest mountain range in the world. He had seen death, illness, accidents and yet, these people outside his home, spitting words of vitriol and damaging his property and shaming him were more frightening than anything he'd ever seen on the mountain. Irrationally she wanted to hug him, but she moved back even further. Hugs were not appropriate for a police officer, and even as a civilian she didn't do that.

Carrie looked around the hallway. The smell of fresh paint lingered, the walls smooth and pristine. The decorator had done a good job, but what else had he been using this house for? She turned back to Ganju. 'Look, Ganju, I'm going to have someone stationed near here, a patrol if you like. In the meantime, please try and think of any details of this decorator that you can, okay?'

He nodded, moved towards the door again. It didn't go unnoticed when he drew back the curtain and peered through before opening it. Carrie felt her lips twist bitterly. He shouldn't be living like this, fearful in his own home.

'Where's your brother?' she asked, suddenly. 'Might he have any ideas on who this decorator was?'

Ganju, caught off guard with the door open, hurriedly closed it again, banging her elbow painfully. He muttered hasty apologies as she rubbed her arm.

'Thaman,' he called. 'Thaman, come out here.'

Movement, scraping from within deep inside the house. Unconsciously Carrie wrapped her arms around herself.

He filled the doorway, Thaman, Ganju's brother. He was as broad as his brother was lithe and slender. Bullish, huge, he stared at Carrie, brown eyes thin, deep-set in his face.

'Yes?' he said, and his whispery voice was such a contrast to his stature that Carrie blinked.

'This is the Detective.' Ganju sounded weary now, and he leaned against the wall as he gestured to Carrie. 'Thaman, please try to remember the name of the decorator, the police really cannot do anything without something to go on.'

Thaman took two steps down the hall towards them. 'I never knew his name, you had me get the payment and put it in an envelope. I did all that, all you had to do was give him the key and tell him where the cash was,' Thaman's eyes slid over to Carrie, 'and remember his name, and yet, you cannot.'

Irritation caught at Carrie. These people wanted her help, but by their own fault they couldn't find the details of the man who she was pretty sure was responsible for whatever had happened here. She threw her hands up, palms to the ceiling.

'I'll station some patrols in the area. Ganju, Thaman, if you recall anything, please let me know.'

She yanked open the door, slipped outside, felt the door against her back as Ganju fumbled to slam it closed against the people he presumed were still outside, waiting to lynch him.

But the street was deserted. Carrie stepped carefully over the broken eggshells and made her way back to her car.

14

The boat was too small for their things, surely, observed Alice as she stood at the cold quayside. But case after case went on, basic bedding, a toolbox, canned goods, bulk-bought bottles of water, all stowed in hideaways that Alice hadn't seen during the brief walk around on deck.

She fingered her iPhone in her pocket. It was fully charged, but once they were across this thin strip of water it would last no more than a day. Sweat prickled between her shoulder blades.

'Harry.' She caught his arm as he strode past her. He stumbled, allowing the box he was carrying to tumble to the ground. A flash of annoyance in the look he shot her as he righted it.

'Harry …' she pulled at his arm.

'What is it, Alice?'

'What if one of us gets ill, or has an accident?' She twisted the material of his sleeve in her fingers. Impatiently he pulled his arm free. 'Nobody can get to us over there, we can't even summon any help.'

He seemed to soften, releasing her grip and moving his hand up to cradle her face. His hand felt ice cold on her skin.

'Alice, we're going to live so healthily over there, no sickness, no illness, I promise you.' He stooped, picked up the box and clambered onto the boat.

She stared after him, no longer feeling cold but suddenly white hot with anger. She hated it when people did that, dismissed her worries and concerns with an airy 'you'll be fine'. She didn't want platitudes or placating, she wanted solutions and suggestions.

'Bastard,' she whispered as tears stung her eyes.

She moved off, away a little from the horrid boat that would take her away from the life she knew into the unknown. Separate from her family and her possessions she watched as Melanie wandered around the boat, running her small hands over the weatherworn wood. Melanie would be all right, with her father, in spite of her concerns that she'd confided to Alice. Harry would be in his element, living the sort of adventure he'd always dreamed of.

Alice looked away, back towards the city. It was early, not even 6 a.m., but already she could hear the sounds of life. A lorry was collecting from the bottle banks, the noise of the glass smashing almost brought a smile. How often did the citizens of Salford complain about that, about the bin men emptying and causing a racket when most people were still in bed? It had always irritated her, but suddenly she found she would miss it. What noise would there be on the island? Birds screeching, Harry's studious voice talking. She rubbed a hand across her face, moved her gaze to her car. A wave of emotion crept over her. Her car, the trusty, new-ish Toyota that Harry had bought for her and which she loved. Harry had driven it here, said he had arranged for someone to pick it up. What did that even mean? Had he sold it, given it away? It wasn't fair; it might be registered in his name but it was her car.

Why do I let Harry get his own way all the time? It wasn't the first time she'd thought it. Every time he had a crazy plan, she caved in. She, who was so strong in other areas of her life.

It was an uncomfortable thought, one she always pushed away whenever it crept into her mind. But this was different, this wasn't arranging a surprise wedding, or buying a house or planning a holiday without her input. This was her life, and he was taking it away from her.

She could walk away, back to her home, back to her bank account and her old, familiar life. She shivered. But what old life? Her job was gone, by next week there would be strangers living in her home. A lifetime's belongings put into storage. Harry and Melanie wouldn't be there, back in Salford.

'You coming now, Miss?'

The deep, gruff voice made her jump. Alice spun around, found herself staring into the brightest, bluest eyes she'd ever seen.

She steadied herself on the wall behind her. The boatman, the man Harry was paying to take them across the water to their new, solitary life. What did he think of them, this young sailor? She grasped in her mind for his name, recalling being introduced to him earlier, but for the life of her she couldn't remember it.

'In a minute,' she said, keeping her eyes on him, taking in all his features, because in a few short hours she would not have any new faces to look at, or any new conversations to be had. Seized with a desperate need to cram in as much as she could she heaved herself up to sit on the wall.

'What was your name again?'

'Ben.'

She thought he was unsmiling, but through his thick, dark beard she realised she wouldn't be able to tell. Hungrily she drank in the sight of him, the facial hair, fashionable once again, she knew, which told her this Ben was younger than she was. But old enough to navigate these waters and their currents which, so Harry had informed her, took experience and many, many years of practice.

'Miss, are you coming now?' he asked again, already taking two steps away from her, back towards Harry and Melanie and the boat.

'Wait.' She climbed off the wall, ungainly, swearing under her breath as she snagged her scarf on the concrete.

He stopped again, turned, waited.

'How much do you charge to take the boat over to Pomona?' He tilted his head a little and she moved closer to him. 'How much is Harry paying you?'

'Fifty quid,' he replied after a beat.

Alice thought quickly. She had a grand in her bag, cash in twenty-pound notes. She didn't know why she'd taken it, only that to go somewhere for a potentially long amount of time with no money on her person seemed wrong.

'Ben, I'm worried.' She stood in front of him, maintaining eye contact as though he were a judge or jury and she was about to launch into one of her closing speeches. 'Over on Pomona we have no way of contacting anybody, no phones, no internet, no way of sending letters. This makes me anxious: I have a small child,' she paused, wondered why she had chosen that phrasing, when Melanie often seemed more adult and competent than Alice herself did. 'If there's illness, or an emergency…' She trailed off, losing her train of thought. 'Can I pay you to come to the island, to meet me, just once a week. I'll pay you, more than Harry is paying you.'

Was he thinking about it? Alice peered at him, but he dipped his head, his hand, as weather-beaten as his face Alice noticed, rubbing at his jaw, the thick, brown bristles of his beard moving slowly underneath his fingers.

'Sixty quid each way,' he said eventually. 'Cash up front.'

A moment of panic; which bag had she put her cash in? She looked towards the boat, saw all the cases and boxes were onboard now. No matter, she would find it, discreetly, without Harry or Melanie seeing.

'Okay.' She breathed out, offered him a smile that felt stretched and false on her face.

'It'll be once a fortnight though, I work away every other week. You need to be getting on board now, Miss,' he said, turning back towards the quay once more. 'It'll be getting busy on the quay soon.' He studied the water, his head moving slowly in a ninety-degree turn. 'We need to hurry.'

For a long moment she considered stalling until it was too late to leave before abandoning the fanciful idea. Harry wasn't giving up on this quest, he would simply insist they come back tomorrow morning.

A siren sounded in the distance, and as they walked towards the boat Alice wondered if she would still be able to hear them from the island. Behind her, a car made its way down the roadside on the quay. She resisted looking over her shoulder, but wondered if it was the police. Would they stop them? Who owned Pomona? Someone must, she should have looked that up. More than likely they would be trespassing if they set up home there.

'Alice, come on!' Harry stood on the boat, the bow, the stern? Alice realised she didn't know and didn't particularly care.

And then another voice rang out in the otherwise still morning. 'Harry, wait up, mate.'

They all turned, Alice, Harry, Ben. Melanie's head popped up over the side of the boat.

'It's Gabe!' said Harry. 'It's Gabe and his family!'

Alice stared, hardly daring to believe it. But there they were, four of them, alighting from a battered old estate car.

'More people going across?' Ben looked at Alice, as though it were her fault, as though she had anything to do with this madcap idea.

She shrugged, turned to him as a thought struck her. 'Do you have room for them, on the boat I mean?' Suddenly she wanted very much for Gabe and his quiet, timid family to go along. They were not who she would have chosen, but at this point she was desperate for some company, *any* company would do.

'It'll be tight.' He glared at Alice. 'It'll cost more.'

Who did he think he was? Alice held his gaze, her nostrils flaring slightly. 'In that case I suggest you speak with Harry,' she said.

As haughtily as she could manage, she climbed down onto the boat, stepping down the small ladder where she nearly landed on Melanie, crouched on the bench, peeping over the side.

'I thought they weren't coming,' said Melanie, without looking at her mother.

Alice held up her hands in a gesture of defeat. Why did it sound like they were suddenly accusing her? None of this was anything to do with her. Harry clambered past them, making his way over to Ben, speaking in Ben's ear before passing him something, money probably, thought Alice, and hailing the approaching Gabe heartily.

Alice moved to the other side of the boat, casting her eye over the crates and bags and cases, trying to remember which one she had put her cash in. She pulled them out, one by one, from underneath the little wooden seats, emitting a small exclamation of relief as she spotted the brown envelope nestled among a pile of towels.

'What's that for?' Melanie bent over her.

Alice crammed the envelope in her coat pocket. 'Ben will need more money if we're taking more people over,' she muttered, pushing herself upright.

'Dad already paid him, I saw him,' said Melanie. 'And besides, shouldn't *they* pay themselves?'

Alice's nerves, already frayed, snapped neatly. 'For God's sake, Melanie, just… just leave it.'

Alice hurried back to the front of the boat. She shouldn't snap at Melanie, but the whole situation was putting her on edge. It was irritating, and it would be a whole lot worse on the island. Taking six notes out of the envelope Alice sidled up to Ben. Keeping it concealed in her hand she shoved it at him. He opened his palm, and lazily licking his thumb he flicked through the notes.

'Don't count it,' she hissed. 'It's all there. Just make sure you are too, a fortnight from today, yes?'

Before he could answer, Harry ushered Gabe onto the deck. 'Look who's decided to join us,' he smiled.

Gabe offered his hand to Alice. She shook it reluctantly, felt her lip curling at his ridiculous gesture. His wife, Liz, followed behind him, head down, the twins silently slipping past her like ghosts. Alice only just managed not to roll her eyes. What a weird family.

'All phones off now,' said Harry loudly. 'We should be able to move away from our old, confined lives. But,' he held up one finger, 'Pomona isn't public property, and though I don't imagine anyone will actually report us as missing, the last thing we want is to be traced to the island.' He smiled at each of them in turn. 'So, phones off now.'

Obediently they did as he asked, one by one their connections to the outside world lost. Alice pressed the button down on her mobile, unable to prevent a shudder as the screen went black.

*

Harry was hardly able to stop himself rubbing his hands together. He stood at the bow of the boat, beside Ben, eager for his first sight of Pomona, for his new life, the life he'd always dreamed of living.

'You ever been there before, not just past it but actually been on the island?' he asked the big, silent Ben.

Ben's beard dipped in confirmation. 'A stag party, a few years ago.'

Harry's face fell. 'A stag party?'

Beneath the bristles he saw Ben's teeth flash in the gloomy dawn light. 'Don't worry, they don't do it anymore.' Resting one hand on the helm Ben turned to Harry. 'Pomona's off limits to visitors now, while they decide what to do with it.'

Harry nodded quickly, casting a glance over his shoulder to make sure Alice wasn't listening in. She was a lawyer by profession, she would never have agreed to this if she knew they were breaking the law.

He touched the bulk in his pocket, the hard edges of the Fluoxetine, and considered hurling them overboard. He wanted nothing like that in his new life. Everything would be natural; from the food they ate to the water they drank from the running stream to the vegetables he would grow himself.

'See that buoy there.' Ben gestured with his head. 'It's a marker, it's at this point I always realise I can't hear the sounds of the city anymore.'

Harry closed his eyes. A smile spread over his face. Ben was right; there was nothing to be heard except the sound of the water lapping in gentle waves. Sweet, blissful, peace. He gripped the cool, metal rails on the side of the boat.

'And there she is.'

He looked where Ben pointed, through the slight mist that clung to the water's surface he saw a grey mass, looming out of the water. The concrete surrounds that protected Harry's new haven. Pomona.

He drank it in before spinning on the balls of his feet, his wife and daughter's names on his lips to call them over and share in the magical moment of first sight.

They sat huddled on the stern of the boat, Alice, Melanie, the strange new family he'd invited beside them, all of them watching as Manchester faded into the distance.

They're not looking forward, he thought to himself, disappointment abundant inside him. *They're looking back. Back to where they were, where they'd always lived, to what they'd always known.*

He turned back to Pomona, no longer wanting to share the moment with those he loved best.

Solitary, he drank in the view himself and held it all inside.

15

Carrie and Hattie– 1998

Mr Lacey's car had a strange smell. Carrie opened the window a crack, lifting her face but the air that came through the window was stale and hot.

She faced the front, and in the rear-view mirror she saw Mr Lacey's eyes, sludge-coloured, like mud. His eyebrows were grey, long threads that almost touched his eyelashes. Carrie looked away, back out of the window once more.

'Mandale Park you say you're going to?' His voice, scratchy and thin, rang out in the silence of the car. Carrie wished he would put the radio on.

He caught her gaze in the mirror again. Carrie nodded.

'Our uncle is meeting us there.' The lie came easily, automatically. She didn't know why she'd fibbed to him, but it was instinctive.

Hattie shifted in the seat beside her. Before she could begin with her endless questions about an uncle she didn't know she had, Carrie gripped Hattie's hand and shot her sister a warning look.

Hattie stared at her, wide-eyed.

'That's nice, is he her side of the family or yours?' said Mr Lacey in a conversational tone.

Carrie felt a dull blush stain her cheeks. People always did that, just because she was white and Hattie was black. She hated it, even though half the time people didn't mean anything by it, but Carrie saw it as a separation. Oddly, it never seemed to worry Hattie, though Carrie supposed it might when she was older.

She looked at her sister, wondering if it would be worse for her in the years to come. After all, Carrie and her mother were a pair; they fitted in. Hattie, without her black father, was the anomaly. Her heart contracted painfully as a rush of protectiveness flowed through her. Moving her hand to Hattie's shoulder she pulled her sister into her embrace and smiled at the little girl's look of surprise.

I need to be nice to her all the time, thought Carrie. *One day we'll be all each other has.* For there was no father, for either of them; no uncles or aunts or cousins or grandparents.

The car slowed to a stop. Carrie had undone Hattie's seatbelt, hoping Mr Lacey hadn't noticed that she'd never worn her own.

'I'd better walk you in, make sure your uncle is there,' he said, eyes on Carrie's again in the mirror.

Carrie averted her gaze and looked out of the window. She craned her neck, held up her hand in a wave at nobody. 'He's there, waiting by the gate,' she said, fumbling with the door handle. 'Come on, Hattie. Thanks, Mr Lacey.'

Dragging her sister across the seat she pulled her out of the car, slamming the door closed on Mr Lacey's somewhat startled face.

'Come on,' she said, and gripping Hattie's wrist she pulled her into the park.

Mr Lacey's car idled on the gravel drive. Out of the corner of her eye Carrie saw the car reverse a few feet.

All the better to view us through the gates, she thought. Moving Hattie in front of her she pushed the little girl gently in her back. 'Run,' she ordered, 'to the playground.'

*

Strangely, for the middle of the summer holidays, the playground was deserted. Carrie leaned over, put her hands on her knees and breathed deeply.

'Go and play for a while,' she ordered Hattie.

Hattie mimicked Carrie's posture. With her head hanging down she said, 'I'm thirsty.'

Carrie straightened up, cast her mind back to when she'd come here with the school. There had been a water fountain, she was sure of it. Looking around she spotted the copse of woods across the uneven football pitch and smiled. That was where it had been, on the sidelines, because they'd all sat down and got told off for getting white paint on their black school trousers.

'That way,' she said. 'We can get a drink.'

'And an ice-cream?' Hattie asked.

Fondness, feelings of wanting to protect her sister vanished, sadness in its place. How many times did she have to tell Hattie there was no money for ice-creams? And just how great would it be if they both could get an ice-cream?

She spotted the patches on Hattie's shoulders, darker than her light brown skin. Sunburn? And she had no more cream and no jacket or shirt to cover her sister. The sun was high in the sky, affording little shade as they walked across the open field. They would drink their fill from the fountain, then go and sit in the woods for a while. Just until the sun moved across the sky a little, Carrie decided. But then they would have to go home, and home was a long way away. She chewed at the skin around her fingernails. What if Mr Lacey was still at the gates, his car engine running, waiting for them to reappear, knowing the story about the uncle was a lie?

But it was too hot to think of a plan, and Carrie wasn't sure why she had taken against Mr Lacey so. He was a nice man at school, everyone seemed to like him. It was just the way his eyes had looked at her, not straight on, but in the mirror in the car. It was like being looked at backwards, and Carrie didn't like it.

The water fountain glinted, the sun's rays catching the silvery metal. Carrie poked at Hattie, ushered her along, hurrying her up, muttering hurried apologies when the little girl stumbled and fell. Her thirst was everything at that moment, and nothing else mattered.

16

The mooring of the boat wasn't as smooth as the journey had been. Harry gripped the railing and stumbled down to where Alice sat with the Hadleys. He looked at each of them in turn, blinking the water away as it splashed up and over the side of the boat.

'Nearly there,' he said with false cheeriness.

They all stared at him with blank, cold eyes. He collapsed into the seat beside Alice.

'Can you try, for me?' he asked quietly.

Before she could answer Gabe heaved himself to his feet and staggered past her. 'Can I give you a hand, mate?' he called to Ben.

Ben raised a hand over his shoulder, an acceptance, a dismissal? Harry wasn't sure. Gabe sat down next to Harry.

'Rough landing,' he said.

'It's hard to dock a boat of this size here. There are these weird currents, all the way around the island and it makes it much more difficult than you might think. Ben was the only sailor I could find who was willing to take us, right Ben?' said Harry.

Ben's hand again, no audible reply. Alice spoke up. 'I think he's trying to concentrate, maybe we shouldn't disturb him.'

It felt like she'd chastised him, and sitting next to Gabe, the all-man, and with Ben at the helm, Harry felt redundant.

Silence descended, the only sound the slap of the water and the boat knocking against the side of the dock. Harry looked to Melanie. 'You okay, champ?'

She nodded at him. Harry looked at the twins beside her, opened his mouth to ask them the same question before clamping it shut. Out of the corner of his eye he saw Ben running up the ladder to lash the boat to the side.

Harry leapt into action, Gabe springing up to assist.

'Everyone up the ladder, Harry and I will get the bags and boxes of supplies,' instructed Gabe.

Harry stared at him. *He* was in charge here, after Ben it was him who should be issuing orders. But there was no time to assert his position, instead he found himself beside the ladder, herding everyone else up to dry land.

He was the last up, and he moved aside as Ben untied the rope and nimbly jumped back into the boat.

'Thanks, Ben,' said Harry.

Ben glanced up at him, shading his eyes from the weak winter sun. 'Enjoy,' he said shortly.

*

They watched him until the boat could no longer be seen in the river mist. Alice shoved her hands in her pocket. She'd not had a chance to speak to Ben before he sailed off. Would he come back as he'd promised, or had he taken her money and run with it?

Slowly she turned to look at their worldly possessions heaped on the quay. She raised her eyes to face the others. 'What now?'

Harry stepped up, grappling with two of the suitcases. 'Now we go to our new home.'

'And our things?' She gestured to the boxes, cases and bags.

'We'll do it in a few trips,' said Harry. A slow smile crept upon his face. 'It'll be safe, nobody is going to steal it.'

She summoned a smile in return, one that was hard to find. As she picked up her own weekender bag she watched as the others began to follow him. She wondered what Harry was thinking, this was supposed to be an adventure, but the tension and uncertainty was palpable. None of them, including herself she admitted, seemed very excited to be here, in their 'new home' as Harry had called it.

She fell into step beside Liz Hadley. 'What's happened to your house, Liz?' she asked conversationally. 'Did you do a quick sale like Harry did?'

'Sorry?' Liz looked startled, as though she'd not realised Alice had been walking beside her.

'Your house, what did you do with it?' repeated Alice.

Liz shrugged, shoulders, bony and narrow, rising and falling. 'Gabe sorted everything,' she replied, a note of apology in her tone.

Alice nodded, waited for something else. Liz remained silent, her eyes on the ground in front of her.

Uncomfortably, Alice fell a couple of steps behind. The twins, Willow and Lenon, walked behind their mother.

'Are you kids okay?' she asked.

The boy remained defiantly face forward, the girl shot a glance in Alice's direction.

'Fine, thanks, Mrs Wilson,' she replied politely.

'Oh, God, call me Alice, please. After all, we're going to be living together.'

Lenon looked up at her for the first time. 'We're going to live together?'

Alice felt herself blushing, there was something in his look, in those dark, brooding eyes that made her look away. 'Not actually together, I understand Harry has got two cottages, adjoining, I think, and we'll take one each of course.' She swallowed, told herself to stop rambling.

She waited for a reply, but nothing was forthcoming. She allowed herself to fall back again so she was now at the back of the small group. In silence they walked on.

*

'Is that it?' Melanie, up front with Harry, tugged on his coat sleeve. 'Is that the house?'

Harry stopped. Pulling his glasses out of his top pocket he slipped them on and squinted in the direction that Melanie pointed.

'Yes,' he said after a moment. 'Those are the cottages!'

She heard the excitement in his tone, saw it on his face as he gathered the others around and gestured ahead to where the grey cottages nestled side by side. Melanie, instead of looking at her new home, watched the others. Suddenly she felt sorry for her father. Nobody wanted this, none of them wanted to be here. It begged the question; why were they here? She knew why she was, and her mother, because Harry wanted this, and it was going to make him better so he never needed the pills again. But Gabe and Liz, and their children, what was their reason?

Melanie slipped her hand into Harry's. 'It's a beautiful house, Dad.'

He looked down at her, a smile crinkling up his face. Instantly she felt better.

'Shall we go and explore our new home?'

His words were just for her, and the others didn't matter. Maybe her and her dad would just let them be miserable, even her mother. But the two of them were going to be just fine.

'Come on,' she said, tugging his hand.

*

'How do we get in?' It was Gabe who spoke up, and Harry turned to him.

'Just twist the handle.' He smiled.

Gabe frowned. 'No key? What about security?'

Harry laughed, long and loud. And it was a genuine laugh, he noticed, just like he used to sound. 'Gabe, buddy, there's no reason to be concerned about security. We are the only people here.' He clapped Gabe's shoulder, in a hard and manly manner, he hoped. 'It's a whole new way of life, but it's all for the better.'

Gabe nodded, lips pinched tightly together. 'How do we decide which family has which house?'

Harry gestured to the cottage on their left. 'That one has three bedrooms, I'm led to believe, so you guys can take that one.'

'How do you know all this?' Gabe stood back, appraised the house. 'Have you been here before?'

Harry shook his head. 'Research, but some of what I read was very, very old, so there might be surprises for all of us.' Catching sight of Alice's face, white and ghostlike, he smiled at her. '*Good* surprises,' he clarified.

'So…' Gabe trailed off, looking a little unsure, Harry thought.

'So we'll go in, settle in, unpack a little. I thought we could meet up and explore in an hour.' He leaned back, raised one arm in the direction of Gabe's cottage. 'The sun will be just above the chimney then, so you know when to come back out.'

He watched as they slipped inside, one by one, a quiet little procession. When the door closed behind the Hadleys, Harry turned to Melanie and Alice, still standing on the path that led to their own front door.

'Did you have to say that about the sun?' Alice said. 'You sound like a bloody pagan or something.'

It hurt, but he managed not to snipe back at her. This was all going to be so new for them, hard for them, much more so than he would find it. After all, Harry had been in the library, on the forums, doing the research.

'Shall we go inside?' He smiled, but it felt stretched and forced on his face.

Alice sighed. Melanie stepped forward. He felt her hand slip into his. Gratefully, he pulled her close.

*

The floors were all concrete, hard and cold underneath Melanie's feet. She frowned, scrubbed the ground with the toe of her trainer. She had expected wooden floorboards, traditional and homely. She moved over to the wall, reached out a hand to touch it. It too, was concrete. Grey breeze block bricks and cement, the jagged points that had not been smoothed away like thorns under her palm.

Melanie drifted around the house, looking into the rooms, waiting for an excitement to come over her. It didn't, but she felt quite tired. Resting her head against the grey wall, she slumped onto an old chest and thought about the day so far.

Alice had barely spoken all day. Harry had attempted conversation, but Alice seemed shut down, mute. Melanie's heart contracted suddenly. Was her mother getting her father's illness; the depression? Melanie was pretty sure it wasn't something you could catch, but wouldn't that just be typical, Harry recovering, her mother failing?

Worry overwriting the tiredness, Melanie clambered off the chest and went in search of Alice. She found her in the kitchen area, staring out of the window. Boxes surrounded her, still taped up. Her suitcases were at her feet, zipped and locked tight.

'Mum, are you all right?' Melanie's voice was sharp with hardly concealed panic.

Alice turned from the window. 'Fine, sweetie,' she replied distractedly. 'Is it time to meet up with the others?'

Melanie went to the open door and stepped outside. 'Yes,' she called. 'The sun is above the chimney now.'

As she went back through the door Alice stared hard at her. 'Come here,' she said.

Obediently Melanie went over to her. Alice swept her up in a hug, holding her tight, so different to the usual cuddles she got from her mother.

'You can still use your watch,' Alice said, and her voice was raw and stripped, and to Melanie she sounded angry.

Later, Melanie sat on her new bed which was actually very old and stroked the thick blanket her mother had placed on top. The meeting hadn't gone very well, after they'd all met up when the sun reached the chimney.

Melanie had hoped everyone might have been a little happier once they'd unpacked their things and made their place. But the twins had been as silent as ever; Liz, their mother, seemed barely there. Half asleep in a false dream world like when Harry had been really bad. Harry had been overly cheerful and Alice had been sullen and sulky. They didn't even get to explore very far before the heavens opened and the rain fell, followed by a sharp snow shower.

'I'd wanted to collect wood for the fires,' said Harry in a worried tone as they all stood underneath a large pine, the spreading branches offering little shelter against the cold and wet. 'But anything we find now will be useless.' He pulled his collar up and regarded the others. 'Tomorrow we need to start finding wood and creating a store. We need to be prepared for next winter, we need to dry anything we find, and it'll need to sit for months.'

'Next winter!' Alice's voice was shrill and angry. 'We need to think about now, tonight and tomorrow, not next winter.'

Harry placed a hand on her arm, soothing, consoling as he had done so many times in the past. 'Organisation is key, Alice. For the future. All wood is wet, even if it doesn't seem like it, it still contains moisture. It needs to be properly cut and stacked before it can burn.'

She'd shaken him off, glared at him. Melanie had looked at the floor, embarrassed.

'Maybe we should start again tomorrow,' said Gabe, the unexpected peacekeeper.

They'd drifted back into their little cottages, out of the grey, sad outdoors and into the grey, desolate interior.

Cold and miserable, she pulled the blanket around her shoulders.

'I'm lonely,' she whispered to nobody.

When the darkness fell and the house grew quiet, Melanie slipped her trainers back on and stood outside the cottage. Next door was quiet too, and she wondered how late it was. She resisted looking at her watch, she wanted to try Harry's thing of telling the time by the sky. But the sun was gone, and she didn't know if she could use the moon in the same way.

She walked away from the cottage, tipped her head back and looked at the sky. There was no moon, only fat, grey clouds. No sun, no moon, no stars.

Despondent, she walked the perimeter of the cottages, coming to a standstill outside the Hadleys' home. A faint light glowed from one of the windows, and hesitantly she stepped up to it and peered in.

The source of light was a candle, she saw with surprise. Harry hadn't packed candles; he had solar powered lamps which would only work with the help of the treacherous sun, of which there hadn't been enough to charge them. Inexplicably she felt shame for her father, and hoped he never found out the Hadleys had candles.

She moved her gaze to the bed, saw the forms of two people entwined, under layers of blankets, their arms around each other as they slept.

Mr and Mrs Hadley's room, she thought, and feeling guilty for spying she went to move away.

One of the figures in the bed moved, turned over. In the dim light that the candle offered, Melanie realised it was Lenon, one of the twins.

Her face grew hot. Lenon slept with his *mother?*

The figure beside him shifted, followed him with arms and legs as he changed his sleeping position. They came to rest, limbs tangled once more, noses almost touching.

Melanie threw herself down to the mossy ground, her fingers at her mouth, her eyes wide.

They were pressed against each other in a way Melanie had only seen lovers doing in movies.

And it wasn't Mrs Hadley in the bed with Lenon. It was his sister, Willow.

17

'How many painters and decorators in the Greater Manchester area?'

Paul looked up. 'Thousands?' he replied.

Carrie sighed. 'Ganju can't find the man's details.'

Paul nodded thoughtfully. 'We should follow up with the girl anyway, try and get some information out of her. What was her name?' He leafed through his notebook. 'Kelly. Kelly Prout.'

'Victoria Prout was leading the vigilante attack outside Ganju's house,' Carrie informed him. 'You should see the mess: eggs broken all over the windows, paint, petrol cans.' Carrie shuddered, remembering. 'It wasn't him,' she said. 'It wasn't Ganju. He wasn't in the country, we checked up on his travel details.'

'Shall we pay a visit to the Prout family?' Paul suggested.

Carrie nodded grimly.

'If this is about the other night, I didn't do anything.' Victoria led them into her spotless, new-build semi-detached house, heels clicking on the parquet flooring. Carrie stared after her, wondering who wore heels in the middle of the day at home. Perhaps the woman was going out.

'I hope we're not disturbing you, are you on the way out anywhere?' she asked, politely.

Victoria appraised Carrie coolly. 'No, I have an hour until I go to Pilates at the leisure centre.'

Carrie suppressed a smile. 'We were hoping to talk to Kelly. In spite of what you might think, we're eager to try and find out exactly what happened to Kelly and I'd like to know if anyone else was with her.'

Victoria's hand came up to her chest; she twisted the long chain she was wearing, dragging it through her fingers. 'Kelly's at school,' she said eventually. 'And Tanisha would have been with her, but I wouldn't expect too much from her mother.'

Paul, across the room studying the photos that adorned the lounge wall, looked over his shoulder. 'Why not?' he asked.

Victoria shrugged. Tanisha's mother is… carefree with raising her kids. There're too many of them to keep a close eye on, if you know what I mean.'

'They run wild?' Carrie asked.

'Pretty much. Tanisha's a nice kid but the father is unemployed, mother is the opposite end of the scale, working all the hours God sends. The kids are left to fend for themselves.'

Carrie pinched her lips together, a scenario of the family running through her mind. The dad, on the sofa all day, cans of beer by his side, the mother working three jobs, in a factory, in a restaurant, cleaning, maybe, all hours of day and night just to make ends meet. Just like her own mother, thought Carrie, minus a husband. She pulled a page from her notebook, passed it across to Victoria along with a pen.

She clicked on her phone, copied a number on the pad and pushed it back across the table. 'You can understand that I don't want this happening again, right? These are *kids*, it's our job to protect them.'

'And it's our job to protect the community.' As Victoria reached out to take the pen, Carrie held onto it until the other woman's eyes met hers. 'No more hanging around outside Ganju Bandari's home, okay?'

Victoria's eyes flashed for a moment. Finally she nodded. 'All right,' she murmured.

Tanisha's mother, Carol, a harassed-looking woman with two toddlers hanging onto her legs, wasn't as forthcoming as Victoria Prout had turned out to be. Behind her, inside the house, more children screamed and shouted unseen.

'Kelly hasn't been round lately,' she said, one arm clinging to the doorframe as the little ones at her feet did their best to unbalance her. 'Tanisha's not back from school yet, she has to be back by dark though,' she said, her eyes wide at her last words, as if realising suddenly who was on her doorstep. 'She's not in trouble, is she?'

'No, not at all,' smiled Carrie. 'We just want to talk to her about an alleged incident which happened a couple of weeks ago.'

'The paedo in Eccles?' Carol frowned, slapped absently at the hands of her children. 'I heard about it, that Prout woman was on the phone, screaming bloody murder. I spoke to Tanisha, she said she didn't go inside the house, only heard about it when Kelly ran out.'

Carrie suppressed a sigh as she handed over her card. 'We'd really like to speak to Tanisha, just to find out what she saw, what she heard, if anything.' She saw the sudden fear in Carol's eyes. 'Don't worry, she's not in trouble, we just want to make sure our streets are safe, you understand that, right?'

Carol nodded, reversing awkwardly back inside, clutching Carrie's card in her fist.

When the door closed, Carrie turned to Paul. 'We're not far from Ganju's house, let's head over there, check everything's okay on the way back to the station.'

Paul nodded, snatched up the keys from Carrie's hand. 'I'll drive,' he smiled.

She grabbed them back. '*I'll* drive,' she said, softening her words with a smile.

'Big difference between those two mothers,' he commented as they pulled away with a final glance towards Carol's home. 'Victoria wasn't kidding when she said Carol had a lot of kids.'

'I know, right?' Carrie huffed out a laugh. 'Victoria and Carol would never be friends, but that's the nice thing about kids, they don't see each other that way.'

'Carol reminded me of my mother,' Paul said, a smile playing around his lips. 'All the kids liked coming to my house; regardless of how many of them were there, Mum would always make sure everyone was fed.' He glanced back at Carol's house. Carrie noticed the faraway look in his eyes before he blinked, looked back at her. 'What about you, what was your house like, growing up? Filled with kids, or was yours more a Prout household?'

Carrie gripped the steering wheel, saw her knuckles turn white. Her home flashed across her mind, not the home of her childhood but the home after her innocence had been snatched away. The silence, the darkness when the electricity went off and the cold when the gas bill wasn't paid. The slumped, immobile form of her mother, in the chair, or, on really bad days, on the floor, curled up foetal-like. The only moving part of her mother her hands as she clenched and unclenched her fists, grabbing on to a memory of a daughter who was no longer there.

Carrie forced herself to relax her fingers until the blood flowed freely again. 'Just me,' she said. 'Just me and my mother.'

He was going to carry on the conversation, she saw it, knew it, because he was relaxed and friendly in nature. And she had to stop him, because that was why she liked working with Paul, because things never got personal, and she didn't want him to ruin that.

'Put Ganju's address in the satnav,' she said, even though she knew the way. Anything to get him off track.

He sensed it, by the silence and the atmosphere that surrounded the sudden wall she'd put up.

He did as she said, falling back in his seat, saying no more about Victoria, or Carol, or his own happy family.

18

'Right.' Harry clapped his hands, turned in a full circle to study his subjects.

That was how it seemed to Alice, and she cringed. Liz stood to her left, swaying slightly, and Alice reached out a hand. 'You all right, Liz?'

The other woman seemed to take an eternity to acknowledge Alice, and when she did, she gave a barely perceptible nod of her head. Alice faced Harry again.

'The rain has stopped, we need to make sure we don't have another night like last night. I'm sure you'll all agree that spending the previous twelve hours without heat and running water was unpleasant.' Harry stopped, surveyed the little group again before correcting himself. 'It wasn't unpleasant, it was a lesson.' He gestured to the bottled water in his hand. 'These won't last forever.'

Alice felt her face flushing with heat. She glanced at Melanie, but Melanie seemed in a world of her own, her eyes fixed on the twins. Alice followed her daughter's gaze. The twins demanded to be observed, she realised. Like an extreme work of art or an animal behind bars in a zoo. What was it about them? They were beautiful beings, she realised. Stunning in their physique, both tall and lean and pale. Their hair was a kind of ordinary brown, which could be boring but just… wasn't. It was the kind of colour that Alice herself sought relentlessly to cover her blonde hair, a shade she could never quite find in a bottle. Their faces were flawless, skin that was clear and healthy looking, matching noses that were straight and a perfect size. It was their eyes, though, Alice realised. Eyes of a slate grey that seemed to see so much deeper that her own ordinary eyes. They were still, unmoving, often silent, but always observing.

Alice let out a little sigh. The pair of them really were extraordinary.

Another clap from Harry brought her back to the present.

'We have a lot of ground to cover. We need to see what is on this island that we can use to live.' He held up a hand, one finger pointing up in the air. 'Not just live, not just survive…' he paused dramatically, 'but *thrive*!'

'Oh Jesus,' whispered Alice.

Gabe, opposite her in the circle, caught her eye. He grinned wickedly, offered her a wink. She smothered a smile in return.

An ally, against Harry and his dramatics that for some bizarre reason nobody else seemed to find amusing.

'Freshwater streams, clear, running water. Alice and Lenon, you're in charge of finding that.' Harry ushered the two to stand together. Alice made her way over to stand by the twins.

'Because as well as finding what we need to, this is going to be a "get to know you" exercise too. Melanie, you're with Willow and Gabe, and firewood and stores is your project. It doesn't matter if you can't carry it back, just remember where it is. Liz and I are searching for food. Pools that might be big enough to hold fish, rabbits we can snare or net for meat; edible plants. Anything that will give us sustenance.'

Alice looked over at Liz, expecting a look of distaste. But Liz remained stoic, a little nod of her head the only sign she'd actually heard Harry.

Harry moved between each group, handing out a bottle of water each. 'Back before it gets dark, everyone. We'll meet here, and I've got something special planned as a thank you for all your hard work.'

Alice raised her eyes in Lenon's direction. In return he offered her a polite smile before turning to his sister. 'Coming?' he asked.

Melanie jogged up beside them. 'Willow is in my group,' she said.

Lenon regarded Melanie through sleepy-looking eyes. 'I don't think we need to worry too much about groups.'

Melanie stood her ground. 'My dad did this because he wants everyone to get to know one another. If we stay with the people we know, that won't happen.' Melanie flicked a glance at Willow. 'He's worked hard coming up with this idea, it would be nice if we do this for him, and then we'll all meet up later and exchange all the information on what we found individually.'

Alice stared at her daughter. It was a diplomatic speech, and Alice the lawyer was impressed. Melanie was all Harry, that much was and always had been glaringly obvious.

Gabe stepped up to the group. 'Ready?' He smiled at Willow and Melanie in turn.

Melanie hooked her arm determinedly through Willow's. 'Ready,' she confirmed. 'See you later,' she called to Alice, and with a little wave the three of them walked away.

'I guess it's just us, then.' Alice turned to Lenon with a smile.

He nodded, an expression on his face unreadable to Alice. 'Let's get this done,' he muttered, and marched off in the opposite direction to the one the others had taken.

*

Beyond the cottages were the woods, so Gabe told them as they walked. Melanie wondered how he knew, had he too done his research on the island, like Harry had? Or had he gone off last night, once everyone had gone to bed, to explore on his own? Melanie risked a glance at him. Did he know his son and daughter slept in the same bed? And why, when Harry had given them the bigger cottage so they would have three bedrooms? She looked at Willow, at Willow's arm which she still held, the same arm that had held her brother close last night. Gently, she disengaged herself from the girl. Willow didn't appear to notice as they walked steadily on.

It was bigger than she'd thought, the copse. Daylight vanished three or four trees in. There was no footpath like in the woods back home, or the forests she'd visited before. It was true wilderness here. The branches were bare, except for a few evergreens. She looked down as she walked, expecting the twigs to crack underfoot. Instead, as she stepped on them, they vanished into a carpet of thick, slushy earth. Willow and Gabe walked to her right, the older man stopping every now and then to inspect something on the forest floor. He picked up sticks, declared them too wet, or 'sodden through' as he put it, before flinging them away.

'It rained really hard last night,' said Melanie. 'Maybe under the firs, where the branches protected the earth we'll find some wood we can use.'

Gabe stopped, scratched his head. 'Wood needs to be seasoned to burn well,' he said. 'Really, I'd be expecting to be collecting for next winter, with this season's stores all built up. I thought Harry might have considered that.'

Melanie frowned, hating hearing her father talked about in a negative fashion.

'Don't get me wrong, Harry's a good man.' Gabe picked his way over to walk beside Melanie. She wondered if he had seen the expression on her face. 'But he's no boy scout.' He smiled at her, a winning, white-toothed grin. 'But perhaps that was what he had in mind; a challenge for us all. We've got a good team, we'll make it work, right?' He reached out his hand, thin and tanned, and Willow moved in to stand between them.

'Not if we stand around talking,' she said as she put an arm around Melanie's shoulders. 'Come on, there must be some dry wood around here somewhere.'

*

'Do you have any idea where the water is?' Alice asked Lenon. The silence had been too long, had gone on since they'd left the cottages, and she was beginning to feel uncomfortable, buried in the quiet. 'There's the water we came in by, of course.'

'We can't drink that.' Lenon's words were quiet, and he didn't look at her, instead remained facing forward as they walked. 'It isn't safe for drinking. We're looking for a stream, a small river, that's free flowing.'

Somehow she felt chastised. Mocked in an extremely subtle way by a boy half her age.

'Well, maybe one of the others will come across one on their jobs they were given.'

No response.

'Your father, probably. He seems very capable,' she tried again.

He gave her a look, loaded with something she couldn't discern. 'He's not my father,' he said.

'Oh.' Alice waited for more, but he offered up nothing else. 'How long has he been with your mother?'

'Ten years,' came the reply.

'Ah, so he's been in your life a long time. Do you have contact with your real—'

'What is this, question time?'

He didn't shout, he didn't even raise his voice, but Alice flinched nonetheless.

'I'm sorry, I didn't mean to pry,' she said softly.

'It doesn't matter.' He stopped at the top of a little hill, looked up and to the left. 'This way.'

They walked on in silence, and this time Alice didn't mind. So Lenon and talk of his father was a no-go area. That was fine by her. On and on they went, until she stopped, leaned over and breathed in deeply.

'Where are we going?' she asked, panting slightly, horrified at how unfit she was.

'Water's this way.' He came back to stand by her. For once he didn't seem off or annoyed, and for that she was grateful.

'How do you know?'

'Do you see over there.' He pointed, a general area. Alice looked, but all she saw were trees and little grassy patches broken up by large bushes.

'See what?'

'Just beyond those brambles, the grass. See how green and thick it is?'

She turned back to look, stared again at where he pointed. 'I see,' she said slowly.

'Vegetation grows like that if it's near a water source. And these, I've been following these for the last twenty minutes.' He went into a crouch, smoothed his hand in the hard, muddy ground.

For a long moment she saw nothing apart from the mud, then, at long last, the shape revealed itself.

'A footprint, of an animal!' She crouched down, grinned up at him. 'What is it?'

'Rabbit, probably. Or a hare.' He offered her a smile in return and it changed his whole face. 'Nothing too sinister. No bears or lions.'

His little joke, as lame as it was, washed away how his earlier angry tone had made her feel.

'Good job, Lenon,' she said, pushing herself to her feet. 'Come on then, let's see this water.'

*

'Have you ever eaten rabbit?'

Liz, shuffling along beside Harry, didn't appear to have heard him. He cleared his throat, waited for her to glance at him, or say something.

Nothing.

'Or pigeon pie? Ha!' He tried again. Liz remained impassive, making her way forward, slowly, too slow for Harry's natural gait. He shuffled around, tried to slow down. 'Of course, if I'd have thought about it, I could have brought some chickens over, we could have used their eggs, the meat.' Harry smacked his hand against his forehead. 'Why didn't I think of that? Everyone likes chicken and eggs.' He paused, stroked his hand over his chin. 'If the guys find a stream, we'll have a hearty diet of fish,' he smiled. 'And rabbits,' he said, stopping for a moment to peer at what looked suspiciously like rabbit droppings by his feet. 'There'll be plenty of rabbits.'

He looked up as Liz shuffled silently past him, moving on, seemingly unseeing, uncaring. Not even looking for signs of wildlife. Not interested in conversing with him, even though the whole idea of this was to break the ice and get to know each other.

Had he ever heard her talk? He thought back to their previous meetings, the dinner party in which she'd been silent.

He waited, watched as she moved over the crest of a small hill and descended the other side until only her head was visible before walking on himself.

It didn't take very long to catch up to her slow, shuffling amble.

They reconvened at the cottages, out the front, in the place where they had branched off in their individual teams. Night had fallen, fast and almost without warning. The heavily clouded day had provided no sunset. Harry arranged the fire, crisscrossing the wood they'd collected, bundling leaves underneath for the tinder. Gabe stood nearby, watching. Reaching into his pocket he pulled out a lighter, flicked it, the flame flashed and burned.

'You all right using this, Harry? Or did you want a go at making your own fire?'

Harry smiled, reached out for the lighter as he mulled over Gabe's words. Was the man teasing him? Making fun of Harry's desire to live as naturally as possible? He decided to be jovial with Gabe.

'How many of these have you got?' he asked, laughing.

'Three or four,' answered Gabe. Slipping a pack of cigarettes from his pocket he offered one to Harry. Harry declined.

'I'll want to practice fire starting,' Harry said, poking at the fire, a flame of happiness within him as it glowed, throwing off light and heat. 'The lighters won't last forever.'

'Yeah, I'd be up for that.' Gabe lowered himself onto a rug that Alice had brought out. Lazily he regarded Harry, the smoke from his cigarette curling upwards. 'Be nice to get back to nature.'

'Girls, Lenon!' Harry called towards the cottages. 'The fire's on, come out here and let's get some dinner going.'

They came out in a procession, Alice in the lead, Liz, Lenon and Willow behind her, all carrying small boxes and plates. Harry clapped his hands together in glee. 'What have we got?' he asked.

They laid their wares on the log by the fire. Tins, mostly, Harry saw with disappointment. Tins were like the lighters, they wouldn't last forever. Soon they would have to find real food, real meat.

'Can you dish it up?' he asked Alice, and then, looking around, 'where's Melanie?'

Alice shrugged. 'Inside, in her room.'

Harry frowned at her, but Alice had turned away to bend over the food stores.

He hurried to the house, dodged inside and over to her open door. 'Melanie, are you coming out for dinner?'

*

Melanie turned away from the window at the sound of her father's voice. It was February, and they were eating dinner from tin cans outside in the garden. She pulled the blanket tighter around her.

As if sensing her misgivings, Harry said, 'We've got a really good fire going. It's warm.'

'Okay.' She walked over to him. He put his arm around her shoulder, pulled her into a hug she knew so well.

'Did you enjoy this morning's activity?' he asked.

Her fingers fumbled for the blanket again, her eyes suddenly full of unshed tears.

She didn't know when she lost Gabe and Willow that morning. At first, for a long time, Willow's arm had been linked in hers. Melanie liked it, the sense that this older, beautiful girl seemed to enjoy being close to her. Gabe had walked behind them, off to one side, and though Melanie and Willow hadn't talked, Melanie had sensed a closeness, a feeling that just by being in the girl's presence she wasn't as alone as she suddenly felt on this strange little island.

Soon they came upon a small valley. It was surrounded by overhanging, craggy rocks which had formed a canopy of cover.

'These are all dry!' exclaimed Melanie, drawing Willow over. 'We should take as many as we can carry.'

A shuffling noise reached their ears. Willow straightened up. 'Gabe,' she said to Melanie. 'I'll go get him.'

Leaving Melanie scooping up the dry sticks she darted up and over the rocks.

How much time had passed when she realised there was no Willow, and no Gabe, and no sound from either of them? She didn't know, not then, not even now, thinking back on it. She dropped her sticks, glanced up at the sun, but couldn't recall where it was when they'd stumbled upon this place.

'Willow?' she called, and stilled herself, listening for an answering shout.

There was nothing, only her own voice thrown back at her, bouncing off the steep, rocky sides.

She picked up her sticks, a pitiful bundle, really, she saw now, and there were many more but too many to carry alone. Stacking them under her arm she clawed her way back up to stand on the lip of the small ravine.

'Willow?' she said again. 'Gabe?'

No reply. And this time, not even her own echo answered her.

She found them near to where they'd started, standing apart, not talking. On Melanie's approach Willow spun around.

'Where were you?' she asked, angrily.

Melanie held the small pile of wood aloft. 'Gathering these,' she said. 'I thought you were going to get Gabe, this is all I could carry on my own.'

Willow sniffed and folded her arms. 'Someone else can get some more tomorrow,' she said. 'It's time to get back anyway.'

'Well?' Harry prompted. 'Did you enjoy it? You found a good store of wood for the fire.'

Melanie offered him as big a smile as she could manage. 'And there's lots more where that came from,' she said.

He seemed pleased that she'd found wood that would keep them warm and heat their food. She thought about the moment when she had found Gabe and Willow, and the streak of colour that had surrounded them, grey and black with hot flashes of lava red, a mist that stood out a foot from their bodies, pulsing and throbbing.

She decided not to tell Harry about that. Instead, she slipped her hand inside his, and followed him outside to the campfire.

19

'Missing twins,' announced Paul as he came into Carrie's office. He balanced two cups of take-out coffee and a brown file.

Carrie stood up, took the paperwork and one cup. Her fingers trembled as she set them down on her desk. Always, when she heard the word 'missing' in conjunction with her work, she showed it outwardly.

'How old?'

'Fifteen.' He gestured to the file. 'The school reported it; absence of three weeks, can't get in touch with the parents, nor the kids. Neighbours haven't seen the family for weeks.'

Two fifteen-year-olds were most likely together. Carrie exhaled. Not young then, not six years old, not the same case, not even really a similar case to… She closed off her train of thought, unwilling to let that name free in her mind.

'And, one more.' Paul pulled a slip of paper out of his pocket and slid it over to her. 'Another child's absence, reported by the school authorities.'

She read the name, tasted it out loud. 'Melanie Wilson.' Sharply she looked up at Paul. 'How old is she?'

'Eleven,' he replied.

She placed the paper on the twins' file. 'Has anyone visited their homes yet?'

Paul shook his head. 'Thought you might like to go now.'

Carrie reached for her coat.

*

The house in Crofts Bank was empty. Carrie cupped her hands to the front window and peered in.

'Furniture still there, there's a coffee cup on the table, and a newspaper. She turned to Paul. 'Someone still lives here.'

He came around the side of the house, looked up and down the street.

'They've been gone a few weeks.'

Carrie turned at the sound of the voice. A woman, old, bent over, stared at Carrie and Paul.

'Weeks?' Carrie moved towards the woman. 'You mean like on holiday?'

The old woman's lips pinched together and she shook her head. 'They took off before it was light, in a hell of a hurry. Woke me up with all the noise. Noise from him, mind, the others never said a word.'

A tingle started on the nape of Carrie's neck and she gestured Paul over. 'Do you know the names of the family that live here?'

'Gabe and Liz Hadley, the twins are Willow and Lenon.' She sniffed. 'Funny names people give their kids these days.' She turned to Paul, her wrinkled face breaking into a smile as she looked at him. 'I'm Sandra. No fancy names in my family.'

'Well, Sandra, we'd appreciate anything you can tell us. I don't suppose the Hadleys mentioned where they were going so early?'

'They never said. They never speak much. Gabe is friendly, actually, but the kids are a bit stuck up and the mother can't string a sentence together. Hammered, I reckon, all the time.' Sandra spoke her last words in a low, conspiratorial tone.

'Do they work, the parents, I mean?' Carrie interjected.

'Liz used to be a nurse, or something in a doctor's surgery. But then…' Sandra mimed a drinking motion. 'I don't know about

Gabe, a building contractor or something, maybe a mechanic. He was always tinkering with his car.'

'Sandra, you've been a great help.' Paul pressed a business card into her hands. 'If you think of anything else, or see any members of the family, will you call us?'

Sandra looked delighted, the smile softening her hard features again. 'I will,' she simpered, eyes only on Paul, Carrie noticed. 'I certainly will.'

Paul mock-shuddered on the way back to the car.

'You're in there,' remarked Carrie. 'Bet she calls you by the end of the day.'

'I won't mind if she has some actual information.' Paul smiled.

Carrie nodded to herself as she clipped the seatbelt on. That was Paul all over. A good, kind man.

'I'll run the names through the computer when we get to the station,' Paul went on. 'And the other family, the Wilsons.' He glanced at Carrie. 'What do you reckon to this?'

She thought as she drove. Missing kids were not so uncommon: custody battles, runaways, one parent leaving with the child. But entire families doing a vanishing act. And two of them at that.

'See if there's a connection between them. Find the registration of the Hadleys' vehicle and run it through, and the one belonging to the Wilsons. We'll get as much info as we can; did they privately rent, have they done a runner on the landlord?' She nodded, the tingling sensation dimming somewhat now she had a plan. 'We'll see what comes up.'

'Did you put the request in for the CCTV at the train station?' Carrie asked as they shed their coats back at the station. 'The caller, the girl who was calling me, did you chase it up?'

'Yeah, I'll look into it while I'm getting the Hadleys' car details.' He gave her a questioning look. 'How long since the last call?'

She pulled her notebook out of her pocket, looked back to the pages where she'd scrawled the call logs. 'About a month,' she replied. 'They've stopped, haven't they?'

It was a troubling thought. The more she contemplated the calls, the more she listened to the recordings, the surer she was that it wasn't a prank. The girl was deadly serious.

'Yes, chase it up,' she said. 'In fact, do it now, then get Gabe's car info, I'll look into the house, if it's privately rented, council or bought. Then we'll try and get some more info on the other family.'

They took a seat at Carrie's desk, she passed over her laptop and switched on her own PC. For long minutes they worked in silence, each pausing to scribble a note. The monitor and laptop pinged occasionally, all the details they requested feeding through the networks.

'Council house,' Carrie announced. 'The rent isn't in arrears yet, not until the first of the month. Gabriel and Elizabeth are the names registered, with Willow and Lenon as minors.' She looked over at Paul. 'What about you?'

'I've repeated my request for the CCTV at the train station. Gabe's registration was easy enough to find and guess what?'

Carrie rolled her eyes. 'Tell me.'

'A Ford Mondeo, registered to a Gabriel Hadley, was reported abandoned on Salford Quayside two weeks ago.'

'Had he reported it stolen?'

Paul shook his head. 'Nope. Uniforms already went round to his house but never got an answer, nor on the phone. No reply to any letters, so they arranged recovery to the car lock-up in Deansgate.'

Carrie frowned. For a family to disappear, a car might be found at an airport or a ferry terminal, but the Salford Quays had not so much as a foot ferry. At least, not in winter. The Mersey Ferry ran boats from Salford all the way to Liverpool in the summer, but they didn't start until July.

The Quays again… she sighed, remembering the previous December, all those days and nights seeking another lost boy.

Her eyes met Paul's. 'Print all that out, then we'll go over to the quays. I want to see where this car was left.'

From Bridgewater Dock, Carrie glanced up at her apartment. What had she been doing when Gabriel Hadley left his car here? Sleeping, probably, or at the gym or the care home or the station. She rubbed her face, cold even though the sun had been shining brightly recently, promising an early spring. It was sad that there were only four places she could ever be.

'Where would they go from here?' Paul's voice broke into her thoughts. 'I mean, it's not far from their home, why drive a few miles and abandon the car here?' Paul turned in a slow circle. 'There's no stations here, no taxi rank or hire car company.'

Carrie looked out over the water. The only way anyone was leaving here without being seen was on a boat.

She shook her head, dismissed the thought and turning she glanced at the apartment building adjacent to the dock. A wide, gated fence led into the underground parking garage. She gestured to the camera mounted for automatic registration plate recognition for the residents who lived there.

'We'll get that CCTV, it should show what Gabe did after he left the car, who was with him, and what they did next.'

Paul was already striding towards the building. 'I'm on it,' he called over his shoulder.

The request for the CCTV was in, the end of the working day was upon them.

'Half hour,' said the building manager. 'I'll burn it onto a disc for you.'

'Very helpful,' remarked Paul as they returned to the quayside again.

'Too helpful,' replied Carrie.

Paul rolled his eyes and laughed. 'You think he has something to hide?'

'Not to do with the case. Maybe elsewhere.' Carrie glanced over at him. 'Don't you?'

'I often find this warrant card encourages helpfulness all on its own.' He smiled. 'Hey, what do you reckon about grabbing a coffee? We've got thirty minutes to kill.'

Carrie chewed on her lower lip. She didn't fraternise with her colleagues. Her thoughts earlier of how little she actually did in her life pricked at her conscience. They were approaching a Costa now, and before she could change her mind, she pointed at it.

'Nice one,' he said, striding towards the door. 'My treat.'

She selected a booth, and while Paul went to the counter to order she pulled out the photos of the three missing children that she'd printed off. The twins, Willow and Lenon, were uncannily alike physically. She wondered if they were close, and as her gaze fell on the lone picture of Melanie she wondered how she felt about being an only child. She wouldn't care, probably, because she'd never known anything else.

Unlike Carrie.

A wave of agony washed over her, and she bit at her finger but it did nothing to stop the tears, sudden and fierce.

'Fuck,' she whispered.

'One Americano, here you go.'

'Oh, cheers,' she said, scrubbing at her eyes with her sleeve.

'Carrie, what's up?' Paul slid onto the seat opposite her, his eyes wide, swimming with concern, missing nothing as always.

She shook her head, attempted a smile. *Don't be nice*, she begged silently, *let it go*.

His hand crept across the table. She watched it with alarm. If he touched her, if he went *that* far, was *that* nice… She pulled her hands back and tucked them in her lap.

'I was looking at the photos, the twins, Melanie Wilson.' She swept her hand over them, knowing it was no explanation.

He sipped at his coffee, all the while watching her.

Carrie sighed, and it felt like it came from the soles of her feet. 'I had a sister,' she said, her voice so soft it was almost inaudible. 'Once, a long time ago.'

Silence fell, along with the scent of misery. It covered their table like a blanket.

20

The weather turned a few degrees warmer as March went on, and it lifted everyone's spirits considerably. The wood, scattered around the island, dried, and every day they went out to collect it. From the stronger pieces, and newly discovered sheets of aluminium found piled against the wall of the boat docking area, Gabe built a store on the end of his cottage. The wood stacked up over the next ten days until it was completely full.

'We need a second store,' proclaimed Harry, observing Gabe's structure and scratching his head.

'The valley where we found the first wood,' suggested Melanie. 'It's sheltered, everything in there was dry.'

He high-fived her. 'Good plan.'

Alice watched them, a true group now, discussing logistics and construction. Only Liz, Gabe's wife, seemed to be the same person as when she'd arrived on the island. Quiet, withdrawn, she never joined in or offered solutions or input. Instead she remained mostly in the cottage, only emerging outside if she were called upon for some chore or another.

After a few attempts, mostly at Harry's prompting, Alice had given up. This whole trip had been Harry's plan, not hers. And besides, Alice now had more important things to do.

With the rest of the group busy at work, minus Liz, Alice backed away from the cottages. She moved slowly, in a relaxed fashion, stopping in the scrublands that bordered the cottages every few yards, casual, meandering. The ground dipped into the grassy place which ran down to the water and the docking bay. Once she was out of sight, Alice ran.

And even though island life wasn't so bad, Alice still hoped Ben would keep his end of the bargain she'd paid him for, and would be there to meet her.

Scrambling over the rocky outlet, she paused to peer over the high stone wall. She felt the first, real smile of the last two weeks break out on her face.

Ben.

'Ben.' She said his name, softly, too quietly for him to hear over the sound of the water lapping against the wall, but he looked up anyway. Perhaps he sensed her presence.

'You came,' she said.

He straightened up. 'You're still alive,' he remarked.

She was taken aback at his words, moments passed before she realised it was a joke. It confused her, Ben hadn't seemed the sort to make jokes.

'Are you coming aboard?'

With a single, fleeting glance behind her, Alice clambered down onto the boat.

It was cold there, on the deck. Alice sat uncomfortably on the same wooden bench that she'd sat on as they'd sailed over.

'Tea?' Ben held up a flask, tilted his head in an enquiring manner.

'Yes, please.'

Alice folded her hands in her lap, covered them with her jacket so he wouldn't see how cold she was. As he disappeared with the flask below deck Alice wondered what she was doing here. She didn't know this man. He was not someone she would come across in normal life, not unless he was in trouble and in need of a lawyer to represent him. But he was someone from outside, someone who wasn't part of the new family she'd been thrust into, and that sort of contact was something she craved.

'How is it, then?' he asked, coming back up from the galley. He passed her a cup, made of tin, and she tried not to make a face at the dark brown liquid.

'Thanks. The island is all right, might have been better in the summer.' She shrugged, sipped at the tea which was surprisingly good.

'Summer will be hard if it's a hot one,' he remarked. 'Not much shade, the rabbits Harry was talking about catching will be hidden until night time. The streams will be lower, harder to collect from. They might run dry.'

She blinked at him, hadn't thought of any of that. To Alice, if the sun shone, everything was easier and better. 'Oh,' she said.

'Are you cold?'

'A little,' she lied; she was freezing.

'You can go in the galley if you want, below deck.'

The air really was biting now, her hands so cold she knew if she looked at them, they would be red and blotchy. She smiled gratefully, slipped past him and down the rickety stairs below.

It was a whole different world down there. She stood in the long, narrow room and looked around. A bed, just enough for one person took up the starboard wall. The blankets were homely, hand crocheted, and looked remarkably clean. The tiny stove was on and heated the room considerably. Pots and pans hung above a sink and a small desk was stationed at the end of the room below a small window that looked out on the deck.

'Do you live in here?' she asked, amazed.

'Sometimes.'

He was close to her, right behind her, so near that his response made her jump. The tea sloshed, spattering onto her hand.

'It's very nice.'

He was trying to move past her, she realised, and she was blocking his way. He came on down the last step anyway, big hands on her shoulders, shifting her gently but firmly. She stumbled and he righted her with a muttered apology.

She watched as Ben moved down to the stove. He told her to sit down if she wanted.

She looked around, the only place she could see to sit was the bed. She perched on the edge, gripping the tin mug, watching him as he busied himself around the cabin.

She relaxed, realising she was warm and safe and feeling that way for the first time since landing on Pomona. The heat in the room settled to a pleasant warmth that blanketed her, everywhere except her shoulders, which burned with an intensity where Ben had laid his hands on her.

*

The wood store was complete. Harry stood back and surveyed it before moving back up. He clapped Gabe heartily on his back.

'It's brilliant,' he said, genuinely pleased with the man's work.

'Not bad, hey?' agreed Gabe. Looking around he leaned closer to Harry. 'Harry, pal, I brought some contraband over, what do you reckon we crack open a bottle, you and me?'

Harry regarded him. 'A bottle of what?'

Gabe grinned, all white teeth. 'Come with me.'

Harry followed him into the cottage. 'Wait here,' said Gabe, and disappeared into one of the bedrooms.

Harry glanced around the room, noticing the difference between Gabe's cottage and his.

This cottage, the one that Gabe, Liz and the twins lived in, seemed not to have changed one bit in the two weeks they'd been here. He crouched down, drew his hand across the floor. The dirt was an inch thick, the lines of his fingers making a trail. He stood up, scuffed his shoe over it. What was Liz doing, all that time when she wasn't with the group, if she wasn't homemaking?

'You got any plans for this place?' he called out to Gabe.

Gabe stuck his head round the door frame. 'What do you mean?'

'Well, Alice and Melanie have made our cottage more… comfortable to live in. Honestly, Gabe, you should see them, tidying, cleaning, moving and shifting stuff.' He laughed but it sounded hollow to his ears. 'Personally, I think the two places are fine as they are, but you know what women are like.'

It was a lie; Harry was meticulous with cleanliness and keeping one's home nice, he had always been more of a homemaker than Alice. It was a trait that endeared him to the other mothers and Alice's friends. Equally, it grated on the husbands, who retaliated by pushing Harry firmly out of their groups.

'Liz isn't bothered much,' said Gabe, vanishing once more into the bedroom.

But if she hasn't been making this place nice, what has she been doing? wondered Harry.

'Ha!' Gabe emerged, clutching a bottle in his hands. He held it aloft. 'Bourbon,' he announced.

Harry hesitated. He wasn't supposed to drink at all on the antidepressants, and he had a feeling that Gabe wasn't a one-glass kind of guy. On the other hand, he had planned to use the island time to wean himself off them. And what better time to start than now?

'Go on, then,' he said. 'Why not?'

Gabe poured in silence and handed a glass to Harry. Harry sipped at it, noted it was a very nice bourbon indeed and threw it back.

Take that, Fluoxetine, he thought.

'Where's Liz?' he asked, settling into one of the wooden chairs by the fireplace.

Gabe cocked his head towards the bedroom he'd just been in, the door still ajar. 'Sleeping,' he said.

Harry was startled, *why was Liz sleeping? Wasn't she feeling well?* 'Sorry, I didn't realise,' he said. 'We can take that bottle over to mine if you like.'

Gabe studied Harry over the top of his glass. With a glance at the bedroom he got up, walked over to the door and peered in.

'Sweetheart, are you okay?' he murmured in a low voice.

Whispered words in return; Gabe opened the door wider and moved across to the bed. Harry craned his neck, watched as Gabe bent over the figure in the bed, tucked the blanket in around his wife, brushed a hand softly over her hair.

He backed out of the room, closed the door quietly and made his way back to the table.

'She's under the weather,' Gabe said, frowning. 'Think she's got a fever.' He shook his head, forced a smile. 'Hopefully a day or two in bed and she'll be right as rain.'

Harry nodded, cast an anxious glance at the bedroom, thinking of Alice's worries of what would happen if someone needed medical attention on the island. He forced her thoughts out of his mind, smiled brightly at Gabe.

'She'll be fine, mate,' he said.

Gabe nodded, but Harry could see the lines of concern etched deeply into his face.

*

'Where were you today?'

Alice, poking at the logs in the rapidly dying fire looked up at Harry. Ignoring his question, she said, 'Fix this, will you?'

He knelt unsteadily down beside her, reaching for the small twigs they kept on the side of the hearth and shoving them under the larger logs. Finally the flames leapt up.

'Thanks,' she said. 'Some of these logs aren't dry enough yet.'

He stood up, using her shoulder as a crutch and dusted off his hands.

'Where were you?' he asked again.

She shrugged, kept her face turned towards the fire. 'Walking, by the water, mostly.' She chanced a look up at him. 'Why?'

He lurched over to the armchair and slumped into it, his hip banging the side table. He shot a hand out to steady it.

'Jesus, Harry.' Alice trailed him, leaned over him in the chair. 'You smell like a distillery, you know you're not supposed to have alcohol on the Fluoxetine!'

He grinned up at her, a lazy smile. 'I stopped taking them.'

Alice fell heavily into the chair next to him. Thoughts rushed at her: Harry, prone in his chair, the curtains pulled across the windows, the room in darkness; her own life, in darkness. As if in answer to her vision, the sun vanished behind a cloud, a gloom settled over the lounge.

'Alice.' His voice made her jump, he gripped her hand, squeezed it and tenderly lay it on his cheek. 'I'm all right, here, I'm okay. We all are.'

She searched his face, reassured herself that here, now, he was the Harry she remembered. The one who was well, who functioned better than anybody she knew.

'If you start to feel bad…'

He kissed her knuckles. 'I'll tell you, I promise.'

Empty promises. She wrenched her hand from his grasp. Had he told her any of the other times that the cloud began to bite at him?

'Because I can't cope with it here, alone, on my own.'

He sat up suddenly. 'That's what I wanted to talk to you about, that Liz, next door. Alice, will you call in on her tomorrow?'

She blinked at him, thrown by the sudden change in topic.

'I already tried, Harry. She's… she's just not interested.'

He shook his head impatiently. 'I was over there, earlier, Alice, she was in bed, it was the middle of the day and she was asleep.'

'Maybe she didn't sleep well last night, maybe she's not feeling very well,' said Alice.

'She's always in bed.'

Alice turned at the sound of Melanie's voice. 'Sweetie, why are you hiding over there?'

Melanie stepped forward from the shadowy corner. 'I wasn't hiding, I was reading.'

'Wait a minute, what do you mean she's always in bed?' Harry butted in. 'Did Willow tell you that?'

Melanie gazed at her father. 'No, I see her when I look through her window.'

An explosion from both of her parents; laughter from Harry, an exclamation of disbelief from Alice.

'Melanie! You can't go looking through people's windows!'

Melanie transferred her glare to her mother. 'What else are windows for?'

Harry let off a peal of laughter. 'She's got you on that one,' he said to Alice.

'Shut up, Harry,' said Alice, unable to keep the laughter from her voice. She turned to Melanie, curiosity getting the better of her. 'Why is she in her bed all the time, is she sleeping, or just, you know, there?'

'Sleeping.' Melanie shrugged. 'Sometimes she's crying.'

Harry's laughter abruptly ended. Alice sank back into her chair.

'Maybe I should try speaking to her again, get her out of the house.' She looked sharply at Harry. 'Did Gabe say anything about her when you were over there?'

'He said she was sleeping and she might have a fever.' He scratched at his head. 'He seemed a bit worried about her.'

'Okay, I'll speak to her, check she's okay. She might be home-sick,' mused Alice.

Melanie stepped closer to her mother. 'Are you homesick, Mum?'

Alice shivered suddenly, in spite of the fire in the grate. She fixed a smile on her face. 'I'm fine, sweetie. I'm just fine.'

*

Melanie knelt beside her father in the mossy grass. She thought about what had been said about Liz, and her parents' concern for her. It was strange seeing a grown woman crying like that, alone in her bed. It made her feel weird, like the times she'd seen her father crying in the same way. Maybe Liz had depression too. And since her father wasn't taking his medication any longer, perhaps he could give it to Liz.

'Dad, if Liz is crying because she's depressed, can't you give her your pills?'

Harry glanced up from the wire he was twisting into a loop. 'It doesn't work that way, honey. The doctor has to prescribe the medication based on what they think from talking to the patient. Pass me that hammer.'

She did as he asked. 'But we have no doctor here on the island,' she said.

'I'm... sure... she's... not... depressed.' He spoke between hammering a stake into the ground. 'Your mother will sort it out, don't worry about it.'

'Gabe isn't helping Liz, though, not like Mum helped you when you felt ill.' It wasn't a question, but Harry put the hammer down and shuffled over to her.

'Maybe he doesn't know what to do. Maybe he's a bit overwhelmed.'

'And Lenon and Willow, they're not helping her either.'

Harry sighed. 'Sometimes people just don't know what to do, so it becomes easier to do nothing.' He went back to the snare trap he was setting, twisted the last length of wire around the thin, grey trunk of a tree.

Now it was time to wait. Melanie sat on a grassy hillock, pulled a notebook out of her pocket.

'What's that?' her father asked.

'I'm recording the birds I see here,' she said.

He came to sit beside her. 'Let's see what you've got then.'

She opened it, read aloud to him the birds she'd spotted so far. 'Swift, sparrowhawk, woodpeckers, plovers.' She closed the book, grinned up at him. 'I saw a buzzard too.'

He smiled in return, their eyes locked together. Happiness flooded her; this is how it should be; her and him, sharing the stuff that nobody else was interested in.

From the corner of her eye Melanie saw movement. Slowly she reached out to lay a hand on Harry's arm. 'Rabbit,' she whispered.

They moved as one, reversing backwards on their hands and knees into the long grass that surrounded the mossy path. Harry stopped and lowered himself fully to the ground to lie on his front. Melanie copied his position.

'Keep still,' Harry said quietly.

The rabbit, fat and brown, zig-zagged in their direction, stopping now and then to nibble at the grass. Sometimes it paused, lifted its head. Its nose twitched as though it could smell them.

'It's coming!' Harry's whisper was hoarse, excitement evident in his voice. Through her chest, Melanie felt her heart banging painfully on the ground beneath her.

The rabbit was at the snare now; suddenly it darted forwards, the entire head inside the loop that Harry had created. Panic, now, Melanie could see by the whites of its eyes. The rabbit lurched forward, tightening the steel. It thrashed, the wire constricted, pinching the rabbit's neck harder.

'Yes!' Harry exclaimed, no longer any need to whisper.

Melanie remained in the long grass, transfixed by the colours that the rabbit threw off. A scarlet red, like blood, which pulsed into a pale pink, gradually dimming to white as the life drained out of it.

Melanie closed her eyes and laid her face down on the ground. The grass was cold against her hot cheek.

21

'How is your mother?'

Alice, who had been waiting for either Willow or Gabe for what felt like an eternity stood up as Liz's daughter appeared in the doorway of her cottage.

Willow, carrying a basket over her arm, stopped. She glanced left and right, seeming to Alice as if she were looking for a way out. Apparently finding none, she walked slowly over to her.

'Getting better,' said Willow, her strange, blank eyes staring at something unseen in the distance.

Alice scrutinised the younger girl's face. It had been two weeks now since anyone had seen Liz. Gabe had told them she had a stomach virus, and she was quarantined for everyone else's safety. When pressed, Willow and Lenon had verified this.

'I think someone needs to see her,' Alice had said to Harry, a fortnight prior, talking in hushed tones in their bedroom. Melanie was there, curled up at the end of Harry and Alice's bed, a place she had taken to falling asleep. More often than not they left her there until morning, Harry covering her with a blanket.

'We don't want to get sick too, though,' Harry had replied. 'I've told Gabe to make sure she has plenty of water, fresh water from the stream.'

'But is that safe?' Alice asked urgently. 'What if she got the virus from it? Bacteria?'

'Then we'd all be ill, and nobody else is.' Harry gripped Alice's leg. 'She will be fine, they're taking good care of her.'

Alice had slapped his hand away and turned to her daughter. 'Have you looked through their window lately, have you seen her?'

Melanie shook her head.

'Melanie?' Alice pressed.

'I haven't, they've put curtains up now anyway,' she protested.

Two weeks had passed, a whole month on the island, with one of the group so rarely seen, Alice could hardly remember what she looked like.

'Are you sure, Willow?' Alice asked now. 'Because if not, I really think we should contact the mainland and get Liz to a doctor.'

Willow stared at Alice. 'We can't contact the mainland, can we?'

Alice gritted her teeth. Today was the day that Ben should be visiting. As yet, nobody knew about her liaisons with him, but if one of the group's health was really at risk, she would get Liz on his boat and take her to the doctor herself. She thought about it briefly, back on dry land, among the lights and the noise and the smells. The vision almost made her mouth water.

'Can I see Liz?' she asked.

Willow shook her head. 'In a few days, maybe. She'll be up and about soon.'

Willow made to move away. Alice reached out and grasped her arm. 'And the rest of you are feeling okay? None of you have caught this stomach virus?'

Willow shrugged. 'We're okay.'

Alice narrowed her eyes at the girl's apparent lack of empathy. 'It's odd, though, isn't it?' she pressed. 'Highly contagious but you three are all fine.'

Willow bared her teeth in what Alice presumed was a smile. 'We're fine,' she said. She pulled away, Alice had no choice but to let her arm go. She watched Willow tread lightly down the footpath, vanishing into the fields that lay below the land upon which the cottages sat.

She looked at the house next door. Gabe was out, checking the snares for rabbits. Alice rolled up her shirt sleeves and picked her way over the thistles to the Hadleys' door.

'Liz?' She pushed open the door, moved quickly inside.

It was the first time she'd been in here, she realised. And wasn't that strange, that they ate around Harry's damn campfire every night, but never entered each other's houses? Alice sniffed. It smelled bad; dry, unclean air and a mustiness that had been present in her own cottage when they'd moved in. But they had cleaned it; even without conventional cleaning fluids they'd scrubbed and mopped and the scent of an unused home had vanished. Stalking over to the windows, she pulled back the rugs that covered the glass. The weak sun flooded in, the shadows disappeared, and Alice looked around in disgust.

Nobody had cleaned here. Dust, dirt and grime covered every surface. How could they live like this? No wonder the woman had got sick.

Spying a closed door, Alice hurried towards it, pushed it open. It was a bedroom, with two mattresses on the floor. A tangle of blankets were heaped on an old wooden chair. Someone slept in here, but there was no sign of Liz.

Alice backed out of the room, tried the door directly next to the one she'd just looked in. Another bedroom; this one had no bed, no mattress, no blankets or sheets. Alice closed the door softly. Harry had given the Hadleys this cottage because it had three bedrooms, yet clearly they were only using two.

Jesus. Alice wrinkled up her nose. What a weird family.

One door left. Wishing she'd left things alone and hadn't started this crusade to check on Liz, Alice stalked up to it and pushed it open.

It wouldn't budge. Alice tried again. Standing back, she looked at the frame. Was it locked? But there were no locks anywhere on this damn place. No privacy, not even on the front doors or bathrooms. She put her shoulder to the door and shoved again, tilting her head back as she pushed.

Then she saw it, almost at the top of the door. A sliding bolt. The door was locked.

From the outside.

Alice lurched back into the main living area, her feet skidding over the dusty concrete. Her fingers flew to her mouth.

Why was there a lock on the *outside* of the door? Was Liz locked in her room? She squinted up, wondering where the lock had come from. Was it old, new? It was coated in dust and grime like everything else, impossible to tell how long it had been there.

A slow burn started within, an anger. She rushed forwards, stretched up and slid the bolt back before reaching for the door handle and shoving it open. The door flew from her grasp, banged back against the interior wall.

Breathing heavily now, Alice headed to the window, yanked the dirty blankets from the glass. She held them in her hand, feeling the dirt encrusted on the material, before screwing them up and clutching them tightly.

Only then did she turn and look at the bed.

Liz. The few times she had seen Liz, Alice had been struck by how thin and gaunt she was. Now, standing by the window, her heart thudded as she wondered if the woman in the bed was even alive.

'Liz?' Her voice cracked and she didn't even recognise it. Who was this shrill woman?

The figure under the sheets stirred. A hand emerged, creeping over the bed cover.

The drapes fell from Alice's hands to the floor. She stepped on them as she walked over to the bed.

'Liz?' Alice's voice a whisper now. Unconsciously she covered the lower half of her face. The smell … earthy and raw and rancid. 'Liz, can you sit up?'

The woman opened her eyes into narrow slits. 'I don't know.'

Her voice was surprisingly strong, and it gave Alice hope. She reached towards Liz, tried not to think about the filthy sheets or the woman she was about to touch who looked like she hadn't washed in weeks. She put her hands on Liz's shoulders and cringed. A memory flashed; Ben's hands on her own shoulders two weeks ago.

Ben.

She glanced at her watch. He should be arriving soon, in little over half an hour.

She had thirty minutes. But that didn't matter now.

Alice slipped her hands under Liz's arms, didn't let herself register too deeply the dampness there. 'You're getting up, we're going to wash you, get you outside in the fresh air. Get some food inside you. Liz, when did you last eat?'

'Don't know.'

Anger, sudden and rich, replaced the feelings of distaste. How could Gabe allow Liz to stew in her own mess like this? And Willow and Lenon, they were practically adults, what were they thinking?

'Can you walk?' she murmured.

Liz met her eyes then, blue on blue, one pair cloudy, unsure, the other, alert, with a quiet fury.

Liz could walk, it turned out. Unsteadily and very slowly, but she made it to the bathroom. No showers here, the same as in Alice's cottage, just a big, claw-footed bathtub. Alice stared at it as Liz leaned on the sink. She wasn't sure about bathing this woman that she barely knew.

And she's not my mother, nor my daughter, thought Alice. *She's not even my friend.*

Bending around Liz, Alice filled the sink from the water bucket on the floor. She wrinkled her nose at the green-tinged water, but deemed it clean enough to do the job. Spying a face cloth on the side she grabbed it up, sniffed it gingerly.

'Wash your face, then we'll get you into the lounge,' she said.

Feeling suddenly drained and rather unsteady herself, Alice sat on the edge of the bath. She watched as Liz mopped at her face, wondering how to phrase a question that hadn't even fully formed in her own mind. The lock… the lock on the outside of the door.

'Liz,' she began. 'Why was—'

The door flew open, Alice shrieked and grabbed at the side of the bath. The door bounced against the wall and flew back. A boot, heavy and black, stopped its progress. A large, masculine hand opened it again. Gabe filled the doorway.

'Liz,' he said. Liz's hand stilled, the face cloth fell with a splash into the sink. 'Liz, are you feeling better?'

She met his eyes in the mirror above the sink. 'A bit.'

'Liz decided to get up for a while,' Alice said. He looked at her again, gazing down at her. Hurriedly Alice stood up to put her on a more even height with him. 'She's feeling a lot better. She decided to have a wash up and get some fresh air.' Alice stared at him the way she'd stared at men in the dock in her courtrooms. She didn't blink. She didn't look away. 'There was a lock on the outside of her bedroom door.'

She let it hang there, a not so subtle question. The echo of her accusation spun between the three of them in the small room.

He cocked his head, gestured for Alice to come out into the hallway. Wiping her hands on a towel she followed him.

'Liz had a bad fever, she got… violent.' His voice dropped on the last word, his eyes downcast. 'She's been really bad, Alice, we… we just didn't know what to do.' He passed his hand across his face, blinked once and shook his head. 'She was scaring the kids, hallucinating.' He turned away from her. 'She went for the knives.'

Alice went cold. She darted a look towards Liz, still hanging onto the sink in the bathroom.

'It's not like her, she's the most placid woman I've ever met,' Gabe said, raising his head to stare at his wife. 'I don't think she even remembers.'

Alice snapped her attention back to him. 'God, Gabe, why didn't you say something? We could have helped you!'

He pinched his lips together. 'It's a bit embarrassing, isn't it? Your family were kind enough to give us this chance, I didn't want to spoil it for everyone.'

Alice reached out, squeezed his arm. The capable, cheerful and charming Gabe had problems. Somehow, it was reassuring. She returned her gaze to Liz, unable to see the normally calm, slow-moving woman as a threat to her family. But fevers and infections did strange things to people, she knew that.

'I'm so sorry, Gabe, but you didn't need to hide it. We're all in this together.'

He smiled, nodded, and raised his hand to touch her hand, still on his arm. 'Thanks, Alice, that means a lot.' He cast a glance back towards the bathroom where Liz still stood motionless at the sink. 'She's much better now, the fever seems to be going, she just needs to get her strength back. I'll take it from here. Liz, let's get you in the bath.'

Alice glanced at her watch, saw the time was ticking fast. Liz, Gabe and their troubles diminished. All was well; Liz was on the mend, Gabe had confided in her. It comforted her, that they'd pulled together a little bit, even if it was only in words. She offered Gabe a smile and moved past him.

'I'll come by tomorrow, Liz. I'll bring some breakfast, we need to start feeding you up.' She darted to Gabe, embraced him in a quick hug, hoped the strange, mournful look in his eyes would disappear once his wife recovered. 'We're all a team here, Gabe, don't forget that,' she said. A quick, embarrassed laugh. 'God, I sound like Harry!'

This time, Gabe joined in her laughter.

She climbed down the rocky inlet, crouched under an overhanging branch that seemed to be growing out of the wall and checked her watch.

Ten minutes to spare. Realising she was shaking, Alice wrapped her arms around herself. Still the tremors rocked her body. An aftershock, she knew, of the horrible state Liz had been in, the thought of Gabe, lovely, genial Gabe and his kids struggling to handle her illness all on their own.

In the distance she saw Ben's boat coming and she let out a breath she hadn't even realised she'd been holding. She stayed where she was, watching the progress of the boat on the choppy water. She wondered if he realised none of the others knew that he came here. She wondered what he made of it, or if he even cared.

When Ben docked, she could hardly clamber down into his boat. Seeing her difficulty he reached for her, helping her off the dockside, and then pushing her down into the little galley.

'Something's wrong?' His voice was clear and loud in her ear, his breath played over the side of her face.

'Liz has been ill,' she said, her words a rush. 'Really quite badly sick, and I didn't know.'

That was it, she realised. *I didn't know.* The fact that she had been so wrapped up in her own loneliness and her own fears that she hadn't paid any attention to anything going on with anyone else.

Poor Liz, and poor Gabe, dealing with it all on his own, not wanting to burden her or Harry.

She leaned into Ben. He didn't seem to mind. His arms encircled her, and suddenly he was closer than he'd ever been. She breathed in deeply. He smelled of sea air and a cleanliness. She inhaled sharply, trying to dispel the aroma of Liz and her room.

After a few moments Ben pulled away. Alice thought about gripping his arms, forcing him to hold onto her, but his limbs slipped through her fingers and she sat back, a blush staining her face.

'Drink?' he asked, roughly, his eyes piercing hers.

Alice nodded, unable to meet his eyes. 'Yes, please,' she whispered.

22

Carrie and Hattie – 1998

The woods were denser than Carrie remembered. Or maybe, when she'd come here with the school, they hadn't really gone into the woods. She slowed her steps as she thought back. The memory was fuzzy; a warm day, childhood friends, ice-creams, laughter, horses. Nothing of the actual park or the attached forest at all. And the field where the horses were seemed to have vanished.

'It's a bit cold,' said Hattie.

Carrie stopped walking and turned around to study her little sister. As she did so, she rubbed her hands over her own bare arms. Hattie was right; the trees were thick here; no sunlight came through. To Carrie it was a welcome change from the scorching sun that had burned down on her pale skin. But Hattie, she noticed, had goosebumps. Hattie's liquid brown eyes stared mournfully up at her. Carrie put her arms around Hattie, squeezed her tiny frame affectionately.

'Walk faster,' said Carrie. 'You'll soon warm up.'

She dropped her arms, walked away, hurrying now, eager to get out of the woods and to the other side. She stopped so suddenly that Hattie crashed into the back of her legs. If they came out the other side of the forest they'd be even further from home, and they were far enough away as it was, much further than Carrie had ever been on her own.

'We're going back,' announced Carrie, grabbing at Hattie's hand. 'Come on.'

Somewhere to their left, the sound of a cracking branch echoed around the trees. Carrie stopped again.

'What was that?' Hattie's voice was high, the hint of a tremble present that promised tears were near.

'A bear,' deadpanned Carrie, stifling a giggle. 'Come on.'

The little girl squealed, pulled her hand out of her sister's and flung her arms around Carrie's legs. 'I wanna go now, I'm scared!'

Carrie nudged her away with her knees, but when Hattie didn't move she grabbed her shoulders and pushed her. Hattie flew backwards, landing on her back on the forest floor. She burst into noisy tears.

'Hattie, I'm sorry, but...' Carrie pulled at her own hair in frustration. 'Please, come *on*!'

The younger girl sniffed, drew in a deep breath and released it in a scream.

'Oh my GOD!' Carrie looked around, mortified that someone she knew might witness her inability to look after her little sister.

What if the cool kids in the years above her at school were hanging out here? She would be so embarrassed. She stamped her foot as Hattie wailed on. It wasn't fair, it wasn't fair that Hattie always did this, it wasn't fair that their mother expected Carrie to do this. Fury, red and hot scratched at Carrie's skin. There were no more words, no more cajoling, pleading, reasoning or bargaining. This was it.

Carrie spun on her heel and stalked away, leaving Hattie still on the ground, the dry, dusty dirt smudging through the little girl's clothes. Hattie's cries followed her. Carrie began to run.

*

She didn't go far, she'd run for less than a minute, she figured, before the guilt set in. And was it guilt, or was it the sudden realisation that she couldn't hear Hattie crying any longer?

She turned back to where she had left her sister alone.

The earth was dry, crumbling under her feet. The ground was split where no rain had fallen for weeks. Brambles snagged her ankles, growing in snake-like trails along the forest floor. Carrie stopped and turned in a full circle.

Am I lost?

'Hattie!' she called, an edge to her voice. 'Hattie, this isn't funny, come out now.'

There was no reply. No sound; even the birds were quiet. Carrie stopped. A familiar smell reached her on the hot air; coconuts; the scent of sunny days.

Hattie's sun cream that their mother had made Carrie put on them both.

Carrie turned, to the left, to the right, but the scent was all around, enveloping, consuming.

'Hattie?' Carrie moved forward on legs that shook terribly. One step, two. With the third she fell to her knees. Frozen, statue-like. Nothing worked any longer; not her arms, not her legs. Her lungs were numb nothingness. She tried to call, to shout, to scream her sister's name but nothing worked, nothing came out.

They found her that way, the dog walker first, who summoned the police who brought along her mother. They picked Carrie up, her legs bent as though she were still kneeling in the under-growth. Her mother, Mary, up in her face, asking for her young-est daughter, over and over again.

A dog brushed past her, a huge tan-coloured Alsatian. It paid Carrie no heed. Its handler held the leash tightly, a crumpled piece of material in his other hand. Hattie's shorts, pink and white and red.

Red?

They hadn't been red, they had been pink and white striped. Red.

Carrie vomited onto the dry earth. She waited for her mum's arms to encircle her, to rub her back. But her mother didn't step forward. Nobody did.

Carrie was alone.

23

Melanie had often felt that her family was fragmented. Different pieces, she'd mused in the past, with her mum being out all the time and bent over her laptop even when she was at home. Harry would be at Alice's beck and call, or 'making life easier', as he'd explained it. And with all his help and all their money, still they were never aligned as a family.

Now, on the island, things were even worse.

Moodily Melanie kicked at a pile of leaves. It was supposed to be different here, no laptops or jobs, just two families working together, enjoying a life free of everyday problems. Instead they spent all their time apart and barely speaking. Willow and Lenon spoke only to each other, shunning Melanie, their mother, their father, and not even sparing a glance at Harry or Alice. Not that Alice was there to be glanced at, thought Melanie.

Where did she go, her mother? Not making friends with Liz, that was for sure. Liz remained unseen, hidden away. Melanie couldn't understand it; was she ill? Was she dying, and that was why her family had brought her here? Gabe seemed to be the only normal person, along with Harry. Together the two men did the everyday chores; trapping, skinning, cooking, collecting. And no matter how hard Melanie tried to lend a hand, she felt pushed out.

Now, standing on the crest of the valley on the north side of the island, she'd never felt more alone.

A flash of movement in her peripheral vision caught her eye. Someone in the distance, amid the small copse beyond the stream. Bored, Melanie decided to follow them. Keeping low, she moved down the dip, past the second wood store and up the small hill. In the distance she saw a movement again, in and out of the trees, too far away to identify.

By the time she reached the copse nobody was there. Melanie's shoulders slumped as she turned in a full circle. Pausing as she stared towards the south she frowned. Was that a boat approaching? Excited now at the thought of company, Melanie broke into a run.

She hooked her hands over the lip of the concrete wall and peered over. The boat had docked, though there was no sign of any passengers. Lying flat on the ground, Melanie waited patiently.

Ten minutes later, boredom set in again. Melanie pushed herself up, walking the length of the dock and scrambling down onto the wet rocks below. She moved carefully along them, out into the water, following the curve of the stones that formed a natural jetty. At the end, she held on tight, went into a crouch and hung on as she leaned out as far as she could to read the boat's name.

The *Barnard Castle*.

Her left hand slipped and wedged painfully in a crevice. She pulled it out and reversed slowly back to the concrete part of the dock.

It was Ben's boat, the man they'd paid to bring them here. Why was he back? And, if he was no longer on board, where had he gone?

Melanie turned towards the cottage, imagined the young boat captain inside, sipping tea or some of Gabe's horrible whisky. With a smile breaking out on her face for the first time in what seemed like ages, Melanie ran towards home.

*

Harry sat in the chair in the cold front room of the cottage. He should be out, checking the traps, but Gabe would have that covered. He glanced at the fireplace, thought about building a fire to put on later in the evening, but it was a warm day, they might not need it.

He poked at the small hole in the arm of the chair. It looked like a cigarette burn, but not from him or Alice. The hole was decades old, like the chair.

His pills sat in his lap and he picked up the bottle, gave it a little shake. Removing the lid, he peered in at the two solitary tablets.

Just two left.

He hadn't taken any for days, and he still felt okay. He checked himself for reassurance. Yes, he felt all right.

Not perfect, a little voice whispered. *But good enough*.

What if it came back?

Alice would leave him, she would take Melanie.

No, she couldn't, he reminded himself. There was no way off the island. He wondered if she fully realised the fact, or indeed if she had thought about it at all. After all, from the docking bay you could see the bright lights of Salford. Subliminally it probably gave her all the comfort she needed.

The door crashed open, startling Harry from his thoughts. He spun in his chair.

'Hey, Melly,' he smiled. A genuine smile at the sight of his daughter. 'Why are you in such a hurry?'

She stopped in the doorway, glanced around the room. Surreptitiously, Harry slid his pill bottle down the side of the chair cushion.

'Is anyone here?' she asked.

'Just me, sweetie. Are you looking for your mother?'

She smiled but to Harry it looked like a grimace. 'Yeah, she's probably...' she tailed off before waving her hand towards the door. 'Out there. See you later, Dad.'

He watched her as she pulled the door closed behind her. His fingers fumbled down the side of the chair until they found the pill bottle. He pushed it in deeper.

Out of sight, out of mind.

*

Melanie circled the cottages slowly, stopping to look left and right. There was no sign of her mother. There was no sign of anyone. *Where were they all?* What did the inhabitants of the island do all day? Why wasn't Harry involved? Why wasn't she included? Where had Ben gone?

She scuffed the toes of her trainers as she made her way back towards the docking bay. If the boat was still there, she would go aboard, find out why it was here. A thought occurred to her: maybe Harry had arranged for him to come, to bring some treats. Wine for her mother, a sweet hamper for her. Melanie jogged onwards, smiling to herself at what lay ahead.

She scrambled down from the concrete platform, brushed her hand along the wooden trim of the boat's starboard side. The boat rocked gently in the water as Melanie swung her legs over the side. She walked around to the little cabin, noted that the door was closed. She pressed her hands up against the small pane of glass above the door and peered in.

For a few seconds she watched the man, Ben, she reminded herself, as he lay face down on the narrow bed. He wasn't sleeping though, she noted as he moved.

She pulled back, her hands flying to her mouth as she realised what she was looking at. Her face reddened as she pressed her fingers to her lips to stop a giggle erupting. Suddenly she wished Tanisha or Kelly were there to witness the boat man having sex.

She went into a crouch, thoughts whirling at her now. Why would the boatman sail all the way over here just to have sex in the privacy of his own cabin? The answer was immediate; because he was sleeping with someone who lived on the island!

Hot now in spite of the cloud cover, Melanie gnawed on her fingernail. It had to be Willow, after all, she was beautiful and the boatman was young. And the other women on the island were married.

Willow…

Just the thought of it made the mysterious girl even more interesting to Melanie than she already was.

On her hands and knees, Melanie crawled to the window at the stern of the boat. She inched her way up and put her eye to the window.

They were finished, she realised, half sorrowful she had missed the finale, half thankful she hadn't witnessed it.

The woman had her back to Melanie, her spine long and strong, her skin creamy and smooth. Her colours were pale blue and a baby pink.

She's happy, thought Melanie. *Those colours are happiness and contentment and love and satisfaction.*

Ben stood off to one side, saying words that Melanie couldn't hear. The woman turned to him, a smile lighting up her face.

Melanie sagged against the side of the cabin, her fingers scraping the wood as she sank to her knees. And even though she couldn't see them, she knew her own colours scraped and shifted to the deepest black.

Ben's lover wasn't Willow.

It was her mother, Alice.

Melanie ran as far away from the boat as possible. On the other side of the island the layout was completely different. There was no bay here, nowhere for a boat to dock, not even a small pebbled beach like there was on the other side.

Melanie passed through the old industrial building, once a factory for the island's workers, now just barren land, graffitied and falling down. Possibly unsafe, Harry had said when they'd explored, poking at the crumbling brickwork. Best not to come here.

Well screw him, Melanie thought now. Irrationally she was angry at him, even though her sense told her that her fury should be directed at her mother.

But it wasn't anger that came to the forefront of her mind when she thought of her mother. She felt hurt, wounded, sick on Harry's behalf.

Harry who didn't have a clue that his wife was cheating on him. *Poor, stupid Dad.*

Melanie picked up a handful of concrete chips and threw them at the wall of the barely-standing underpass. Her anger faded before coming back strong, directed at Ben this time. Ben the boatman was on her mind too. He knew Alice was married. She kicked at the loose gravel, sent it spraying in all directions. A glass bottle lay discarded near the underpass entrance. Melanie picked it up and smashed it against the wall. Flinging it to one side she came out into the sun, moving uphill now, to the very edge of the land.

She sat down on the mossy grass, moved over her front to peer over the edge. It was the high point of the island here, a thirty-foot drop onto the rocks and water below.

Melanie laid her head on her hands as she stared down. It was nice here, better than the network of canals back home, where the rubbish collected and the dog owners failed to pick up after their dogs. This was nature, she decided. And it was a little bit sad she had nobody to share it with.

Melanie pushed herself up and walked away from the water. It was *too* nice there, she decided, and it was being spoiled by the knowledge of her mother's betrayal. She picked her way into the woods, crashing through the trees, moving faster and faster until she was running. When she reached the new, secondary wood store she stopped and slipped inside.

It was dark in here, and smelled of old, still damp, dank wood. She stared at the huge log pile, her angst about her mother replaced with pride that she had helped create this store. Through the dark brown, something glowed red near to the back of the stack. Melanie blinked, moved closer and put her eye to the pile.

There was something back there, a bag, or a piece of clothing. Melanie slipped her small hand in the gap, her fingers closing around something, not a bag, not material; it felt rubbery and hot. She pulled at it gently, yanking harder as it caught on a small branch, wiggling her hand as much as the space would allow to free it.

It popped out, sending her stumbling backwards. She landed on the dirt floor, the red thing flopping onto her chest.

Melanie stared at it until her vision went funny. A scream threatened, tears pricking at her eyes. With a yell she flicked it away to land in the far corner of the wood store. It sat in the shadows. Melanie turned on her side and screwed her eyes shut.

All the while her heart thumped in her chest and the tears spilled over to her cheeks.

*

His body was hard and firm. So unlike Harry's, Alice mused, as she ran her fingers up Ben's naked leg. She said Harry's name inside her head again, wondering why she didn't feel the need to snatch up her own clothes and run from the boat back to him.

She had never had an affair. There had been opportunities; countless colleagues and fellow lawyers and even clients, but she'd never even contemplated it before. And perhaps this wasn't an affair. Maybe it was a need for comfort, for her body had been in some sort of shock, and Ben had seen and had tended to her in a way which had worked.

'I can come over every week, now, if you want.' Ben's voice was muffled by the pillow. 'My job on the east coast has finished, I've got more spare time.' He raised himself up on a forearm and regarded her. Lazily he traced a finger over her stomach.

'Yes,' she said.

She smiled at him, went to get her clothes. He came at her again. Her shirt dropped to the floor and she opened her arms.

Harry was napping in his chair when she slipped inside the cottage. Melanie was nowhere to be seen. Alice breathed a sigh of relief; sometimes her daughter seemed to see right into the very core of her. She moved silently past Harry into the bathroom, tearing off her clothes and leaving them in a pile on the floor. Ben's sperm ran a track down her leg. As she heaved the cold water from the waiting buckets into the tub she caught sight of her reflection in the mirror, marvelling at the woman who peered back at her. Her skin was glowing, her cheeks red. She moved back, cast a critical eye over the rest of her. What did Ben think of her forty-year-old body? She pinched at the skin on her stomach, looked backwards at her legs. Twenty years of wearing heels had been her cardio workout, and those years had served her well. All those long days meant she'd barely had time to eat, not like Harry who snacked at home all day. Nothing had spread, things were mostly nice and tight.

She sank into the cold water, thinking back over what she had done. How old was Ben? His own face was somewhat weathered, but being outside in all seasons on a boat would do that. His eyes were old, but his body was youthful, strong and supple. He was a contradiction, and she couldn't remember the last time a man had consumed her mind the way Ben had.

Alice burst out of the water, reached for the sponge on the side. He was late twenties, she imagined. Not so young that it was indecent or wrong.

She closed her eyes, draped the sponge over her face. What had the job been that he'd had on the east coast? Where on the coast? Whitby, Scarborough or Hartlepool? Was it on another boat, a fishing contract perhaps, or something else, a handyman job, like Gabe? She shook her head, not wanting her neighbour and her new lover in her mind at the same time. And why did he no longer have to go east? Had the contract finished, or had he made the decision that he'd like to see her more than once a fortnight?

Teenage dreams. She allowed herself a small smile. She was behaving the same way that Melanie would soon behave. But, like thoughts of Gabe, it felt wrong to include Melanie in her musings of wantonness. Instead she turned her thoughts back to the mainland and home. Maxine was on her mind now, and she missed her former friend with a sudden and deep passion. Not the Maxine of recent months, the one who was a back-stabber and a job stealer. But the Maxine of old, the one whom Alice could have told about Ben. She imagined it now, their whispered conversations, giggles, serious discussion of what Alice should do next.

Alice struggled upright in the bath. Maxine wasn't here, she wasn't even reachable on a phone. Alice couldn't pop to the mainland to visit her.

Maxine was gone. Alice's old life was gone. Those that were still present were caught in a no-man's land. All that remained was Ben. It was a dangerous thing to cling to.

*

In the dark of the woodshed Melanie tried to talk herself down. There was no immediate danger, she realised that, and to calm herself she visualised all of the beautiful colours she'd ever seen in different people.

After what seemed like hours spent lying on her side with her eyes closed, it worked.

She rolled over onto her front, planted her hands on the floor and pushed herself to a standing position, and moved over to where the red thing sat, deep in the shadowy corner.

She stared at it for a long moment, before lurching forward and picking it up.

She turned it over in her hand, her eyes locked on the awfulness of it.

The colours of this monster: dark red, edged with black.

It dropped from her hand, landing with a soft flop on the ground.

The naked leg. The grubby T-shirt. The horribly deformed face.

Melanie curled her head to her chest. She remained like that until her knees protested and the tears that flowed from her eyes seeped into her mouth which hung slackly open.

Think, Melanie. Wake up and think! she hissed at herself from some deep part within; all the while sirens flashed red in her mind, danger, danger, danger.

Kelly, her head back at a painful angle as someone gripped her hair.

Dark red, edged with black.

Melanie turned and retched. Spent, she cracked one eye open and looked over at the piece of black and red material.

It was the mask that the man had worn in the house of horrors back home. It had been on his face when he had attacked Kelly. The man had been naked on his bottom half, his intentions clear to Melanie, and no doubt to Kelly who had been touched and grabbed and held against her will by this masked man. *Or maybe more...*

And now the mask, red and black and rubbery, lay a few feet away from Melanie. Miles away from the house where it had been worn.

Melanie shivered.

If the mask was here, on the island, did that mean the man who had worn it was here too?

24

Paul stared at Carrie. She smiled, to let him know it was okay, that she was okay. Even though she wasn't.

'Carrie…' He breathed her name. 'I'm so sorry.'

She shrugged, glanced over at the counter. 'Do you want another coffee?' She looked at her watch. 'The CCTV won't be ready to collect quite yet.'

He nodded, and relieved to get away from the intensity of his concern she hurried to get a refill for each of them. As the barista set about making their drinks she looked back at Paul, still motionless in the booth. What had made her spill her guts to him? She'd never done that before, in spite of them working together for five years. She'd never told anyone before, apart from the police. Not that she had actually told him the whole story, just the bare facts, recited in an unfeeling monotone, like a news reporter. Uncaring, unfeeling, the only way she could tell it. She hadn't even told him Hattie's name.

And it always stopped there, the memory of that day. She had been pressed by the police, by social services, by her mother – until her mother stopped talking altogether. Later the professionals had changed; doctors, psychologists, therapists. None of them could ever get past the block. Dissociative amnesia was the label they had slapped on her. She blinked tears away, remembering the horror once she was old enough to understand it, once they had deemed her mature enough to deal with what they were telling her.

She had seen it happen.

It was what they'd said, the likelihood was she had witnessed whatever had happened to Hattie. And whatever it was had been far too traumatic for her young brain. Her mind had blocked it, thoroughly and totally. And for that she was ashamed. Her body, her brain had let her down.

She had let Hattie down too.

She scrunched her eyes closed and rubbed at them with balled fists. How could she tell Paul that? She could barely admit it to herself.

She looked at Paul once more. When she returned to their table, he would have collected himself, his policeman's mind would have come to the forefront. He would continue talking, questioning. She would have to tell him that she couldn't remember.

She was a rank above him; she shouldn't have divulged something so personal in the first place.

'Hey, excuse me,' she called to the barista. 'Can we get those to go, please?'

Paul said nothing about the sudden change of plan and for that Carrie was grateful. She suspected he noticed the wall she'd put up, her usual armour, and he slipped back into colleague mode easily.

He's had a lot of practice, she thought ruefully.

They took the DVD from the building's garage CCTV back to the station. Shrugging her coat off, Carrie peeled the lid from her coffee as she sat in front of the DVD player and Paul selected the date for the morning that the Hadleys had left their home in the early hours.

'What time did Sandra say they left?' he asked.

'Before the sun came up, she said. Start it at five a.m., there shouldn't be much traffic on the quay at that time.'

Paul did as she asked and took a seat next to her. Silently they watched, sipping at their coffee. At 5.15 the odd jogger started to appear, a blur of fluorescent clothing flashing past the docks. At 5.25 a car drove up.

'Here it is,' said Paul. 'Gabe's car.'

Carrie leaned close to the screen. 'No, it's not,' she said. 'That's a Toyota. Gabe had a Ford Mondeo estate.'

Paul blinked and made a face as he flipped through his notes. 'You're right,' he replied. 'So, who's this then?'

'Run the reg,' said Carrie as she continued watching the tape.

The film was high resolution, a decent security system for the expensive building, back-lit so that even when dark the figures were clear. Three of them; man, woman, child. Paul leaned in.

'They're unloading the car,' he said. 'Suitcases, couple of boxes.' He looked at Carrie. 'Are there coach pick-ups from there?'

Carrie frowned. 'We'll soon see.'

After five minutes, a boat appeared at the quayside and the three headed straight for it. A man hopped easily up onto the quayside, shook hands with the father. The woman and child hung back. At that moment a car came out of the underground garage, the camera's motion sensor moved, away from the people on the dockside, towards the car's journey. Frustratingly, it didn't move back.

'So, we don't get to see Gabe's car,' said Paul as the DVD ended. 'And who are the people who *were* there?'

Carrie pulled her hands through her hair. 'Play it again,' she said. 'Slowly, and zoom in, I want to see their faces.'

He set it to play, moved to another monitor to enter the registration of the mystery car. Carrie leaned in, pressed pause, zoomed in on the woman.

She didn't look happy, thought Carrie as she set it to play again. Arms crossed as she leaned against the car while the man moved around the quay, smiling, rubbing his hands. Carrie watched the child.

She's torn, thought Carrie, watching as the girl hovered between her parents, her movements stilted, caught between the apparently warring couple.

Pause. Zoom. Carrie stared at the screen before turning and picking up one of the photos in the file.

'Paul?' she called.

He came back across the room, a page from the printer in his hands. 'Yes?'

She held the photo up next to the screen. 'I think we've located Melanie Wilson,' she said grimly.

He slapped the paper down on the desk. 'The Toyota is registered to Harry Wilson,' he said. 'That's the Wilson family all right.'

Carrie moved back to sit in a chair. 'What are they doing? Where are they going?' She tapped her pen thoughtfully against her lips. 'And did the Hadley family go with them?'

Carrie scribbled furiously and passed a piece of paper to Paul, never taking her eyes off the paused CCTV. 'Find out who this boat is registered to,' she said.

Paul squinted at the sloping writing. '*Barnard Castle*,' he said. 'Odd name for a boat.'

While she waited, Carrie played the short section of tape again. She should be looking at the adults, she knew, after all they were who she was seeking. But she couldn't take her eyes off the young girl. Dragging her eyes away she concentrated on the man: Harry Wilson, according to her notes. He was in fine fettle, bouncing around the quay, excited, buoyed. A complete contrast to his wife, Alice, who seemed deflated, hesitant.

A sheet of paper floated to land on her desk. Carrie looked up at Paul.

'The *Barnard Castle* is registered to a Mr Ben Keller. Home address in Latchford. Born in a little town with a population of just over five thousand.' Paul raised his eyebrows. 'A town called Barnard Castle.'

Carrie stood up. 'Well I guess that answers your question of where the boat name comes from.' She picked up her keys. 'Feel like taking a drive to Latchford?'

A closed book. Her initial thoughts on Ben Keller. She glanced around his apartment that overlooked the river. She could be in her own home. Impersonal, simply a functional place to sleep and eat. She turned her attention back to Ben.

He sat on the window seat, legs apart, hands hanging loosely in between them. Relaxed, casual.

'Do you offer a boat service?' Carrie asked. 'Ferrying people around, up and down the water?'

'Yes,' Ben said. 'I work out of Salford, canal cruises, tours of the old docklands.' He leaned back, folded his arms. I also work on the Mersey ferry tours to Salford in the summer season. The rest of the year my Salford work is self-employed. All my taxes are up to date, so are my licences and permits.'

Carrie suppressed a smile. 'I'm sure you're as scrupulous with your paperwork as you are with your boat.' She looked down at her notepad. 'The *Barnard Castle.*'

She waited for him to ask how she knew the name of his boat, but he challenged her with his silence. She changed tack, pushed the photos of Alice, Harry and Melanie Wilson across the coffee table towards him. 'Do you recognise these people, maybe passengers of yours at some point?'

He lingered over the photo of Alice, swept his eyes over the other two before looking up at Carrie. 'I see a lot of people, hundreds of passengers, thousands in peak season.'

'So you don't recognise these people?' she pressed him.

Ben held her gaze. 'No.'

'What about these?' Willow and Lenon stared up from the pictures she passed him.

Ben shook his head.

'Where were you on the seventeenth of February?' she asked.

'Working, probably.'

'Here, or in Salford?' she shot back. Behind her, Paul prowled casually around the room. He seemed bored, but Carrie knew from experience he was taking in every question from her, every answer from Ben.

Ben appeared deep in thought. A false reaction, noted Carrie, as everything else she'd asked him he had answered seemingly without thinking.

'Probably Salford,' he answered carefully.

'And you don't remember meeting these people, talking with them on Bridgewater Dock?'

He shrugged. 'I meet a lot of people in my job, I talk to a lot of people.'

Somehow, Carrie doubted that. He didn't strike her as the chatty sort. She flipped her notebook closed and stood up.

'Thanks for your time, Ben,' she said. To Paul, 'Come on.'

In the hallway they made their way down the stairs to the lobby of the apartment building.

'Let's stop at that underground car park again,' she said as they walked to the car.

'What for?' asked Paul.

She fixed him with a gaze. 'The Wilsons left their car there that day. It's not there now. I want to look at more CCTV from the days following that particular Sunday. Maybe the Wilsons came back, or—'

'Or maybe someone collected the vehicle for them,' finished Paul.

*

Back in Costa, Carrie led Paul to a different table than the one
they'd sat at previously. The helpful building supervisor was preparing them another DVD from the security camera, spanning
the evening of 17 February through to the next day. A twenty-
four-hour window to see what had happened to Harry and Alice's
car. After all, it hadn't been reported abandoned on the quayside,
not like Gabe's.

Paul sat quietly across from her, cradling his coffee. He seemed
reflective, and Carrie realised he was probably trying to find a
way to pick up their last conversation where they'd left off. Panic
filled her. She pushed it down.

'What else do we have on Alice and Harry Wilson?' she asked.
'Friends, work places, social commitments.' Before he could reply
she pulled out her notepad. This hadn't been an investigation about
missing parents; it was a missing pair of twins, and an absence
reported by the school about a young girl. Her thoughts drifted
before she pulled herself back to the present. 'Mobile phones,
social media activity.' She scribbled furiously before putting the
pen down. 'And seeing who went off in the Wilsons' car.'

Paul glanced at his watch. 'Shall we hurry up the CCTV guy?'

Carrie drained her coffee and stood up. 'Let's go.'

It was clocking-off time when they had the newly burned DVD
from the underground car park supervisor. Carrie tapped it
thoughtfully as they walked back to the car. Across the water,
her apartment beckoned her.

'Paul,' she said. 'We're only a few minutes from my flat,
I've got my laptop at home, do you want to come up and view
it?' Her mouth was dry, she never invited anyone back to her
home. Worry tugged at her, that he might have misconstrued
her invitation. 'I'm only thinking if we go back to the station,

watch this and then I've got to come all the way back here again
to go home.'

His answer was friendly, casual. 'Sure, sounds like a plan.'

The elevator swished silently up to the fifth floor. As they
exited and Carrie opened the door to her apartment, Paul
stepped inside.

He whistled. 'Nice,' he said.

Carrie threw her keys into the ceramic bowl next to the door.
A clay pot, mottled pink and red and blue, made by Hattie when
she was tiny, glazed and fired by Carrie at an activity day just
months before Hattie vanished. It was one of the only personal
items Carrie kept in her home. It was one of the only personal
items that had survived the aftermath.

'You're over by the park, right?' she asked as she flicked the
kettle on and drew back the drapes to the balcony doors.

'Yeah, Jubilee Street,' he answered with a backwards jerk of
his head.

Carrie nodded. They were nice houses, terraced, modern,
homely she imagined. She busied herself with her laptop, skirting around him, wondering what he saw when he looked at her
sterile, impersonal home.

The kettle boiled and clicked off.

'Shall I make myself useful?' he asked, heading towards the
kitchen.

'Thanks,' she said, grateful for their ease with each other.
'Mugs are in the cupboard over the cooker, coffee's by the kettle.'

By the time he returned with two steaming mugs, she had
the DVD playing. She watched it intently, one eye on the time
stamp, the minutes clicking by.

'Headlights,' Paul said, sitting forward suddenly.

Carrie looked at the time. 'Seven a.m.' She hit the pause
button, turned to Paul. 'Not headlights, a boat light, see?'

She sat back, satisfied as the side of a boat came into view. The security lights from the camera didn't pick it up, and she squinted uselessly against the darkness on the screen.

They waited in silence again, the time ticking on, the boat in the background swaying softly in the water. In a blinding flash the security light clicked suddenly on and a man stepped into view, walking with purpose towards the Wilsons' car.

With a cursory glance around he unlocked it, started the ignition, and drove the Toyota away and out of view.

Carrie looked at Paul.

'Did you recognise him?'

Paul nodded grimly. 'I think tomorrow we need to pay Ben Keller another visit.'

25

The next morning, Paul caught up with Carrie in the station kitchen.

'We'll have to wait a bit before we go and see Mr Keller.' He jerked his head to the interview suite. 'You might want to sit in on this one.'

Taking a single sip of coffee, she put the mug in the sink and followed him down the hallway. 'Fill me in,' she demanded as they walked.

'Your friend has been missing for almost two months, but you're just reporting this now?' Carrie knew she sounded agitated, a thought confirmed by the look Paul shot her.

The woman opposite Carrie glared. 'She wasn't a friend. I mean, she was, once, but we parted on… let's just say not the best of terms.'

'You had a fight?' Paul interjected. He looked down at his notepad. 'Ms…'

'Maxine Cooper.' Maxine looked down, took a deep breath before starting again. 'We were work colleagues, friends, too, but Alice was letting things slide. She had a lot going on in her personal life—'

'Like what?' interrupted Carrie.

'Her husband was depressed, he'd had it before, major depression. It was weighing Alice down and, in our jobs, we can't allow personal stuff to get in the way.'

'Alice was a lawyer?' Carrie flicked through her file, that much she'd already found out. She looked at Maxine curiously. 'What did Alice's husband do?'

'Nothing.' Maxine shook her head, checked herself. 'Not nothing, he was a house husband, he raised their daughter.'

'A stay-at-home dad?' Carrie raised her eyebrows, exchanged a glance with Paul. 'And they could afford to live on one wage?'

Maxine waved her hand. 'They didn't need money. They had it, both Alice and Harry were orphaned really young, they had a fortune in trusts, asset, property. I don't even know why Alice worked, she didn't need to.'

Carrie noted the bitterness in Maxine's tone. 'When did you last see Alice?'

'The day she got fired.'

'And why was she sacked?' asked Carrie.

'Actually, she was about two seconds away from being fired and she jumped before she was pushed. She messed up one too many times. Like I said, she'd let things slip. Despite how we left things, I thought she'd contact me, but I heard nothing. I went round to her house when she didn't return my calls and there are new people living there.' Maxine slumped back into her chair. 'She doesn't have many people in her life, neither of them do, and with what happened to Melanie—'

'What happened to Melanie?' Carrie leaned forward, alert now.

'She got caught up in some paedo's house, a girl she was with was attacked; from what I gather Melanie managed to get the girl free and they escaped. Alice didn't tell me, I heard on the grapevine. Now I understand why Alice was so…' Maxine took a deep breath. 'She was shaken, something else that was on her mind that led to even more errors at work.'

Carrie felt Paul bristle beside her. She scribbled an illegible note to remind her to call Victoria Prout and ask why she'd never mentioned there was a third girl. A wave of horror crept though her: what if this unknown man had Melanie? She shook her head sharply, no, the parents were missing too, not just the girl.

Not just the girl; two whole families. This was not Hattie, this was nothing like Hattie's case.

She blinked. An awkward silence had fallen on the room. Both Maxine and Paul were looking at her. Paul cleared his throat and took over with ease.

'You have no idea where the family have gone? Alice never mentioned anything, a house move, an extended holiday?'

Maxine shook her head. 'It's possible Alice didn't know if Harry had planned a move.' She shrugged unhappily. 'Harry was like that, always going ahead with plans and stuff and not consulting Alice.'

'Like what?' demanded Carrie.

Maxine took a long sip of water. 'He arranged their wedding without her knowledge, just pulled up at the registry office one day, witnesses were waiting, wedding was booked. He bought their home without her knowing.' Maxine fixed her gaze on Carrie. 'She always made it sound romantic, but I thought it was a bit creepy. Controlling.'

'All right.' Carrie stood up, gestured for Paul. 'Thanks, Maxine, you've been a great help.'

Maxine pushed her chair back and hurried around the table, blocking Carrie's route to the door. 'Will you let me know if everything's okay, when you track them down?'

Carrie softened at the genuine concern in the other woman's eyes. 'Of course, and thank you for coming in.'

*

'Get that Prout woman on the phone, I want to know why she never mentioned Melanie was in that house.' Carrie said once she was alone with Paul again. 'And then we're going to pay another visit to Ben Keller. He took the Wilsons' car, he clearly lied to us when he said he didn't recognise Harry or Alice.'

He nodded. 'I've got something you might want to see first.'

'What?'

In response he beckoned her over to the laptop set up on a corner desk. 'It's the CCTV from the rail station, at the time you received the last contact from our mysterious caller. I haven't seen it yet, it just came in.'

She slipped into the chair, waited while he set it to play. She caught her breath at the sight of the four public call boxes clearly in view of the camera.

'This is less than one minute before the call came through,' said Paul, hanging over her shoulder.

Carrie shifted discreetly. A few seconds later a young woman came into view, just the back of her as she made her way to the phone box. Carrie flicked her eyes up and down her form. A nice pea coat, light-coloured, a leather shoulder bag and shoulder-length brown hair. Her age was impossible to tell from this angle.

She looked furtively around before picking up the receiver and dialling. The call lasted less than a minute, and from the high-resolution CCTV Carrie watched as the young woman in the pea coat became more agitated, her left hand clutching the phone in a tight grip, her right arm gesticulating wildly. Finally, she seemed to slump as she replaced the receiver back in the holder. Carrie closed her eyes, remembered the soft click, the dead line, her own feeling of helplessness. Snapping her eyes open she looked at the figure on the screen, her shoulders hunched now, her head lowered. Looking as hopeless as Carrie had felt on the other end of the line.

'Turn around,' she urged in a whisper. 'Let me see your face.'

Paul shot her a look, Carrie leaned her elbows on the table, her nose inches from the screen.

'Come on,' she murmured. 'Let me see who you are.' She spoke again, without taking her eyes off the screen. 'This footage is good quality, if we get a clear view we could put it through the AFR.'

'The Automatic Facial Recognition system?' Paul said. 'The trial's over, you know it's going to be quashed, for the foreseeable future at least.'

She nodded grimly. The six-month-long trial had enjoyed some good results, the stations being set up in local football grounds and in the Trafford Centre, but Civil Liberty groups had pounced on it, complaining and protesting about innocent civilians being under surveillance.

'Would they be so up in arms if it found one of their loved ones who was missing?' she snapped, glaring at him now. 'Or identified a criminal on the run?'

Paul held up his hands in mock surrender. 'Hey, no need to convince me, I'm all for it.'

Carrie turned her attention back to the screen.

'Come on,' she implored.

She held her breath as the woman backed away from the phone. She envisaged the train station, knowing the woman could exit to the left or right without ever showing her face to the camera. She swore softly, deflated as the figure on the screen moved to the left. Carrie raised her hand, ready to slam it down on the desk in frustration, when suddenly, the woman switched direction, spinning on her heel and walking sharply towards the CCTV camera.

Carrie stilled, hand still in the air, her eyes widening as the woman's face came ever closer.

Only when she moved underneath the CCTV did Carrie release the breath she'd been holding.

Silence in the room, until Paul spoke up.

'Well, I guess we don't need the AFR then,' he said, and his voice was startled, shocked.

Carrie sank into a chair, nausea sweeping over her in waves. 'She was warning me about a man, a man she had reported before, and we did nothing to help her.'

Paul lowered his eyes. 'And now she's missing.' He glanced up, briefly at the frozen screen. 'Are we sure it's her?' he asked.

Carrie reached for the mouse, rewound, zoomed in on the figure, hit the pause button just before the young woman walked out of view.

'It's her,' she said. 'It's Willow Hadley.'

The feeling of sickness passed. Carrie lifted her eyes to meet Paul's.

'We need to look into the parents, both sets. I want their pictures. Look into their past, any arrests, court appearances, anything on file. I want to know if any of the adults have had so much as a speeding fine.' She rattled off instructions, speaking quickly as thoughts piled on top of each other in her head. 'Pull them up on social media; Facebook, Instagram, all of it, see if the Hadleys and the Wilsons are friendly.' She paused, flipped back through her notebook. 'Give it to someone on the desk, you and I are visiting Ben Keller. And tell them to ring Mrs Prout too,' she called after him.

She let Paul drive for once as she scribbled down a timeline of everything they had so far.

'So we've got a missing eleven-year-old girl, who was last seen dockside a few weeks ago and hasn't been heard of since. Her mother also appears to be missing, and who, along with her husband and daughter seem to have left their house. We've got fifteen-year-old twins also missing, their parents are also no longer residing at their known address. We've got a flow of calls from a previously unknown woman or girl, accusing a man of doing something… and speaking as though she is now taking action against him. We know now this caller is Willow Hadley. These families seem unconnected to each other, but nobody seems to know where either of them went.' She tapped her pen against her chin, glanced over at Paul. 'What else?'

'We've got a man who appeared to have picked up the car that the Wilsons abandoned at the quayside, though he has denied knowledge of knowing these people.'

'He's the only one who can give us information,' Carrie said. 'We need him to talk this time.' She pursed her lips, deep in thought before shooting a glance at Paul. 'We need to treat Ben Keller as a potential suspect, a person of interest.'

There was nobody at Ben Keller's home, despite them hammering on his door for a full five minutes.

'He's not there,' said a neighbour, brought out by the constant knocking. 'Went off early this morning.' The neighbour, a middle-aged man, looked them up and down. 'Can I take a message for him?'

'Do you know where we might find him?' Carrie asked.

The man, bored suddenly, shrugged. 'Work, probably. Out on the boat.' He backed into his apartment, the heavy door closing behind him.

Dejected, Carrie pushed her card through Ben's letter box before she and Paul returned to the car.

'Back to base,' said Carrie as Paul pulled out onto the carriageway. 'At least we can see if they found out anything further on the Hadleys.'

'Wait,' said Paul, as he accelerated into the fast lane.

'What?' asked Carrie impatiently.

'The CCTV from the quayside; he always docks the *Barnard Castle* in that same spot, what is that, do you need a permit, is it like a registered space where he always docks, rented, like?'

Carrie sat up. 'Yes, go there, we'll ask to see the camera footage from the last couple of days, see if Ben's been sniffing around the area again. It could be that he's meeting Harry there, or Gabe or one of the others.' She sniffed, sighed deeply. 'Something's off on this one, Paul.'

He nodded grimly and the rest of the journey passed in silence, each lost in their own thoughts about the anomalies of this strange case.

'Here we go.'

Paul's voice pulled her out of her reverie and she looked up as he swung the car onto the quay. Through habit Carrie looked up at her own apartment. Her safe place. Why had these families left their apparently comfortable homes?

'Look!' Paul's exclamation startled her out of her musings.

She looked where he pointed, out to where the water opened up. A boat came smoothly towards them.

'Is that…?'

'The *Barnard Castle*,' said Paul, unclipping his seatbelt. 'That's our man.'

Carrie waited off to one side, loitering behind a boulder with Paul, not wanting to give Ben the upper hand in knowing they were waiting for him. When he docked and jumped off the boat she stepped forward.

'Mr Keller,' she smiled, taking delight in his brief expression of surprise. 'Where have you been?'

Ben glanced at Paul and in a single moment he appeared to gather himself. 'Just a sail for pleasure,' he responded. 'How can I help you?'

Carrie walked to meet him, Paul one step behind him. 'You said you didn't recognise any of the people that we spoke to you about the last time we chatted, Harry and Alice Wilson?' She raised her eyebrow, waited for him to nod before continuing. 'But we've got you on camera moving the Wilsons' car on the day the family vanished.'

Underneath his tanned skin, Ben's face visibly paled. His gaze went from Carrie to the building behind her. She almost smiled as she watched the moment he clocked the CCTV mounted above the parking garage.

'Did you steal the car, Ben?' she asked, frowning, mock-concern on her face.

He sighed audibly. 'No.'

She nodded. 'Want to tell us what's going on?'

Ben glanced at Paul, back to Carrie, his stance dejected now, caught in the act. 'They paid me to take the car,' he said quietly.

'Take it where?' she asked sharply.

For a moment he looked surprised. 'Anywhere,' he replied. 'Harry said I could do what I liked with it, sell it, keep it.' He stopped abruptly, as if suddenly realising how unlikely his explanation sounded. 'Alice asked me to keep hold of the car for a while, in case she changed her mind.'

'Changed her mind about what?' Carrie was lost.

'About living on the island. It wasn't her idea, it was Harry's, and she went along with it because she wanted to make him happy. That's why she's been paying me.'

Paul stepped forward. 'Ben, can you come along to the station? I think we've got a lot of questions that only you can answer.'

'Voluntarily, right?' Ben shot back. 'Because I haven't done anything wrong. I'm just a boatman, paid to take passengers from A to B.'

'Voluntarily, yes, for now,' confirmed Paul.

Carrie narrowed her eyes as she watched Paul lead him to the car. As she followed them, she had a feeling Ben Keller was going to tell them a lot more than just taking passengers from one place to another.

Carrie grew more incredulous with each sentence that came out of Ben's mouth. She scribbled frantically on her pad, blinking as she read it back. She looked over at Paul.

'Have you heard of Pomona?' she asked him.

'Yeah, didn't think it was somewhere people actually went.' He scratched his head, shot a disbelieving look at Ben. 'The Hadley family and the Wilsons are all living on Pomona?'

Ben nodded.

Carrie rubbed her hands over her face. *Why*, was the resounding question? What would make two seemingly different families up sticks and move to a place where nobody else lived? She voiced her thoughts to Ben.

'Why? Did any of them give a reason? This is a major lifestyle change, after all.'

'Alice… uh, Mrs Wilson, mentioned something about Harry becoming increasingly paranoid, something to do with his health, up here, I mean,' he added, tapping his finger to his temple.

Carrie turned to Paul. 'Is it legal to live there? Who does the place actually belong to?'

Paul shook his head. 'No idea, but even if you can live there, it's illegal to withdraw your kids from school without showing some sort of home-schooling plan.' He laid his heavy gaze on Ben, as though he were responsible for both families' actions.

Ben snorted. 'Man, I'm just the taxi.'

Carrie stood up, laid her hands flat on the table between them. 'That you are, and I imagine you'll have no issue with taking us to this island, then?' She walked to the door, shrugging her jacket on her shoulders. When neither man made a move to follow her, she fixed them both with a steely stare.

'Well,' she said. 'What are we waiting for?'

26

Carrie and Hattie – 1998

The police wanted to take Carrie and her mother home. Mary howled and screamed at the officers that she wasn't leaving while one of her children was still missing. Carrie watched as they surrounded her mum, forcibly leading her away from the forest area where she'd last seen Hattie.

Carrie remained where she was, pressing her back into a tree trunk, until one of the officers realised they were one short and came back to claim her.

She walked along with them, resisting a little; surely they should wait for Hattie to be found? The piece of material flashed into Carrie's mind, pink and white and red. Blood, turning a rusty brown as it dried. Her knees buckled and the woman police officer leading her by the elbow chivvied her along.

No words were spoken. Carrie was used to stern, tough women. Her mother rarely comforted her, it wasn't Mary's way. But Carrie had thought that was just her mother, not all women. She glanced up at the policewoman who led her towards the gates of the park. Her face was steel, frozen, a grimacing mask. Carrie's heart, already beating in double time, jumped at the thought of the woman's disapproval of her losing her little sister. It would be years later that she would realise it had been shock, horror. After all, the policewoman would have seen the pink and white and red clothing too.

'Will my…' Carrie trailed off, unsure of the question she was about to ask.

She was put into the backseat of the police car with her mother. Mary still shouting, barking, twisting in her seat, her hands scraping the inside of the door, seeking for a handle that wasn't there to open the door and run and resume the search for her missing girl.

At home, Carrie watched as they surrounded Mary and led her into the house. Five of them, forming a fence around Carrie's mother, moving like sheep herding. Carrie stood by the police car, forgotten for the moment.

She looked left and right down the road, gripped with an overwhelming desire to see Hattie hurrying towards her, coming home.

The white and pink and ghastly red material came into her mind, followed by the realisation that Hattie would never return home again.

And it was all Carrie's fault.

Carrie sagged against the next-door-neighbour's car, the heat of it scorching through her clothes. The bodywork burned her side but still she remained as hot tears simmered in her throat.

'Miss Carrie, what are you doing out here?'

She looked up at the voice, into the kindly, crinkled eyes of Doctor Joyce. Carrie blinked. What was their family doctor doing here? A thought caught at her, made her gasp. Had they found Hattie and instead of being dead and cold she was just frightened and injured?

'Have they found my sister?' she demanded of the doctor, pushing herself off the neighbour's car. 'Is that why you're here?'

And even though he remained smiling gently, his eyes began to water. 'No, Carrie, I'm here to see your mother.'

Carrie frowned. Her mother wasn't ill or hurt. She forced a smile. The doctor had been called by the police, maybe they had mentioned that her mother had been shouting and screaming and Doctor Joyce had misunderstood, thought there was something wrong with Mary. But it was Hattie who needed him, although she wasn't here, was she? Carrie glanced around, wondered if there was any way Hattie could have been brought back home without her seeing. Maybe she'd got here first! Perhaps she was inside right now, with grazed knees (which would explain the bloodied clothing, thought Carrie sagely) and whimpering and whining in that annoying way of hers.

There was only one way to clear it up. Carrie plucked at the doctor's sleeve and pulled him towards the house.

'It's not my mother, it's my sister, Hattie,' explained Carrie as she led him through the back gate. 'She was hurt while we were out in the park, she was bleeding, I think.'

Doctor Joyce resisted against her grasp. 'How do you know that, Carrie?' he asked. 'Were you there?'

Carrie yanked at his sleeve impatiently. 'The police found her shorts, they had blood on them.' She resisted the urge to stamp her foot. 'That's how I know she was bleeding, she's probably fallen over or something.' Carrie recalled the amount of red on the material and she bit her lip. 'Do you think she'll need stitches? Hattie won't like that.'

Doctor Joyce turned his back, through the glare of sunlight now low in the sky Carrie saw his sleeve scrub at his face. He stayed with his back to her for a long while. Carrie, suddenly afraid of his silence, looked down at the ground.

He shuffled, came back to face her again. 'Come on, let's get inside and see your mother.'

Mary was in her chair, the armchair she never usually sat in during the daylight hours. Daylight hours were for working, cleaning, cooking, ironing. Mary didn't get a chance to sit down until it was dark and she spent an hour or two with her children until they went to bed.

The vision of her mother slumped in a chair in the early evening was more disconcerting to Carrie than the tears that streamed down Mary's face.

'Mary, I've come to help you.' The doctor's voice wavered a little as he made his way through the five police officers that surrounded Mary's chair.

Mary looked at him through blazing eyes, nostrils flaring, a strange sound in the back of her throat, like a scream waiting to emerge. Carrie braced herself, but nothing came out of her mother's mouth.

'Just a little something to help you relax,' the doctor said, as he opened his case and lifted out a small glass bottle. 'A little sedative,' he said, though who he was speaking to Carrie didn't know.

'A little pinprick,' he murmured, pushing up Mary's sleeve.

Anger flared in Carrie. Fury at the doctor, at his patronising tone, as if he said the word 'little' enough it would minimise the situation.

For this wasn't a little problem, Carrie realised. It was very real, very big, and their lives would never be the same again.

Carrie expected her mother to go to sleep when Doctor Joyce withdrew the needle, but Mary stayed awake. She stared around the room, landing accusing glances on the officers. Her eyes narrowed when her gaze landed on Carrie. Mary said nothing, but her look spoke a thousand words to her daughter.

'Carrie, can we have a word with you for a moment?' One of the female officers moved to stand in front of Carrie, blocking Mary's view of her. Carrie was grateful for that and she nodded.

In the next room, the officer closed the door, gestured for Carrie to sit at the dining room table. Obediently Carrie took her usual dinner time chair.

'My name is Lisa Michaels, I'm a police officer, and I'd like to ask you some questions about what happened today, if that's okay?'

Carrie nodded, watched as Lisa took a notepad and pen out of her deep trouser pocket. Lisa Michaels seemed young, Carrie thought as she took in the woman's long, swishing blonde hair, pulled back in a ponytail. She had cheeks like apples, a healthy glow to her make-up-free face. *An English rose*, thought Carrie. A phrase she'd heard and often wished her mother would use to describe her. But Mary didn't make observations about Carrie. She saved all her compliments for Hattie, detailing often how she, Mary, had learned how to tame Hattie's afro hair, how it was nothing like her own, how special it was to have a bloodline like she did.

To Carrie it seemed like an awful lot of work. It was a lot of work, but unlike the other chores Mary had to do, she seemed to take delight in Hattie's hard-work hair.

'Carrie? Carrie?' Suddenly the policewoman's voice was very far away.

Carrie put her hands on the table, pressed her fingers into the Formica. Still the world turned, spinning around her, and Carrie swayed against the sudden pressure in her head. Her mother's gaze in her mind, those narrowed eyes.

Your fault… your fault… your fault.

Lisa Michaels, still saying her name, urgently now, bordering on a shout.

'CARRIE?'

Carrie gave in to the spin, she released her grip from the table, tilted sideways. Her last thought was of her sister as the carpet rose up to meet her and Carrie closed her eyes as she passed out into blissful oblivion.

27

On the eighth week of island living, Alice awoke to fat, bulbous clouds of grey and black that brought with them the distant rumble of thunder. She drew back the curtain in their bedroom and felt her heart sink at the lack of sun.

Fearfully she glanced at Harry, still sleeping. He struggled with bad weather, she'd been sure for years that along with the sporadic depression he suffered from Seasonal Affective Disorder. While most people, like her and Melanie, used a rainy day as an excuse to curl up under a blanket with a hot drink and a film, Harry fidgeted and withdrew into himself, only seeming to wake again when the sunshine reappeared.

Alice snapped the curtains closed before Harry woke up and saw the dismal day. Slipping her housecoat on she quietly left the bedroom, wincing at the cold tiles on her bare feet as she made her way into the kitchen.

She stared at the copper kettle on the fireplace, not sure if she could be bothered to start a fire in order to make a coffee, remembering wistfully the days when she could flick a switch and have boiling water in a matter of minutes.

Rain spattered against the window pane, heavy drops that abruptly hammered the thin glass as the heavens opened. Alice moved to the window, staring out of the front, stepping back behind the drapes as three people left the cottage next door.

Willow and Lenon, she noted. Both of them in waterproofs, heads down against the driving rain, baskets and buckets in hand. They'd really taken to island living, she realised. Possibly even more so than Harry, which was ironic, considering this madcap idea had been all his.

Gabe emerged, pulling the hood of his mac up, hoisting a backpack on. Hunched against the rain he moved in the opposite direction to the kids, disappearing over the field, heading towards the woods. What of Liz? wondered Alice. And, not wanting to be there when Harry woke up and saw the disappointing weather, Alice pulled open the door, slipped outside and ran the few feet to Liz's cottage.

To her surprise, she saw Liz moving around the kitchen, and Alice banged on the glass, raised a hand in greeting.

The door was ajar, and Alice pushed it open, leaned into the room. 'Hi, are you all right? I just thought I'd pop round, so little to do in this crap weather,' she said.

Liz stood by the sink, a glass in her hand, gazing silently at Alice. Alice swallowed, the rain hit the back of her dressing gown and it lay uncomfortably damp against her skin. She inched further into the room, lost for words now. Did Liz even know who she was?

'Liz, you okay?' she managed.

Liz blinked and the strangeness passed.

'Hello,' said Liz, and her words were slow and careful. 'Would you like a drink?'

Alice smiled, spotting a jar of coffee on the side which made her practically salivate. 'Love one, thanks.'

'Sit down.' Liz waved a hand vaguely around the room and Alice, her bare feet sodden, tip-toed across to a chair.

'Foul weather,' she said.

Liz made no reply and Alice stared uncomfortably down at her feet. They were muddy, there being no path between the two cottages, just a strip of grass. She folded her ankles together, reminded herself next time to put shoes on before she went out. A lump came to her throat as she caught sight of her own reflection in the glass of the door of which she'd just come through. Dressing gown, bare feet, she hadn't even dragged a comb through her hair or washed her face. How had she become so feral in such a short amount of time?

Harry, spat a vicious voice in her head. *This is all his fault.*

She became aware of Liz lurching across the floor towards her, walking unsteadily, holding two mugs. Alice half rose, ready to intercept the mugs of coffee from the woman who looked increasingly unsteady on her feet. But Liz made it without incident, and with shaking hands she placed the two drinks on the table.

Alice stared down into the chipped mugs. Water. Liz had served them both water. Alice floundered. 'No coffee?' she asked eventually, her voice falsely bright, gently mocking.

Liz shook her head.

Alice's eyes went to the coffee jar on the counter. Liz followed her gaze, but made no comment.

Alice gave up, sipped at the water. 'Where have the others gone?' she asked politely.

Liz blinked, drew in a deep breath. 'I'm not sure,' she said, and then, 'which others?'

'Your husband and kids,' said Alice.

'Oh.' Liz nodded, and to Alice her head was like a pendulum, heavy as it tipped up and down. 'I'm not sure,' she said again.

Alice sighed. 'How are you feeling, Liz?' she asked, with genuine concern tinging her irritability. 'You were really quite ill. You've lost weight, are you eating?'

'Yeah, you know.' Liz smiled weakly, pushed herself up from her chair and sidled back to the kitchen. The counter underneath the window was cluttered, noticed Alice, pots and jars and bottles. Liz's hand danced among them, her fingers tapping each container before she pulled out a small, white bottle. Unscrewing the cap she tipped something into her hand, threw it in her mouth and dry swallowed. Placing the container back where she'd plucked it from, Liz walked unsteadily out of the room. When Alice heard the bathroom door close she jumped up and hurried over to the counter.

Diazepam, she saw was printed on the bottle. Liz was on Diazepam. Valium! But *why*? What was her story?

'Liz, I have to be going now, I'll catch up with you later, okay?' Alice called in the direction of the bathroom. She waited for a moment but when there was no answer, she slipped back out of the door and tripped back over the grass to her own cottage.

When she darted inside, Harry was in the kitchen, looking anxiously at the sky out of the window.

'Morning,' he said, and then, 'Oh, you'll catch your death going outside like that.'

Alice shrugged off the now soaking dressing gown and snatched up yesterday's shirt and jeans from the back of the chair. 'I went over to see Liz.'

'How is she?' Harry asked, moving over to the fire clutching a handful of tinder.

'Same,' said Alice.

She watched him painstakingly arranging the wood in the hearth. Bitterness flowed in her again, that she had to go through all this hassle just to get a morning coffee. And what would happen when the coffee ran out? What then? She could ask Ben to bring some, she supposed, but no, she would have to explain it to Harry. He had no idea Ben was visiting her, he would be horrified that she wasn't going along with his 'living from the earth on a deserted island' dream.

One thought led to another: *what if Ben decided to stop coming? What if he had to go away on his boat, work miles and miles away, or,*

God forbid, met a woman and settled down? Alice's heart thumped painfully in her chest.

'What are we doing here, Harry?' she asked as she yanked her jeans on. 'I mean, really, are you enjoying this?'

'Are you not?' he sounded aghast, disbelieving. 'This is a once in a lifetime opportunity, Alice, we need to appreciate it, not fight it.'

Alice opened her mouth, prepared herself to say the words that she had spent years suppressing. 'It wasn't my choice.'

Harry carried on, as though he hadn't even heard her. As though Alice hadn't even spoken.

'Living from the land, getting back to nature, doing away with all false substances, that's what it's all about, Alice,' Harry went on, 'A safe place to raise our child, away from the streets, away from the drugs and the booze and the youth culture.' He leaned close to her, spoke his next words very quietly. 'Away from men who snatch our kids off the streets. Melanie had such a narrow escape, Alice, surely you see that?'

Alice swallowed. Harry had missed it, he'd missed entirely the words she'd spoken which she'd thought silently to herself since the day Harry had arranged their wedding without even telling her.

'It wasn't my choice,' she said, stronger, slightly louder. 'So much of what we've done wasn't my choice, Harry.' She swallowed again. 'Out here, I'm starting to realise it.'

Her words were huge, bigger than her and Harry and Melanie put together. She had imagined saying them so many times over the years; always, in her head they were accompanied with a fanfare that finally she had broken out of herself and told him the truth. Never, in all her daydreams, had Harry dismissed her feelings as easily as he did now.

'It'll be better in summer,' he said, craning his head to look out at the black sky. 'Everything seems so much better when the sun is out, the mornings are lighter, the days last longer—'

'No, Harry, that's JUST YOU,' Alice shouted, her words came out in a bark, clipped and fierce with the hysterical edge of threatening tears. 'You have no idea of anything, of how I feel, how Melanie is feeling, this wasn't our choice, Harry, you never gave us a choice. Liz next door, this wasn't her choice, it wasn't her children's choice. It's you, you men, forging ahead to give your own masculinity a hard-on that it can't achieve in normal life.'

Harry turned his head to look at her, his eyes grew very small as he grimaced. 'Alice, there's no need for talk like that—'

'There is!' she slapped her hand on the table, hard, and it felt good, and it sounded good and she did it again. *Bang, bang!*

'I always let you work,' Harry said, quietly now.

She pushed her palms flat into the table top, pulled back her right leg and kicked the leg of table hard. The table screeched across the tiles. 'Who are you to *let me work*?' she spat. 'Who the fuck do you think you are to *let me work*?'

She spun away, her bare toes throbbing, not daring to look down, knowing her foot would soon be as black and blue as the swollen clouds outside.

'…and Gabe would have talked this over with Liz and the twins,' Harry was saying in an infuriatingly mid-mannered tone of voice. 'Just like we did, he would have answered any concerns, discussed it in a civil and adult manner just like we—'

'Oh, Harry,' Alice breathed his name, all the fight gone as she sank to sit on the cold concrete floor. She laughed, but it was mirthless, dry and brittle. 'If Liz is so happy to be here why is she next door tanked up on Diazepam?' She glared at him.

His mouth worked before settling into a thin line. 'She's taking Diazepam?'

Alice nodded wearily. 'I can't go on like this, Harry. We need to talk, to decide what we're going to do, how we can get home… Harry, Harry? Where are you going?'

But he was gone, slipping out of the house and into the driving rain.

Alice stared after him and covered her mouth with her hands.

*

The door to the cottage next door was ajar and Harry pushed it open. Through the gloom he could see Liz in the bathroom, the door ajar, she stood at the sink. Harry opened his mouth to call her name, but closed it again.

Was there something very wrong with Liz? He thought back to the times they had interacted, and his lips pinched together. They had never interacted, she was spaced out all the time, even back in Manchester. His gaze went to the worktop, the plates and cutlery and pans and the small pill bottles nestled in the mess. He glanced back towards the bathroom. Liz hadn't moved.

She had no idea he was standing in her doorway.

Harry edged to the kitchen area, plucked out a bottle at random. Not Diazepam, he noted, but Zopiclone. Lightly, he touched the lids of the other pill bottles, half a dozen in all, different brands of sedatives and tranquilisers. He thought of his pill bottle, with two tablets left. The bottle wedged down the side of his chair. Those two pills that he hadn't yet taken, because he'd weaned himself off the medication, because he wanted to live normally, naturally, among people who wanted the same kind of life as him. But here was Liz, moving around like a zombie, carelessly leaving her pills out where anyone could find them.

She had been careless. And since Harry was the leader of this expedition, he figured it was up to him to dish out the lessons. He slipped the bottle of Zopiclone in his pocket and exited the little cottage soundlessly.

He wasn't going to take any of the pills himself. *No*, it was just to make people realise they couldn't leave things like that around where children, or rather, his child, could find them.

And if Liz and Gabe had any sense, they would put the rest of the pill bottles away in a safe place, like the bathroom cabinet or a high cupboard. He nodded to himself, fingering the outline of the bottle in his pocket.

It didn't solve the bigger issue though, Harry admitted. The discord in the group, the fractures and splinters that were preventing them from fully realising how successful they could make this life. What to do about that? He thought of Alice's words, as painful as they were to recall. *This wasn't my choice.*

Harry sat down on the bench outside the Hadleys' cottage. Perhaps she meant to say it hadn't been her idea, which was true, it was his idea, but he'd only mentioned it and gone ahead with it because he knew best. He was older than she was, he'd always known what was best for his family. He thought back overall the decisions he'd made in the past that Alice had been reluctant about. Melanie, for one. Alice hadn't wanted a baby when she'd got pregnant, but Harry had made her see how perfect it would make their little family. And she would agree with him now, wouldn't she?

Their wedding was another one. Back then Alice had been all work and study, and Harry had known she would never have the time to plan a wedding. So, he had planned it, booked the registry office and found the witnesses. He'd even planned the little wedding tea that they had after the ceremony. A ghost of a smile caught at Harry's mouth as he remembered. She had wept, Alice had, tears of joy he was sure, that someone loved her so much to do all of that for her. And the house he had bought, equally split with his money and her own. She hadn't been too sure of that, he remembered, because she fancied herself living in one of those penthouse apartments that had gone up at the waterfront, with elevators and marbled floors. But Harry knew that somewhere slightly out of the main city streets would be better suited to them, somewhere with a garden that they could enjoy as a family.

Harry had known what was best for them. Alice just pushed against it because she liked to think she was independent. But she'd got used to everything he had done, and seen that it was in their best interests, and she would get used to this too. Island living.

He pushed himself up off the bench. Moved backwards out of the rain. He glanced at his cottage, knowing Alice was still inside, remembering her earlier angry words.

Probably best not to disturb her yet. The rain lessened to a light mist. Pulling up his hood he moved off towards the copse of trees, hoping to stumble upon one of the other members of his team.

As he walked the pills in the bottle rattled in his pockets

They hummed out a tune. *Take one... take one... take one.*

*

Alice had been nervous that Harry would stick by her side the day after their fight, but he'd been surprisingly easy to dodge and avoid. He hadn't mentioned their argument when he returned to the cottage, and Melanie had come back home even later than Harry. They had eaten a meal around the table, rabbit trimmed with wild garlic and tinned potatoes, just the three of them, and it was filled with an awkward tension. Melanie refused to even look at Alice, and Alice had neither the patience or even the desire right now to find out what was going on with her daughter.

Instead she thought of later, Ben's visit, and how much she wanted to see him.

Alice unbuttoned her shirt and it was halfway off her shoulders before Ben held his hand up. Feeling foolish she held it closed to cover herself.

'What's wrong?' she asked.

'The police came to my house,' Ben said. He sat on the little bed, rubbed his hand over his beard. All the while his blue eyes pierced hers.

Alice sank onto the wooden bench. 'What did they want?'

'They want to know if I've seen you, or your family, or the other lot. They know you're here, they wanted me to bring them over, but I dodged them this morning.' He grinned at her, suddenly, out of keeping with his serious nature. A smile so bright she couldn't help but smile back.

We're both dodging people, she thought. She Harry, he the police. And at the thought of them again Alice felt the blood drain from her face. *The police?* Why did they care? She voiced this thought.

Ben shrugged. 'Someone probably reported you missing.'

'But we haven't done anything wrong!' she exclaimed. Immediately she thought of Melanie, who should be in school. But Harry was home-schooling her, insistent she would learn more over here than in any classroom. The laws were pretty relaxed on home education, though she knew they hadn't gone through the correct channels of actually informing Melanie's school. And who on earth would have reported them missing? They had no other family, no real friends to speak of. The immediate neighbours would know by now that the house had been sold with a quick sale company.

Maxine.

Her former friend's name flashed into her mind, a sense of warmth along with it. Did Maxine still care? Was there someone who didn't live on this godforsaken island who still gave a damn about Alice?

Ben cleared his throat. 'Just thought I'd better let you know.'

Alice breathed deeply. On the table in front of her sat a bottle of whisky. Expensive stuff, she noted, the sort the partners at work had in their office. She grabbed it, unscrewed the cap and swigged directly from the bottle. It went down well, and she realised suddenly how much she missed the good stuff.

'Have you got time?' she asked Ben, made bolder by the liquid fire that burned down her throat.

He nodded. Alice slipped her shirt off her shoulders and walked over to him.

*

Melanie positioned herself behind a huge oak tree and poked her head out to check she had a clear view of the wood store. The mask was still in there, horrible, red and black.

Somebody very dangerous was out there, and they were on the island with her. It was a man, she deduced, because this very mask had been worn by a man and back then, when it was on his face Melanie had seen his legs and his arm and they were masculine.

And there were four possibilities.

Gabe, Lenon, Ben the boatman, and her own father.

Melanie hung her head. Could she really put her father on that list of potential suspects? It hurt her to, but she couldn't discount him simply because she loved him, and he was her dad.

But you know him, a little voice whispered in her head. *You know he could never hurt anybody.*

But that wasn't true, not really. He was on medication and she knew from the list of side effects she'd read that pills could sometimes make people do things that they wouldn't normally do. Medication could make them angry, or sick, or lower or raise their libido in ways which were unusual. She hadn't known what that meant when she'd read it, and she'd Googled it later, then wished she hadn't. But no, she couldn't discount him. She couldn't disregard any of them.

She considered Ben, the sailor, the man who had brought them over on the boat. The man who came to visit and sleep with her mother. Melanie's lip curled with distaste and she made

fists with her hands and held them tight against her head, trying
to rid herself of the vision, of the memory. She waited for long
moments, crouched in the undergrowth until her mind cleared.

She would stay here, she had decided. Eventually someone
would come along to collect the horrible mask and when they
did, Melanie would have her answer.

'You'll have your answer,' she said out loud. 'But then what
the hell are you going to do?'

For that question, Melanie had no reply.

28

Carrie had been eager to go, right that very second, but Ben Keller had held up a commanding hand.

'No can do,' he said. 'The engine's been playing up and the boat's in dry dock just now for checks and maintenance.'

Carrie had tilted her head. 'When can we go then?'

He appeared to have been thinking. 'In three days,' he said. 'I can take you.'

Now, one day later, and Carrie had watched his little boat as it vanished from the Bridgewater dock, heading, no doubt, to Pomona.

The sound of running feet, she turned to see Paul, clad in active wear, jogging over to her.

'Got your message,' he said, leaning over and breathing hard. 'What's going on?'

Briefly she felt bad about calling him on a weekend, but he didn't seem to mind and, it appeared, he was already in the area.

'I saw Ben Keller's boat sailing away,' she said, shading her eyes although the *Barnard Castle* was long gone. 'Heading towards Pomona.' She fixed her gaze on Paul. 'Even though he said his boat was out of commission until Monday.'

Paul slumped down on a concrete plinth and massaged his calves. 'He lied to us. Why?'

Carrie looked across the water in the direction of Pomona. 'To warn them?'

'What do you want to do, get another boat? The canal police or the divers' division?'

Carrie softened somewhat and forced a brittle smile. 'It'll wait until Monday. I'm sorry, you're not on duty, I shouldn't have called.'

'It's no bother, I was here anyway. Had the same thought as you by the looks of it.' His eyes travelled over her own workout clothes.

'I usually go to the gym, but this is perfect running weather, it's a pity to waste it.' She gestured to the cloudy sky before looking back at him. A genuine grin broke out on her face. 'Want to run with me?'

He pushed himself upright, his smile matching hers. 'Do you think you can keep up?'

'Detective Constable Harper!' she exclaimed. 'Do you even know me at all?'

She turned, broke into a steady run, heard his yell of surprise, running feet, catching up and settling comfortably beside her.

After five kilometres they stopped, breathing hard, clinging onto the railings under the Centenary Way Bridge. Silently Carrie stretched, feeling good as the blood pumped around her body.

'Juice?' panted Paul, gesturing to a pop-up bar under the bridge.

Carrie nodded and together they made their way over. A cluster of tables, all empty, sat in the sunshine and Carrie pulled five pounds out of her pocket and handed it to Paul.

'Surprise me,' she said. 'I'll get us a table.'

As she waited, she surveyed the water. A different water to where Ben Keller was headed. And yet again she wondered why he had lied to them.

'I shouldn't have taken Ben's word about his boat,' she said as Paul came back with two plastic cups with straws, and two big glasses of tap water. 'I should know better by now than to take people at their word.'

He shrugged as he passed a cup over to her. 'You had no reason to disbelieve him.'

Carrie eyed her green, iced drink suspiciously. 'Wheatgrass,' said Paul.

She sipped at it, trying not to wrinkle her nose at the taste. 'What did you get?'

'Mango,' he said. 'Delicious.'

'Swap?' she asked hopefully, only half-joking.

In reply, Paul drew his drink closer to himself.

'Did we get anything more about looking into Willow Hadley, anything in her past, reports or allegations she'd made?'

Paul shook his head. 'Nothing, not a single thing on any of the family. Nothing on Harry Wilson or his wife or daughter either.' He took a long sip. 'So, the mystery caller is Willow.'

Carrie nodded. 'That CCTV, it sure matched her.'

'From what we know of her, we've only got a photo supplied by her school, and it wasn't the most recent photo.'

Carrie suppressed a smile. Paul, the rational to her haste. And it wasn't a bad thing, it was why they worked so well together.

She drained her vile drink, washing it down with water, and stood up. 'Want to go back to the dock, see if our Mr Keller has reappeared yet?'

Paul tightened his shoelace before standing up. 'Race you,' he said with a wicked grin.

But the spot where Ben's boat usually stood was still empty. Carrie scanned the shore both up and down river, disappointed.

'Have you ever been to this Pomona?' she asked Paul.

'No, never. In all honesty I didn't think you could still access it. I think it used to be open to the public, but the docks have been crumbling away for a while now and it put an end to visitors.'

'Ben knows a way,' she remarked. 'I can't believe he's the only boatman round these parts who can get us there.'

'Maybe we can find out if it really is as tough a job as he claims,' said Paul, walking a few yards down the quay to where a small barge was tied up. 'Excuse me, sir!'

Now this man did look seasoned, thought Carrie as she regarded the man's weathered, lined face.

'We were wondering how we could go about getting to Pomona,' she said. 'Is it easy to get there?'

The man's bottle-green eyes stared at each of them in turn before he broke into wheezy laughter. 'Whad'ya wanna go there for?' he asked. 'S'nowt there anymore.'

'Just for a visit,' said Carrie. 'Are there boat trips there, anyone you know of who can take us?'

The old man slowly shook his head. 'They closed down the docking bay years ago. It's nigh on impossible to land anywhere else.' He narrowed his eyes as them, looking as though he considered the pair to be challenged in their intelligence. 'Why d'ya think they've done nowt with it? Given a bit of green land someone will build on it, don't you wonder why they ain't?'

'You don't know of anyone who takes their boat there?' Carrie pressed.

The man turned back to his barge, climbing aboard with difficulty, his gnarled fingers gripping the rail and he cast the pair one last glance over his shoulder.

'You don't want to go there,' he rasped, and then he was gone.

They hung around the quayside until it got decidedly chilly.

'Guess we'll have to catch up with Mr Keller on Monday, as planned,' said Carrie.

Paul nodded. 'I'd better head off then,' he said. 'But this was good fun, it's been nice to have a running buddy, maybe we should do it again?'

He looked anxious, noted Carrie, as though he was overstepping some sort of boundary. She considered her musings the other day, how few people she let into her life, and how she should start to change that. She nodded firmly at him.

He waved goodbye, and Carrie headed in the opposite direction, eager to get home now the sun had cooled and get in a hot shower. As she passed the old man's barge her phone vibrated in her pocket.

'DS Flynn,' she said as she answered.

'Detective Sergeant, this is Ganju, from Eccles,' he said. 'Miss Flynn, I found the information on the builder man who decorated my home. I have the paper here, with his details on it.'

Carrie stopped walking. 'Are you home now?' she asked. 'Can I come and get it?'

'Yes, Ma'am,' he answered, polite as ever. 'I will be waiting for you.'

Carrie hung up and turned around. She saw Paul's running jacket in the distance, a dot of blue in among all the black coats. She cupped her hands around her mouth.

'PAUL!' she yelled, and when he turned around she waved her phone in the air. 'Fancy a drive to Eccles?'

It wasn't a business card, as Ganju had originally said. It was a scrap of paper, with untidy writing on it. Not professional, not business-like. Carrie strained to see it; infuriatingly Ganju held it tight, as though worried he would lose the information again.

'My brother told me he was a decorator, this man,' said Ganju, waving the scrap of paper that he held in his fist. 'But he wasn't, not really. He painted, as you can see,' Ganju swept his hand around the freshly decorated lounge, 'but it wasn't his job, wasn't his business. He's an odd-job man, so my brother says.'

Carrie turned to face the man slumped in a chair in a darkened corner of the room. Ganju's brother, the hot-headed Thaman, looking as furious and edgy as the last time she'd met him.

'We should have done the work ourselves.' Thaman's voice rumbled out and he glared at his brother.

'Could we have the details?' Carrie asked politely, stepping closer to Ganju and the paper he clutched in his hand.

'He seemed all right, when I saw him in the pub. We got talking over a game of darts.' Thaman mimed throwing a dart, his hand stilled in the air before falling back to clutch the arm of his chair. 'More fool me. He said he was capable, and his quote was far less than some we'd had. I trusted him to be in my home while I was away, without even knowing him. But he was friendly, normal, you understand?' Thaman's eyes flashed, he curled his hand into a fist and thumped his leg. 'Now we know why he was so cheap, now we know he just wanted a house to bring defence-less, underage girls to where he wouldn't be disturbed.' Thaman snarled as he pushed himself out of the chair and snatched the paper out of his brother's hand. 'You find this monster, you find him and you lock him up and you tell those people outside that this was nothing to do with us.'

He leaned close to Carrie. Every instinct told her to back away, but she held her ground, wishing for the armour of her uniform instead of looking like a normal woman in her running gear. She felt Paul's arm brush hers as he moved closer to her. Instantly she breathed, relaxed, and nodded at Thaman. She held her hand out, her eyes locked on his.

He pushed the crumpled piece of paper into her palm and she closed her fingers around it, resisting the urge to open it up and read the name of the man which would be written there.

'Thank you,' she murmured to the brothers'. 'We'll get this sorted, I promise.'

She let Paul drive for once, the folded paper throbbing in her hands. The car pulled away from Ganju's house, and Carrie smoothed out the paper. She stared down at the cramped, untidy writing, read over and over the name and telephone number and address of the man who had put his hands on the young girl that he had found in the house.

'Oh my god,' she murmured.

What?'

'Oh my god,' Carrie said again, and she leaned her head back against the seat rest. 'We need to call on Ben Keller, *right now*.'

29

Carrie– 1998

Life went on.

It was the general, if unspoken, consensus that Carrie learned. The police and social services visits tailed off, Carrie went back to school and spent the whole day pretending not to notice the stares of the kids and teachers. Previously a high achiever, she lost her ability in lessons, whole hours swallowed up with concern about what she would find when she got home.

Her mother never returned to her after Hattie vanished. She was there, Mary, in her chair, sometimes, but more often than not in her bed. The pills the doctors had given her lay unopened on her nightstand. The house that Mary had taken such pride in grew dark with dust, the windows lost their shine, became grey pools which one could barely see in or out of.

Mary was supposed to take Carrie to an appointment every Tuesday after school with a trauma counsellor. The first few times somebody called a Family Liaison Officer took her, until Mary was deemed fit enough to do it herself.

Mary didn't take Carrie on that first Tuesday she was supposed to, and Carrie had nobody to tell that she had missed the appointment. She waited for the Liaison Officer or the nice policewoman or the social services lady to telephone or call round so she could bring it to their attention, but no calls came. Nobody visited.

Carrie and Mary had fallen through the cracks of an overworked system.

They had a talk at school about 'stranger danger'. The children sat agog, listening wide eyed as the teacher told them the rules they needed to survive.

'You must not get in the car of somebody you don't know,' Miss Graff intoned. 'You must also not get in the cars of people you *do* know,' she went on to emphasise.

'What about if my dad picks me up?' called out Noah, a boy in Carrie's class.

Miss Graff looked confused for a moment before saying sharply, 'Well that's okay, he's your dad.'

'But he's not allowed to see me, my mum has said that.' Noah fixed his blue-eyed stare on Miss Graff. 'She's got a paper, a r-r-restrained order…' He stuttered over the legal word.

Miss Graff sighed. 'Then no, Noah, you shouldn't go with your dad if he tries to pick you up.'

Carrie was as confused as the rest of the kids. She had gone in a car with Mr Lacey, a man she knew, and nothing had happened. But alone in the park with Hattie something had happened, something terrible, but she hadn't got in a car with the person who had stolen her sister.

She burned hot with an anger which had no outlet, sitting cross-legged on the cold floor of the assembly hall. These adults didn't really know what they were talking about, they didn't have all the answers, they couldn't protect the kids.

Carrie stood up. Two hundred little faces turned to watch as she walked out of the hall, out of the school, and went home.

Nobody stopped her.

*

Carrie heard the shallow breathing of her mother as she stood on the landing. Disappointed, Carrie drifted back down the stairs. There would be no dinner served up tonight.

She dragged a chair into the kitchen from the dining table and looked in the cupboard where the tins were kept. She pulled out a can of beans, the same supper she had made herself for days and weeks. Once they were a treat. Now, just the thought turned her stomach. She craved something else, something delicious, substantial. Something like chips. Hot with vinegar and salt, where the grease stained her fingers and she sucked at them long after the chips were finished.

Carrie practically salivated at the thought.

But Mary's purse was empty, not even a few pence. Carrie rummaged around the back of the sofa, the place where people always found money, but her hands came out with nothing except a thick coating of dust on her fingers.

She pulled out the wire vegetable rack. Soft carrots, a single, brown parsnip, and a handful of potatoes. Carrie fingered the white roots of the potatoes before pulling open the pantry and looking at the rarely used deep fat fryer.

There was smoke first, thick and cloying, and Carrie, unable to reach the top kitchen window even with a chair, opened the back door wide. She flapped with her tea towel, the way she'd seen her mother do on the occasions when something burned under the grill.

It looked like it was clearing, she thought with relief, as the smoke thinned. She moved away from the door, into the room to figure out how to turn the fryer off.

A pop, subtle but distinctive, a split second before the flames came.

Carrie ran to the door and jumped outside, her hands on her face, her mouth open in a scream that wouldn't come. But her mother was upstairs, the telephone was in the hall, she couldn't even call 999.

And Hattie's pictures, those nonsensical crayon drawings that Mary had pinned up all around the kitchen. They would burn, they would be gone, and they were all that was left of Hattie.

Her mother would never forgive her.

Carrie moved to the fence, saw her neighbour's patio door stood open. She found her scream as she yelled their names, relief as her shout brought their dog running, in turn its barking brought its owners, and Carrie sagged as they saw the plume of smoke pouring out of the kitchen door.

'Jesus, Karen, call the fire brigade,' her neighbour instructed his wife. 'Carrie, come over here.' He held his hands out to lift her over the fence, but Carrie backed away.

'Mum's inside, she's in bed,' she said. 'I have to get Hattie's drawings.'

She heard his shouts, heard his curses as he tried to vault the waist-height chain link fence but got his jeans caught on the little metal spikes.

Carrie darted back inside the kitchen.

It was all over, less than an hour later. The kitchen black, Hattie's drawings burned to ashes. Her mother lay on a bed in the back of the ambulance, not really aware that her home was gone. Carrie rubbed at her face and studied the black that came away on her fingers. Pete, the neighbour, an oxygen mask on his mouth and nose, leaned his hands on his knees while his wife rubbed his back. His wife, Karen, her eyes red and watery, darted glances at Carrie, sitting alone in the driveway.

Blaming me, no doubt, thought Carrie, for almost getting her husband killed.

Carrie thought about apologising, admitting her mistake, that she should have been content with having another can of beans, shouldn't have wanted the fancy chips.

They took her away for good, that night. Before she went, a small crowd of official people arrived and stood in groups. Carrie wandered among them, listening, unnoticed as always.

'But she never looked neglected,' hissed a voice she recognised.

Carrie glanced up. Miss Graff, her school teacher, her face red, her voice defensive.

Miss Graff went on, 'Her hair was always neat and tidy, she was clean, showered, I wouldn't have known what was going on, not by looking at her.'

The slow burn of fury again.

Of course I never looked neglected, she thought. *I've been doing my own hair and washing myself since Hattie came along. Hattie was the one my mother chose to look after. I looked after myself.*

But she didn't say anything. Through her eight-year-old eyes she could see Miss Graff needed to feel better about herself. And even though her inner irritation wanted to punish Miss Graff, a little bit of Carrie felt sympathy for the older woman.

They had all failed, she realised, and by looking at their faces, their quiet, hushed whispers, they all knew it.

Carrie allowed herself to be led away.

She didn't look back at the house that she would never live in again.

Ten years later she went back to the house where she had grown up. A new family lived there now, evident by the bikes abandoned near the gate. The windows sparkled again, the way they used to when Carrie and Hattie were little.

Her therapist had thought it might be a good idea to return when she was released from care. It was her first stop on her new journey as an independent adult.

The front door of the house beside Carrie's old home opened. A woman stepped out, tall, blonde, instantly recognisable. Her eyes darted to Carrie, just the way they had a decade ago.

'God, little Carrie, oh, look at you.' Karen smiled, but there was something in her eyes that Carrie couldn't identify.

Carrie walked over to her. 'I…I wanted to say sorry, for what happened, for making your husband come in the house after me. I was stupid, I could have killed him, and I don't blame you for being angry at me.'

Karen blanched, and her eyes grew rapidly red. 'My God, Carrie, I wasn't angry at you. I was angry at myself, for not realising that your mother was in such a bad way. I was furious with myself, not you.' Karen took a deep breath and shook her head. 'Never you.'

'Oh.' Carrie scratched at her head, unsure what to say. 'Thank you.' She forced a smile on her face. 'Please give my best to Pete.'

She walked away, raising her hand in a small gesture of goodbye. She was almost at the end of the road, heading towards the bus stop when she heard pounding feet behind her. Stopping, she turned.

Karen halted, her face red, as she stretched out a hand to Carrie's shoulder.

'We asked the authorities if you could come and stay with us, fostering, like, after that night.' Karen let go of Carrie, twisted her hands together. 'They said it wasn't a good idea, being so close to your old home. I just wanted to let you know that we tried, once we realised, we did try.' She paused, her words thick now. 'We did care, Carrie.'

Impulsively Karen moved forward, Carrie's hands shot out and she gripped the older woman's elbows to prevent her arms encircling her. 'Thank you,' she said simply.

She walked away, past the bus stop, back to the little council flat that served as her own halfway house.

She didn't visit the old house again.

30

Melanie slipped out of the cottage before anyone woke up and made her way to the wood store where the mask still lay. Someone had to come for it, she theorised. Someone had put it there for a reason, it hadn't been discarded. If the owner had wanted to throw it out, they would have set it on fire, buried it, or tossed it into the sea where the tides would have taken it far, far away. It had been in the wood pile, *hidden*.

It had to be Ben the boatman, Melanie reckoned, because if it were her father, or Gabe or Lenon they would have returned to the store to collect it by now. It was strategically placed, she deduced, not carelessly dropped or fallen from a pocket. It had been deliberately hidden.

She'd had an idea of searching the men's colours for the culprit. They would stand out, she imagined, they would tell her the truth. And so she did; she stared at each of them every time she saw them, but to her horror her father's and Gabe's and Lenon's colours, all of them, were muted, dull. Grey and a deep, dark purple, shot through with flashes of scarlet. She turned to the women, and to Willow, and saw fear and depravity in them, apart from her own mother. Alice was a marbled grey with the occasional pulse of pink excitement.

Melanie turned away in disgust. Everyone on the island was unhappy apart from Alice. And Alice was only happy because of the man who would come and visit her.

Melanie wondered what her own colours were, and not for the first time she was dismayed that they were never visible to herself.

She looked over her shoulder as she sat in the shade of the oak tree to wait for the mask-wearer to put in an appearance. Would today be the day she identified him? Maybe, but it occurred to her then, once she did know who it was, what would she do then?

*

'I'm sleeping with the man who brought us over here on the boat.' Alice said the words out loud, turned to Liz next to her on the bench to watch the woman's reaction.

Liz said nothing. Her eyes remained fixed on a point in the distance.

Alice leaned closer to her, the unwashed scent of Liz heavy in her air. 'I'm fucking him,' she said.

Nothing.

Alice felt her own face redden, scandalised by the words that had come out of her own mouth. She looked down at her feet, bare still, because the second toe on her right foot was too swollen to fit into any of her shoes. She reached across the bench and found Liz's hand. She held onto the other woman's fingers, squeezed them a little.

Sometimes Alice felt like she was losing her mind. She knew how Liz must be feeling, or must have felt. It no longer occurred to Alice to wonder why nobody was doing anything. Nobody was doing anything for Liz, that was just the way it was. Alice considered how long it would be until she, too, no longer spoke and nobody spoke to her. Already it had started. Melanie had been aloof for days, Harry was quietly angry about her outburst. And the other kids, Lenon and Willow, had never spoken to her anyway.

We will be an island community that doesn't communicate and we will carry on living here until we all quietly die, she thought.

She raised an imaginary glass in a silent toast to Harry and his island living.

'Cheers,' she said to herself.

She looked at the arm of the wooden bench, and the scratches she had made to mark the days. It would be another day before Ben came to visit. She needed to have a bath before then, maybe wash some clothes and try and force her foot into a shoe.

Her heart thudded at the thought of him, of her, of all of them. In her mind the clouds parted, the sun beamed through and Alice sat up straight.

She could sail back to Manchester with Ben.

She slumped. Melanie wouldn't go with her, Melanie would never leave her father here alone. And Alice couldn't leave Melanie here.

Could she?

The thought made her shiver.

*

From the lounge window Harry watched his wife as she sat on a bench with Liz. They had their backs to him, and he wondered what they were talking about. Alice spent a lot of time with Liz now, more than she did with him, her own husband, or even her daughter.

He frowned in annoyance. It was what he had wanted, for Alice to strike up a friendship with Liz, but not like this, not to the extent where it shut everyone else out.

He saw a smudge on the window pane, rubbed at it with his sleeve. They'd cleaned this house from top to bottom when they moved in, but it was dirty again, and Alice seemed to have lost interest in cleaning. He supposed it was to be expected, he had always been the home-maker, not her. It wasn't in her nature, really. But it was something he'd hoped would change about her out here on the island.

He squinted at her, at the cut-off jeans and grubby T-shirt and the bare feet. He used to love looking at Alice in her heels, in her crisp, designer suits.

She's changed, he thought, a*lmost beyond recognition.*

Harry moved into the bathroom and slipped the bottle of pills from the little ledge behind the toilet tank. He shook them, enjoying the satisfying rattle.

They were no Fluoxetine, but they were good pills. Relaxing, he'd found, when he took the first one the evening of the big fight with Alice. And every time he found himself growing concerned with his island community and the fractures, he took another one.

He thought of the dirty mark on the window pane, and Alice's dirty clothes and bare feet and he tipped a pill into the palm of his hand and swallowed it down.

*

It was much warmer now, decided Melanie as she shed her cardigan and let the sun blaze down through the trees on her bare arms. She hoped the good weather would bring everyone out of their moods, including herself. They were like hibernating animals, she realised, waiting for something to bring them alive again.

She blinked as she considered that the revealing of the masked man might do just this. They could banish him, whoever he was, and the island would be a better and safer place.

A worry niggled, *who would believe her?* She'd been accused of fantasies before by her parents, Alice more than Harry though. Her colours, for one thing. Her mother worrying that it was some sort of medical concern, like a brain tumour or something, but really knowing deep down that it was actually a part of her. Alice's warnings not to speak of the colours she saw. It would make people look at her like she was different.

Melanie pouted. She *was* different, and she didn't speak of the colours, yet still she didn't fit in anywhere. Not back at home, not with Tanisha or Kelly, and not here on the island.

The sound of a twig snapping brought her out of her reverie. Melanie gasped as she threw herself to the mossy ground. A memory caught at her, down on her stomach as she watched her dad trap the rabbit. Melanie closed her eyes briefly.

'Please don't let it be my dad,' she whispered.

And taking a deep breath she opened her eyes and watched as the man emerged from the shelter of the trees and made his way into the wood store.

It took hours for Melanie to move. She stayed concealed behind the tree, scrubbing at her face with her hands. A little part of her had thought it might be a fantasy, the 'creative side' of her, but it was real, the mask was real, and the man who wore it was real.

And he was here.

And she knew who he was.

When the sun moved in the sky to beat down upon her Melanie struggled to her feet. Putting her head down she ran, jumping over hillocks and scraping her knees as she slipped on the uneven earth. She slowed unwittingly as she recalled the man, dusting off the mask, fussing over it, stroking it fondly. She gagged, thumped at her chest and forced her feet to run faster.

She knew where she was headed, to find the twins, and she knew where they hid out all day, in a rocky cave underneath the highest point of the island. It was a place she had followed them to before, but she hadn't let them see her. They seemed to want to be alone all the time, and she'd thought – after that first night of looking through their window and seeing the way they slept together – that they had something going on like her mother and Ben. She had respected their privacy, embarrassed for them, and ashamed. But not now, because she needed them now, because the adults were falling apart, and the twins were the only people left on the island who could actually do something.

They were there, huddled together, joined at some part of their bodies like they always were. And she realised this was the first time she'd seen them in days.

'Willow?' Melanie craned her head into the darkness, could just about make out their silhouette. 'I need to talk to you.'

Two pairs of eyes turned to her, gleaming in the darkness. Melanie moved into the cramped space. Her eyes adjusted to the gloom and she frowned.

'What's wrong with him?' she asked, her discovery forgotten for a moment as she peered at Lenon, doubled over, one hand on Willow's arm, the other clutching his stomach.

'He's not well,' snapped Willow.

Melanie took a deep breath. More sickness: first Liz, no, before that her father, his illness, the whole reason they were here. Now Lenon.

'I need to talk to you,' Melanie whispered again, urgently this time.

Willow glared at her. 'Lenon's ill,' she hissed.

Melanie sat back in a corner. Normally she would leave, run, for Willow scared her, more than Tanisha or Kelly ever had. But now, with this news and with nobody else to turn to, she stayed put.

'I'm all right.' Lenon's voice was weak, stilted.

'Can I bring you anything, some water from the stream?' Melanie whispered, ignoring Willow's harsh stare.

Lenon shook his head, muttered something that might have been a 'thank you'.

'I found something,' Melanie started, 'I think we're in danger.'

The temperature in the little cave seemed to change. The space grew lighter, Melanie's eyes widened as she realised that Willow was aglow. Suddenly, Melanie understood so much.

'It's why Lenon's ill, isn't it?' she exclaimed.

Willow shushed her. 'Quiet,' she murmured. 'Keep your voice down.'

Melanie stared at Willow, lost in her light. 'What did he do?'

Willow's eyes bored into Melanie's. 'He doped him. He needs him calm, disabled, pliable. Lenon thought he'd avoided it, he never ate or drank anything *he* made, neither did I, but something must have slipped through the net.'

It was the most words Melanie had ever heard Willow say at any one time. And she wasn't yet finished. 'What did you find?' she asked, as if only just remembering what Melanie had said.

Melanie closed her eyes before slowly opening them. 'A mask, one that he wore, when he…' she tailed off, unable to finish.

Willow nodded, and her mouth twisted bitterly. 'That fucking mask,' she spat.

Willow knew about the mask. 'Why does he wear it?' Melanie whispered. 'Is it like a disguise?'

Willow uttered a humourless laugh. 'It's part of his game. It scares the kids, literally makes them freeze.' She concealed a shudder which made her colours tremble and shake. 'If the kids are frozen by fear, they're easier to handle.'

Melanie remembered inside the house, Kelly, above her on the landing, moving in slow motion. She remembered herself, immobile on the stairs. *Frozen.*

'Why is he doing this?' Melanie burst out, her voice scratchy and thin as though tears were close to the surface.

'He wants me.' Willow tilted her head to one side as she regarded Melanie. 'He probably wants you too, actually.'

Melanie gulped, her fingers worked at her mouth. Words, for the time being, were lost to her. All she had were memories; the hand grabbing her friend, and visions; of what could become of her.

Willow moved, gently shifting Lenon to lean against the wall as she reached across to Melanie.

'It'll be okay,' she said softly.

Melanie's eyes filled with tears which she let fall. 'How?' she asked, her voice grew louder and louder. 'We're trapped, he's getting to everyone, one person at a time, soon there'll only be you and me and—'

A hand clapped across her mouth, Melanie struggled against it.

'Quiet,' demanded Willow. 'He's been wanting me for ages, but me and Lenon we knew what he was doing, what his plan was. And he's not got me yet, has he?'

Melanie felt her breathing return and she nodded to indicate Willow could remove her hand.

'If you knew what he was doing, what he plans to do, why did you come here?' Anger flared, directed at the girl sitting across from her.

Willow smiled, though it never reached her eyes.

'I brought him here,' she stopped, reached for Lenon's hand, '*we* brought him here, because we're going to stop him, for good this time.' She paused, let her eyes settle on Melanie's. 'We're going to kill him.'

Silence that stretched on, broken only by Lenon's wheezy breathing. Melanie sat back, and watched as Willow's colours shone like the sun, while Lenon's thinned and turned to a deep, dark, grey.

31

Ben dithered, making calls, consulting his tide app on his phone, checking maps in the hull of his boat.

Carrie stood behind him, clutching tight to a shelf in the hull of his boat, staggering slightly as the water beneath them rocked the boat.

'It's going to be tight,' Ben said from between clenched teeth. 'The wind is getting up. I wouldn't normally risk it.'

Paul, perhaps sensing that Carrie was near to exploding, stepped up to Ben. 'We really have no time to waste, lives may be in danger.'

Ben put his phone down, his blue-eyed gaze pierced Paul. 'Alice is in danger?'

Carrie regarded the change in Ben, as soon as he thought that Alice might come to harm. *Interesting*, she thought. *Why fixate on Alice, rather than the children, or any of the others that were on the island?*

'You know Alice?' she barked. 'As something other than a passenger, I mean?'

Ben tugged at his beard. The moment was gone, he turned his back to them again.

'Ben?' Carrie prompted, her tone firm.

'We're having… an affair I suppose you'd call it.' Ben spoke but kept his back to them.

'Ah.' Carrie exchanged a glance with Paul. 'How, if you're not living there? Do you mean you *were* having an affair until she moved here?'

Ben shook his head. 'I go over to see her, she gets away from the others and spends an hour on the boat.' His face reddened and he glanced down at his feet. 'It wasn't planned.'

Carrie didn't know what to say. *Keep focused*, she reminded herself, and sensing an opportunity she moved to stand next to Ben. 'So you understand our concerns, that we don't want any harm to come to Alice or anyone else.'

'Right.' Ben started the motor, flicking instruments and craning to look out of the small window in the direction they were headed. There were a few, long moments of silence before Ben spoke again. 'What sort of danger?'

His voice was almost fearful, and to Carrie he sounded very young all of a sudden.

Carrie didn't answer his question, instead she asked, 'What did they seem like to you when you sailed them to the island the first time?'

Ben looked at her sideways on. 'I barely spoke to them; they were just passengers, paying a fare. Then the other family arrived, they weren't even supposed to come but they turned up on the quay, literally moments before we set sail.'

'Did they say anything to you?' asked Paul.

He shrugged, repeated, 'They didn't speak, any of them. I thought Harry was mental for wanting to do this, and I think Alice and Melanie weren't too keen. They were hostile, you know?' he glanced at Carrie. 'The other guy seemed okay, his family were… quiet.'

Carrie looked at Paul.

'Were they in on it together, some of them, *all* of them?' Carrie thought out loud, the terrible idea springing to mind.

'Like a paedophile gang?' Paul spat the words.

The boat lurched, Ben cursed, swung it back on course before staring at Carrie. 'A paedophile gang?'

'We don't know that,' said Paul, hurriedly. 'We're just trying to get information on how many people are involved.'

'But we need to get there as quickly as possible to figure this whole thing out, before someone gets hurt,' said Carrie.

'Fuck,' muttered Ben.

And it seemed to Carrie that the boat suddenly began to move a lot faster.

'You'll have to be quick, I can't keep her steady for long in the current unless we tie up,' called Ben as he inched the *Barnard Castle* as close to the quay as he could. 'The cottages are straight over the field above the dock, that's where they're all staying.'

There was a hint of worry in his voice. To hear that from the unflappable, stoic Ben chilled Carrie. She lurched out of the cabin, pulled herself up and onto the quayside, waited impatiently for Paul as he stepped up to join her.

'Wait here!' said Carrie, but Ben, down in the hull, didn't acknowledge her.

'Did you call this in?' Carrie asked as they made their way off the concrete platform.

'No, there wasn't time.' Paul pulled his phone out, glanced at it once before slipping it back in his pocket. He swore. 'No signal,' he said.

Carrie turned back to the *Barnard Castle*. 'Wait here!' she shouted again.

There was an answering shout from the boat, but the wind whipped Ben's words away.

'Hopefully this won't turn out to be a *Wicker Man* situation,' commented Paul as they reached the edge of the field.

'Huh?'

'You've not seen the film?'

Carrie shook her head. 'What's it about?' she asked.

Paul snorted a laugh. 'I'll tell you when this is all over.'

It was an eerie feeling walking through a meadow towards the two grey breeze-block cottages. Not a soul in sight, and not a sound either. Carrie looked back towards the city, but the field had dipped and neither the skyscrapers nor the water were in view. *I can't see Ben's boat*, Carrie realised. She hoped he'd wait for them, for there wasn't likely to be any other traffic passing by Pomona.

The cottages were in surprisingly good condition, despite being abandoned for so many years. She voiced this thought to Paul as they approached the front doors.

He raised a fist and hammered, while Carrie moved to the second little house and knocked. They waited, exchanged a glance. Nobody home.

Carrie lifted her hand, twirled her finger in the air, a signal for them to circle the cottages. He nodded, moved to the right, she went left. They met in the middle of the back of the houses, stopping to peer in the windows. Both houses were lived in, one of them tidier than the other. Carrie tried the handle on the back door of the house she'd walked around, pulling it closed as it opened.

'Not locked,' she said. 'Shall we go in?'

'You stay here,' Paul said. 'I'll do a quick recce.'

She watched through the open door as he moved quickly and quietly around the cottage, holding her breath as he darted in and out of the rooms leading off the main living area.

'Nobody,' he said as he slipped outside. 'Definitely people living here though.'

'Any signs of... anything?' Carrie finished lamely, unsure of what she was asking.

'Nothing out of order.' Paul looked at his watch. 'What do you say we get back to the boat, come over here with a team?'

Carrie looked around, nothing but fields to see and some trees on the horizon. No massacre, no blood-thirsty murder. Just an uneasy feeling that caught at her over and over again. But Paul was right; Ben had been concerned about docking the boat. They needed to come back prepared, with a team like Paul said. She nodded once, sharply.

'Let's go.'

She could hear the water even before they'd got halfway across the field. Carrie stopped for a single moment before breaking into a run.

'Carrie?' Paul called behind her.

'The water!' she said, but the wind whipped her words away.

It sprayed up and over the concrete docking platform, so high, so ferocious Carrie couldn't even get to the dock. Paul came up behind her, breathing hard.

'Is he still there?' he asked.

A spray of fine water hit them and they staggered backwards a few feet. 'I doubt it,' said Carrie grimly.

They moved to the side, away from the concrete but where they had a clear view of the water. Carrie, fearful of the sudden strong winds, went into a crouch, digging her fingers into the mossy grass as she peered towards the dock.

'He's gone,' she said. 'The boat isn't there anymore.'

Paul knelt beside her, pulling the hood of his fleece up. 'Will he come back?'

'He'd better,' Carrie said. She gestured to Paul. 'Come on, let's get away from the water.'

*

They stopped at the edge of a small copse of trees. Carrie held back, cast her eyes over the trees, their branches only just coming into bud, limbs held aloft, twigs like claws. She concealed a shudder.

'Were we stupid, coming here?' she asked Paul.

He stopped, sat down on a gnarled root as he pulled his phone out of his pocket. 'I don't think we expected Ben to abandon us,' he said.

'He knows he left us here, he knows Alice is in danger. Once the wind drops he'll be back.' She sincerely hoped this was true. 'Anything?' she asked, nodding towards his mobile.

He shook his head. 'Nothing. No signal.'

'Ben said he comes over to see Alice,' she remembered suddenly. 'How often do you think he sails here? Daily? Weekly?'

Paul gave up on his phone and shoved it back in his pocket. 'I really fucking hope it's daily,' he replied morosely. 'But what do we do while we wait for him?'

Carrie pushed herself off the tree trunk she had been leaning against and zipped up her coat.

'We try to find the kids, that's our first priority.'

She turned a full circle, saw nothing but trees, and under her feet the ground shifted, soft mud, scattered with stones, twigs and dead leaves.

It was all too familiar, though it was a memory she rarely allowed herself to recall. She shivered, violently.

'Let's get out of these damn woods for a start,' she snapped, and without waiting for Paul she hurried away from the copse.

*

Alice ran, legs pumping, breathing wheezy, in and out, all the time a grin stretched across her face.

She'd been on the most northerly point of the island, on the high ground, walking, deep in thought when the approach of the

Barnard Castle caught her eye. She'd watched in shock, amazement and happiness spreading throughout her body.

An unscheduled visit from Ben!

As she dashed back across the island she wondered what would have happened if she hadn't glanced up and seen the boat. Would he have come ashore looking for her? The thought of such a chivalrous and knightly act made her shiver in anticipation.

Alice didn't glance at the cottages as she ran across the field, and when her bare feet pounded the concrete dock she pulled up sharply as an unexpected wave came up, up and over. She held her arms out, the shock of the wind-blown water and the slippery dock stunning away thoughts of Ben. *How had he even docked?*

But the thought of him misjudging the current, sailing away from her wasn't an option. Gathering her full skirt to bunch at her waist she went down on her knees, crawling along the dock to the edge, thrilled and horrified in equal measure at the danger.

Digging her fingers into the concrete she peered over the edge. The *Barnard Castle* was gone.

'Ben!' she called, but her shout went unheard against the wind.

She whispered his name instead, tasted it in her mouth. She put her hand on her face. Her fingers were wet.

The spray of the water, she told herself as she crawled back off the dock.

32

She returned to the high point of the island. Did the others know that from here the whole of Pomona was visible?

Probably, Alice concluded. They were all into exploring. The others knew every square foot of the place. Apart from Liz, of course, Alice acknowledged to herself. Liz knew nothing other than the cottage and the bench outside.

'Ben,' she said out loud. 'Please come back.'

Alice picked up a small, white stone and scraped it across the boulder next to her. She stared at the jagged, chalky line.

'I'm so lonely,' she said to nobody. 'I have to go home.'

She turned around, swivelling on her knees to look across at the skyline of Manchester. What was home? Not the house that Harry had sold. Maybe not Salford, perhaps not even Manchester.

She waited for the hope to spring forth, that anything was possible, that she could go anywhere. Instead a crushing weight came to rest in her throat.

She had spent too long being quiet, she realised. A quiet girl, just like Liz, like Willow, like Melanie. Quashed into keeping quiet to placate the men. And it was a new realisation, because always she had applauded herself for her feminism, for being the money-maker, the breadwinner, while Harry tended house and raised their child. And in the court rooms and in the office she hadn't been a quiet girl, she had been outspoken and strong and loud.

Until the men in that office decided that she was no longer needed.

It was all of the men.

And even Ben had sailed away.

Alice pressed the white stone to the boulder again, so hard that it snapped in her fingers.

She stood up, wiping her hands on the front of her skirt.

Enough. The island life was over. She was taking Melanie home. And simmering with long-overdue fury she went to find her daughter.

*

'How are you going to kill him?' Melanie whispered into the darkness of the cave.

Lenon leaned over and retched in the corner. Willow absently rubbed his back.

'It might be best if you don't know too much,' said Willow. 'We're not planning a prank, this isn't some kids' game, you know.'

Melanie blinked as Willow's colours glistened when she spoke.

'Does… anyone else know?' Melanie asked.

Willow's glittering aura dulled to a deep, dark green. She shrugged, sulkily. 'Can't depend on anyone else. Can't tell our mother. She doesn't know anything anymore.'

Her words were matter-of-fact, her tone flat and dead, her voice hoarse with a love lost the only sign of any emotion.

Melanie moved slightly so she was fully in the shadows. Willow's sadness caught at her, but it also frightened her.

'We can tell *my* mother,' said Melanie. 'She's a lawyer, she knows all the legal stuff, she's protected loads of innocent women and she's put a lot of bad men in prison.'

Suddenly Melanie was hopeful. They could hand it over to the adult, the way kids were supposed to when they had a problem.

Her mother could sort it out, make an arrest, she had the power to do that, didn't she?

'You're not telling your mother anything.' Willow's voice was loud, echoing around the rocky chamber. Willow pushed Lenon off her and crawled over to Melanie. 'You don't tell your mother anything, okay?'

Melanie shifted as far back as she could, away from Willow's wild eyes, fierce breath and exposed teeth.

A rustle at the entrance, a shadow moved across the room.

'Tell me what?' said Alice. And then, as her gaze landed on each of them in turn, she said, 'what the *hell* is wrong with Lenon?'

*

'Has the wind changed?' Carrie asked Paul as they walked back towards the concrete dock where Ben had dropped them.

He moved close to the edge to check, and even the movement confirmed to Carrie's that she was right. The wind was not as strong here; the water was still agitated, but it was no longer coming over. Paul wouldn't have been able to stand that close to the quayside an hour ago.

'Do you reckon he'll come back?' Paul asked as he came back to walk beside Carrie.

'If he doesn't…' Carrie didn't finish her sentence. Instead she paused, sinking down to sit on the concrete edge now it was no longer covered in water.

She rubbed at her temples, fighting off the panic of being lost. She'd been lost once before, and terrible, life-changing things had happened. How was she here again?

Paul sat down beside her. 'You okay?' he asked quietly.

She forced her head to nod, still massaging the sides of her face.

'Is this…' Paul hesitated, shot a single glance at her before trying again. 'Is this what happened to Hattie? Someone like this, I mean.'

She sucked in a breath, not enough air, nothing coming in, and a steel fist gripping her chest. She panted, suddenly, leaning over, feeling even more constricted, changing to tilt her head back. A hand on the back of her neck, moving to snake around her shoulders. She shrugged Paul off her, shook her head fiercely.

'I never told you her name,' she hissed the words, the only way to get past the blockage in her chest. 'How do you know her name?'

He moved away, giving her one last uncomfortable pat on her shoulder. 'I looked up the case,' he said.

She glared at him. He had the good grace to look embarrassed, but he pressed on regardless.

'The newspapers said you saw it, witnessed it, but you couldn't recall it.'

Carrie stared at him in disbelief. What did he want her to say? *Yes, Paul, you're correct, I failed my baby sister, my stupid, idiotic brain blocked it, so there was no chance of catching the man who killed Hattie?*

And, *oh God*, what else had he read? What else had the newspapers said? Did they report that her mother had slumped into a living, breathing coma, unable to care for herself or her one remaining child? Carrie swallowed. She genuinely didn't know; she'd never read the reports, never looked back at them, even when she was an adult.

'We need to find the girls,' she said, pushing herself to her feet. She hooked two fingers into the neck of her T-shirt, pulling it away from her neck.

'Carrie—'

She spun to face him, barely resisted the urge to plant her hands on his chest and push him into the water. 'What?' she snarled. 'What do you want from me?'

He held his hands up, and his brown eyes locked on her, sad, filled with a sympathy that she hated. 'I don't want any—'

She moved closer to him, covered her mouth with her hand so he wouldn't see her lip trembling.

'I can't go back in time, but we've got young girls here, on this island, with a man who is going to hurt them. Those girls are here, and they are alive, and it's our fucking job to get to them before he does.' A jagged, internal breath escaped from her, like a gasp, and she walked backwards, away from him, away from the possibility of losing herself so completely that she did something she would regret.

He nodded. 'Yeah,' he said. 'Let's go.'

*

Melanie closed her eyes and pinched her lips together. In the darkness behind her closed lids she heard the shifting ground, felt it underneath her as her mother wedged herself into the already cramped cave.

'Willow?' Alice's sharp voice rang out. 'What is wrong with your brother? And what are you not supposed to tell me?'

It was Alice's courtroom voice, Melanie realised. One rarely used at home, one hardly ever used against Melanie or Harry. At home Alice's voice was a soft murmur, usually in agreement to whatever Harry was suggesting.

'Melanie?' Alice, unaccustomed to the dark, stumbled over to her daughter. 'What's going on?'

I won't tell her, thought Melanie. *It's not my secret to tell.* She clamped her lips even tighter together, knowing they were white as the blood drained away.

'Lenon is sick.' Willow spoke up suddenly. 'He's been poisoned, just like my mother. Just like all of you will be if you stand in my way.'

'What?' A half-laugh came from Alice. 'What are you talking about?'

More noise as Willow stood up. She was as tall as Alice, Melanie realised, as the two of them stood face to face. Suddenly Melanie had a terrible thought, a vision, almost, of the cold, uncaring, unfeeling Willow, producing a knife, the sound of it as it swished through the air towards Alice.

Melanie's heart pounded furiously. She pushed herself up, darted out of the cave, and ran as fast as she could towards the cottages.

'Dad!' Melanie burst into the cottage, scanned the room. Even before she darted into her father's bedroom she knew he wouldn't be in there. 'Dad.' She spoke desperately. 'Where are you, Dad? I need to know it isn't true. I need you to tell me that, Dad.'

The stillness of the deserted cottage mocked her in its silence.

She walked towards the door, stopped in her tracks. Colours coming around the edge of the frame, seeping into the house, black and grey, reminding her of smoke.

Melanie ran to the door, peered outside, the low sun beating down in her face, blinding her. She shaded her eyes.

'Dad?' she called, a tremor to her voice now. 'I'm scared.'

The colours, their source unseen, juddered towards her, followed by a figure.

'Melanie.' He said her name once, smooth, like caramel, friendly and normal-sounding, just like he always had been.

But before she could speak he moved again, his colours settling around his physical form, as he lurched towards her, clamping his hand roughly down across her mouth, stopping the scream before it had even begun.

*

Silence stretched, the only sound an occasional groan from Lenon.

Lenon. The boy was sick. Alice blinked rapidly, pushed her hands through her hair. It felt greasy, dirty, and unconsciously she rubbed her hands on her skirt.

'Who has poisoned your mother?' she asked, sure she'd misheard, misunderstood, praying unconsciously that she'd got it wrong, that Melanie had got it wrong, that Willow was making it up. She looked at the silent boy, his white, damp face. 'Who has done this to Lenon?'

'He feeds my mother pills, he started a while ago, now she can't cope without them. He must have given Lenon some too.' Willow turned to face her brother, put her hands on either side of his face. 'What did he give you, a drink, food?' she asked urgently.

Lenon shook his head weakly. 'I never accept anything he's prepared, he must have put something in a drink, maybe that coffee this morning, I might have turned my back for just a second but…I don't know.' His last words came out in a rush and he slumped back against the rocky wall, exhausted from his speech.

'But *who*?' Alice snapped this time, looking from Lenon to Willow. 'And *why*?'

'To stop them interfering, to stop my mother and Lenon being able to stop *him*,' said Willow impassively.

Alice's mouth fell slackly open, part disgust at Willow's words, part horror in the emotionless way in which the younger girl spoke.

'Where did Melanie go?' she asked, and without waiting for an answer she bent over and darted from the cave.

In the open air, in the bright sun, she breathed deeply, in and out, hissing on the out breath to dispel the smell that seemed to have cloyed in her nostrils.

'Melanie?' she called, and then, louder, 'MELANIE?'

The twins followed her and she rested her eyes on Lenon. 'Tell me everything,' she demanded.

'He's grooming me… trying to.' Willow corrected herself. 'I think he's done it before, he was in that house with Melanie and her friend. He wants the kids, he's… sick.' She moved her hand to rest upon her brother's shoulder. 'There's no way out, he needs not to be here any longer. He needs to be nowhere.' Her hand kneaded her brother's arm. 'He needs to die.'

Alice drew in a shuddering, ragged breath. 'Who?' she asked, quietly this time.

Finally Willow raised her eyes to meet Alice's.

'Gabe,' she said. 'Gabe needs to die.'

But he's so nice. It was the first thought that sprung into Alice's mind. She swallowed the words before they came out of her mouth. It was a ridiculous thing to think. She, better than anyone, knew the cloaks and disguises people could wear. She saw enough of them facing her in the courtroom. She flicked her gaze between the two teenagers in front of her. And as she studied them, the pair of them, looking so much older than their actual age, she realised they were telling the truth.

'Willow.' She moved forward, ready to pull the girl into an embrace, but Willow scooted backwards.

'Where did Melanie go?' she asked, turning to Lenon, as though he had the answer.

Her words were the jolt that Alice needed.

The danger, her daughter, a paedophile, loose on this island from which there was no escape.

'We need to find her, we need to stay together,' she said. 'Where is he?'

There was no need to ask who *he* was. Willow shrugged.

'Right,' said Alice from between gritted teeth. 'Come on.'

Willow placed one hand under Lenon's arm as they began to walk. Alice sucked in a breath. The boy was pale, clammy, practically green. Alice moved to walk beside him, hooked a finger under his chin and forced his face up to hers.

'What's he had?' she snapped to Willow. 'The same pills as your mother?'

Willow glared at her. 'Probably, I don't know, like he said, we thought we were careful, we never had anything he cooked, or foraged for, or collected, but something got through.' Willow looked long and hard at her brother. 'Not the same pills, maybe, because it took weeks to get Mum like she is, this is sudden, in the last couple of days.'

Alice suppressed a moan. What was happening here? How were they talking so normally about something so terrible? A man had been grooming his child, her own child too, and poisoning his wife, and the boy whom he had raised as his own son since childhood.

'Jesus fucking Christ,' Alice swore. 'I can't actually believe this is happening. This man is your *father*.'

Lenon raised his head, his eyes, pale and watery fixed on Alice. 'He's not our father,' he said weakly.

His tone served only to irritate Alice further. She inhaled, held it, and blew it out slowly. *I'm just scared because this is so huge, and so dangerous, and we're fucking well trapped*, she thought. *I just need to find my girl and then I can think, I can come up with a plan.*

But rational thought deserted her. All she had were more questions.

'Why didn't you report him, Willow?' she asked, her voice high with fright. 'Why didn't you tell someone, a teacher, or the police?'

The sound of twigs cracking, of footsteps approaching stilled any answer that Willow may have given. Unconsciously the group moved closer together, Alice moved in front of Lenon and Willow.

Her heart pounded, and she realised for the first time in maybe all of her adult life she felt the deep, maternal instinct that she had always been chasing. A realisation like a shock jolted through her.

I'll kill for my daughter.

And it wasn't dramatic, or hysterical, simply pure and true.

They waited, and two shadows emerged from the trees. Two people, a man and a woman, casually dressed. Alice's heart hammered in her chest. Strangers. Were they here at Gabe's behest?

'Who are you?' Her voice was a shout, ragged and trembling, fear-filled, angry.

The woman stepped over to them, her blue-eyed gaze holding Alice's for a long moment before flicking over each of the twins.

'I'm Carrie Flynn,' she said. 'Detective Sergeant Carrie Flynn, this is Detective Constable Paul Harper.' Carrie rested her gaze on the group of people in front of her and took a deep breath. 'Willow did tell us what was happening. That's why we're here.'

33

He didn't speak as he forced her to walk. Once they were into the woods, he took his hand away from her mouth.

'You're not going to scream though, are you?' he asked.

Melanie shook her head. *No*, she wouldn't scream, not yet. You had to judge these things, she knew.

'Good girl,' he said, and his words made her shiver.

'Who are they?' he asked now, quietly, his eyes cold but glinting with a hidden danger.

His question threw her. 'Who?' she asked.

'Those people who've come here, they're police, aren't they?' He pushed on, not waiting for an answer. 'I can tell by the way they move.'

Melanie's lips moved soundlessly. There were no other people on the island, nobody could come here.

Ben comes here, a little voice in her head told her.

But he's not the police, her mind hissed in return.

'I— I don't know what you mean,' she whispered, but he had turned his back on her again.

He hadn't talked to her face on, she hadn't even seen him before when he pounced on her. She wondered if he had the mask, if he were going to slip it on. Melanie began to shake, and she wrapped her arms around herself to try and stop the tremors.

She thought of Willow, cold, hard, brittle Willow, and wondered what this man had done to her to make her that way. She thought of Liz, slowly and regularly drugged by this man, and Lenon, pale and sick. She thought of Kelly, the way this man had held her hair so tightly that it had streamed out behind her like a ribbon. She wondered what this man planned for her. He gave nothing away as he stood beside her, silent and brooding, his shoulders hunched over.

'You— you could let me go,' she said, her voice brave but small.

He laughed, pushed her in her back, his fingers leaving an ice-cold trail on her spine.

*

'My daughter has vanished,' blurted Alice to the officers. 'She was here, then just… gone.'

'Is she with him?' Carrie asked as she jogged the last few feet over to the little group.

'I don't know! I don't know where he is!' Alice's voice rose, high-pitched, frantic.

Carrie nodded as she cast her eye over the cluster of frightened people in front of her. 'Who else is here?' she asked.

Alice swallowed. 'My husband, Harry, somewhere.' She gestured helplessly.

Paul stepped up and addressed Lenon directly. 'Do you know where Gabe might be? Where he might have gone with Melanie?'

Alice staggered where she stood. 'Do you think he's got Melanie?' she cried.

Paul held up a hand. 'We don't know that, how long ago was she here? Which direction did she go in?' He turned to the twins. 'Where does he usually spend his time?'

'The woods,' said Willow doubtfully. To Carrie her answer sounded like a question.

'Let's go,' she said. 'Stay close. Willow, tell us the way.'

*

They traipsed along, Willow in the lead, Carrie and Paul bringing up the rear. Alice fell in step beside Carrie.

'Did Ben bring you here?' Alice asked quietly.

Carrie exchanged a glance with Paul. 'Yes, he did,' she said.

'Where is he?' Alice stared straight ahead as she spoke, Carrie noticed the blush that stained her face. 'I thought I saw his boat, but when I got there it was gone.'

'We think it was the water conditions, docking here's not easy for a small boat at the best of times,' Paul answered. He waited a beat, then said, 'but I guess you know that.'

Alice's spine straightened noticeably. 'I do know, he told us all about the currents when he brought us over. Harry knows too, he researched it all.' Alice hissed out a bitter little laugh. 'Harry researched everything except the people he brought over with us.'

'So, you had no idea about Gabe?' At Alice's fierce look Carrie hurried on. 'What do you know now? What has Willow told you?'

Alice pushed her hair back with her hands. 'Apparently he's been doping Liz, he's given something to Lenon, he's sick.' Alice stopped abruptly and turned to face Carrie. 'He's been, what do you call it, grooming? Grooming Willow, whatever he did to the girl in that damn house back home, and… *oh God…*' Alice covered her face with her hands, her shoulders shook.

'Alice, what is it?' Carrie leaned close to the woman.

Alice dropped her hands. 'I thought he was charming!' she said, her voice hoarse. 'I thought he was the only person on this island who was *normal*!' Alice grabbed blindly at Carrie's sleeve and pulled at it. 'Now I don't know where Melanie is, she could be with him! What sort of a woman am I? What sort of a *mother* am I?'

Something splintered at Carrie's memory, that word, *charming…* but as soon as the feeling came it was gone. Carrie extracted her arm from Alice's grip. 'People like Gabe are clever, they seduce everyone, even their victims to a point. Please don't blame yourself. We'll locate your daughter, that's our priority.'

Paul moved up ahead of them, gesturing for Carrie to hang back while he took the lead from Willow. She glanced back, made sure that Lenon was still with them.

'Stay close,' she called to him.

'What are you going to do?' asked Alice fearfully. 'Are we all in trouble?' Without waiting for an answer she shook her head, rubbed at her face again. 'It doesn't matter, as long as the kids are safe, as long as Melanie is okay.' She paused, turned and stared at Carrie, a piercing glare. 'You will make sure the children are okay, won't you?'

Of course, Carrie wanted to say. *This is why I do this job, to save children before it's too late, to make up for the time I didn't save the most important little girl. That's why I'm here, and I'll do anything to make sure these kids get off this godforsaken island and have a normal, safe life.*

Instead, she swallowed hard and whispered, 'Of course we will.'

A shriek, piercing the air, startling a flock of birds as Carrie and Alice entered the underpass.

'What was that?' Alice hissed, frozen beside her.

Before she could reply Carrie heard footsteps pounding, a silhouette at the end of the tunnel. Carrie shot out a hand, dragged Alice to remain beside her, braced herself, planting her feet solidly on the concrete ground, finally relaxing as the person got closer.

Paul.

He stopped, locked his eyes on Carrie's. 'He's down on the rocks,' he muttered. He cast a single look at Alice. 'Melanie is with him.'

'Stay behind me,' said Carrie to Alice. Alice shoved Carrie, ran after Paul who had already jogged halfway back down the underpass.

They were practically on a cliff top, she realised, as she emerged from the underpass into a howling wind. Ahead of them, Paul paced back and forth, his stance stiff, his movement jerky.

'Where is she?' Alice cried. 'Where are they?'

Paul gestured over the cliff edge. Carrie inched towards him, peered over. The water slapped against the rocks below; beyond them, to the right of the water, two figures walked a winding path towards a small wooded area.

'Where does that path lead to?' Carrie called to the twins, her voice straining against the wind.

'The east side, through the fields. It forks off, you can double back to the fields from there too,' said Willow, gesturing to the side of the underpass they'd just come through.

Carrie turned to face Paul. 'Take them back to the house, I'll follow this trail.'

He shook his head. 'We shouldn't separate, we don't know—'

She cut him off. 'No time, Paul. I'll meet you at the cottages.'

And before he could protest, she darted off towards the rocky shelf, and vanished from sight.

34

Harry sat in his window seat, periodically switching from peering outside from the lounge window, and shuffling across the room to look out across the back fields.

Where *was* everybody? He scratched at his head, wincing at his tender scalp from where the sun had caught his head through his thinning hair.

He hadn't seen anyone all day long. He hadn't seen Gabe for ages. Liz hadn't emerged from her cottage; the kids could be anywhere. And Alice.

Where is Alice?

She hadn't talked to him properly since their fight. Harry sighed, stuck his hand down the side of the chair and pulled out the medication bottle. Unscrewing the cap he looked inside, comforted slightly by the sight of the little white pills. There were many in there now, and Harry tipped two into his palm and dry swallowed them.

With another heavy sigh he leaned his head against the back of the chair and closed his eyes.

Where was everyone? After fifteen minutes or so, his question didn't seem very important anymore.

'Harry? Harry!'

Alice's sharp tone pulled him from his slumber. He raised his hand, wiped at his damp mouth.

'Baby,' he said, but his voice was thick and his tongue felt too big for his mouth. He smiled regardless; he felt happy.

He reached his hand out, hooked his fingers around hers. 'Come sit with me,' he murmured.

Alice slapped his hand away. 'For God's sake, Harry, will you wake up?'

Someone else stepped into view, a man. Harry squinted.

'Gabe?'

'Mr Wilson, I'm Detective Constable Paul Harper with the Greater Manchester Police, Salford Division. We need to speak to you, we need your help, or some way of communicating with the city. Mr Wilson, do you have a working mobile phone?'

Harry felt the saliva dribbling from the side of his mouth as he stared at this stranger. Police? Manchester police? And he wanted a… *mobile phone*?

He tried to push himself upright in the chair but his arms were soft and liquid. He gave up, gazed open-mouthed at the man, before turning his attention to Alice.

'What?' he managed.

He saw Alice's clenched fists, the red rash on her chest and neck, the fury in her eyes. He remembered their fight, her kicking the table, not seeming to feel the pain in her bare foot.

She pounced, suddenly, and Harry tried again to lift his arms to protect his face, certain she was going to scratch his eyes out. He let out a thin wail as her fingers grazed his leg, felt the breeze as she spun away from him.

He blinked through sleep-encrusted eyes. She stood in the centre of the room, holding something, looking triumphant, almost.

'Liz's fucking pills!' she spat, holding the bottle aloft like a prize, rattling it. The noise cut through Harry's fog.

'Hey,' he mewled, reaching for them, struggling once again to stand.

Off to one side, the police officer blew out a frustrated breath of air.

Alice threw the bottle behind her. 'He's no help,' she hissed. She made to leave, before turning back to Harry. Crouching down, she put her face very close to his. 'Gabe is a paedophile,' she hissed. 'He's got your daughter.'

At her words Harry felt panic manifest in the room. It touched him, worried at him, even though he didn't understand what his wife was saying. A terrible lie, an *awful* thing to say about a man.

Alice stormed past him, headed towards the door. The police officer, the strange man who didn't belong on the island, followed her.

And was it Harry's imagination or did he throw a filthy look in his direction?

The door opened, a breeze ruffled the curtains. Moments later it slammed shut. Harry swallowed past the lump in his throat.

'Wait,' he called, weakly.

But they had gone.

*

'He's a fucking liability, I can't fucking believe it.'

Alice felt the heat of her anger threading through her body. She turned to Paul, suddenly furious that he was standing there, scanning the horizon for his partner, while her daughter was in the hands of that man. At her glare, he seemed to snap to attention. He turned to Willow, standing like a sentry in front of the door to the second cottage.

'Your mother is in there?' he asked.

Willow nodded.

'I looked in there earlier, I didn't see her,' he said.

When neither of them replied, he stepped closer and peered at Lenon.

'What about him?' he asked. 'Can we find out what he took?'

'It could have been anything, mushrooms, berries, pills. Anything.' Willow slipped her thin arms around her brother's shoulders. 'Watch it,' she said to Paul as he stepped closer.

Alice saw it then, the splash of vomit that Paul had nearly stepped in. Grimacing, Paul moved carefully around it.

'It's probably good, if he's vomited,' he said cautiously.

Alice let out a grunt of fury. 'This is…' she tailed off, closed her eyes before opening them wide. 'Liz, Lenon, Harry, all drugged up to the eyeballs. I need to find *Melanie*.' She wrenched Paul's sleeve, a plaintive plea for him to help.

Paul set his mouth in a firm line and walked up to the door. Hesitating for just a moment, he pushed it open and walked in.

Alice paced around, darting fleeting glances at Willow and Lenon. She wanted to run, sprint and find that son of a bitch and wrench him away from her little girl. A part of her knew she needed these officers. And couldn't Melanie be inside that house right now? Quietly, making no sound, she slipped through the cottage door after Paul.

It was gloomy in this cottage, the drapes always closed. Dust mites made an arc in a strip of sunlight from a rip in the material that hung at the windows. It smelled real bad, Alice noticed. Even worse than the last time she'd been in here.

She could make out Paul's shadow in the bedroom through the open door, and eager to stick close to him, she padded across the room.

Liz was on the bed, Paul bent over her. At first she thought he was crying, chest heaving, rubbing at his eyes, before she realised the stench was attacking him.

She heard two sets of breathing and she held her own breath to make sure one of them wasn't her. Paul, steady, noisy, inhaling though his nose. Liz, jerky, in spasms with an accompanying wheeze.

'Jesus Christ,' muttered Paul.

'She's no better then?' said Alice.

Paul lurched forward at the sound of her voice, reaching out to steady himself on the bed post. He turned to face her.

'How long has she been like this?' he asked.

Alice shrugged, holding on to the door frame, peering inside, looking at the wall, the ceiling, anywhere except at the inert woman.

She heard Paul swallow as he looked back at Liz. 'I looked in here earlier, she was so quiet and still under the bedclothes I didn't even notice her.' He straightened up. 'Can we get her some water, please?'

Alice nodded and slipped out towards the kitchen. When she came back Paul was bent over Liz, one hand taking her pulse, the other on her forehead.

He waited while Alice lifted the bottle to Liz's dry, cracked lips before asking, 'Are there any phones that work on this island?'

Alice shook her head.

He nodded, as though he'd been expecting that answer.

'No internet? What about 3G coverage?'

'No.' She pushed herself upright, turned back to the door. 'I need to find my girl,' she said.

'Right.' He backed out of the room. 'Let's move outside,' he said, and he jogged back to the door.

*

Carrie saw the look of pure relief on his face when she came around the corner.

He stalked up to her, his face closed and cold. 'Don't ever do that again,' he murmured in a clipped tone.

She restrained herself from reminding him who was in charge. She let it go, knowing she would have said exactly the same if he had done what she did.

'I didn't see where they went,' she said before turning around to face Alice. 'Where else have we not covered?'

Alice began to speak, rattling off the points of the island she was familiar with. She stopped suddenly as the cottage door creaked open and Harry emerged.

'W-what's happening?' he rasped. 'Where is Melanie?'

Carrie stared at him, something tugging at her inside at the sight of his watering eyes.

'Are you saying that man has got my daughter? But you called him a-a…' He tailed off as though repeating Alice's words would make it all so real. Suddenly to Carrie he looked as sick as Lenon.

Carrie glanced at the boy, drew in a sharp breath.

'Lenon,' she said. 'Where is your sister?'

'I don't know,' he said, and his slate-grey eyes glinted.

Carrie breathed heavily. 'Stay here,' she said to Alice. 'Stay together and don't *move*.' Turning to Paul she said, 'come on.'

'What're we going to do, walk round and round the island until we stumble upon them?' Paul asked.

'If we have to,' replied Carrie.

'We need help, we need to get—'

She raised a hand. 'Shh.'

'What?' he whispered back.

Footsteps behind them. Carrie turned, visibly relaxed as Alice came into view.

'We really could do with you staying with Harry and Lenon, and keeping watch over them and Liz,' said Carrie.

Alice raised her chin. 'I need to find my daughter,' she said. 'If you were me, if the missing were one of your own, would you stay put?'

It was like a knife through Carrie's heart.

I did worse than that, she thought. *I turned away, I walked* away.

'Stay behind us,' she ordered as she began to walk again, faster now, the sense of urgency pulling her along.

'Look,' said Paul, pulling up so abruptly Carrie almost collided with him.

She looked to where he pointed, saw the blossom, a trail of it, stretching ahead of them on a beaten path. Bright pink; a beacon against the dark brown earth.

'A trail?' she wondered aloud.

Alice looked up at the sky. 'There's no trees here where it could have fallen from.'

They were like breadcrumbs, like the fairy tale, thought Alice as they broke into a run. Only they were flowers, not crumbs, and they were leading not to the witch, but to someone far worse.

'Where does this path lead?' called Carrie as they jogged along.

'Back to the cliff top, where we were earlier,' Alice huffed. 'Oh God, the cliffs.'

What was he planning? He would be feeling cornered, with no route for escape. Her daughter would be his bargaining chip, or, if he were truly mad and he had nothing to lose and he liked the idea of someone else's fear and suffering… The frightening thought pierced at her along with the vision of Melanie, held hostage above those deadly rocks. One push and it would all be over.

Alice began to sprint, easily passing Carrie and Paul as her fear lent her wings.

*

'What did she say to you?' Gabe asked, his tone just as it always was; conversational, pleasant.

Melanie gasped a breath, heard it rattling in her chest.

'N-n-nothing,' she managed.

They had stopped walking after what felt like day, though in all probability it was only an hour or so since she had been sitting in the cave after discovering the terrible truth. She remembered

Willow, her awful dead eyes, the cool way she had spoken of killing this man, her own fear that Willow would hurt Alice.

Now she saw the girl wouldn't. The girl was after one man, and one man only. And that man was on the run, and Melanie was stuck with him.

She glanced around, realising for the first time they were on the cliff top, the sound of the water slapping on the rocks below.

He sat opposite her, his back to her, trusting her not to move, not to run. Briefly she considered it, after all she knew this island as well as he did, knew where the paths were, the obstacles, the holes which the animals dug to get to their burrows and the traps which she had laid with Harry.

The traps!

Melanie envisaged the last one she had watched Harry make; the steel he had found in a part of the old industrial building, the spring he had fashioned, the jaw trap it had become. She closed her eyes, the scene playing out in her mind, darting along, leading Gabe towards the trap, him lumbering, moving clumsily, not knowing where to step and where to avoid like she did.

She closed her eyes, stared at the back of the man who was not who he seemed.

His colours were those that she'd never seen on him before. Red and silver, edged with black. Excitement, she realised. And another thought struck her; *maybe Willow had the right idea in what she had planned to do to him.*

She stood up, her eyes never leaving him. Was this what he relied on when he preyed on girls? That they would be immobilised by fear? That they wouldn't run or scream or try to escape him?

But you're different, she whispered to herself inside her head. *Everyone's always told you you're different. Use it to your advantage.*

Melanie turned and ran.

35

It wasn't far from the cliff top, a hundred yards or less in the opposite direction from the underpass, but to Melanie it seemed like a marathon. She didn't dare glance behind her, or try to listen for his footfall, sure if she did she would be caught.

Instead she put her head down, pumped her arms and legs, and ran as fast as she possibly could. A flash of white in her peripheral vision, a face, a shape in the long grass. Melanie didn't stop until she was almost at the trap and she leapt, clearing it easily, already imagining him when he followed her and put his foot in those steel jaws.

Ten more feet and she flung herself down to the ground, pushed herself up, enough to be seen, understanding the need to draw him in, knowing she was his bait, sensing now she had stopped running that he was close.

She screamed as she turned, the sight of him, literally on her tail, so close, the tears rising and spilling over that he was faster than she'd realised, that she'd barely had a head start. Did he know the trap was there? Had he seen her leap? Had Harry shown him the steel jaws he'd constructed?

She moaned as Gabe closed in on her, grinning now, his mouth stretched in a smile that was terrible, worse than the mask he'd worn.

Bearing down on her, looking bigger than she'd ever seen him, and Melanie sank back to the ground, not wanting to see when he reached her, not wanting to look at his face, not wanting to see his colours that danced around him, bright red and orange as his excitement grew, like a fire surrounding his body. *He enjoys the chase*, she realised. The danger of her almost-escape had only made it better for him.

She closed her eyes.

A snap, the sound of metal on metal, a thump, a yell that grew into a panicked shout. Silence, and then, another noise, something crashing through the grass, a crack and then… nothing.

*

They heard the scream, all three of them, and while she sensed Alice slow down, Carrie ran faster, not caring when Paul overtook her, silently urging him on towards the sound of the awful cry that had pierced the air.

Carrie chanced a look behind her, saw Alice moving again, gripping her skirts, her mouth moving, soundlessly repeating her daughter's name. Ahead of them, the trail opened up into a field, Paul striking at the long grass, creating a makeshift path which Carrie followed.

The pink blossom stopped suddenly, heaped in a small pile. She caught up with Paul, nudged ahead of him, horrified at what she might see, remnants of clothing, just like before.

She wilted with relief at the sight of Melanie emerging to her right, staggering, legs shaking. Carrie opened her arms, a natural motion, but Alice shoved past her, grabbed at Melanie, sinking to her knees, pulling her daughter with her.

Carrie blinked, lowered her arms, hoped that Paul hadn't noticed. She was the officer here, not the mother, not the comforter. Never had she been those things.

'What have we got?' she asked, treading where Paul had, her words sharper than she had intended.

She saw the foot first, a boot on the end of an outstretched leg. An arm, and then, the man, spread-eagled, face down in the dirt. A chain, rusty brown snaked around his leg. She followed it to see the spiked metal that enclosed his shin. Blood pooled around his head. Next to him crouched Willow, a rock larger than her fist in her hand, the fingers that clutched it white down to the knuckle.

Carrie darted past Paul, skirted around Willow, shooting a look at the girl's expression; stoic, unfeeling, unmoved.

Gabriel Hadley's face was totally concealed, but she noted the movement of his torso, the chest that rose and fell.

'Are you both okay?' she called to Melanie and Willow.

Melanie, her head tucked into her mother's chest, moved her face at the sound of the unknown voice. Her mother murmured to her, and they got unsteadily to their feet. Carrie cast one more glance at Gabe. Satisfied he was out of action for the moment she walked over to Willow.

'Come with me,' she said, but the girl moved sideways, away from Carrie, never taking her eyes off the man on the ground at her feet.

'You left the blossom trail,' Carrie said to Willow. 'That was a really good move. Clever.'

Still no response. Carrie walked smartly over to Alice and Melanie. 'Alice,' she said. 'Can you stay with Willow? I think she needs a familiar face,' she said.

Alice stilled, her hands on her daughter's shoulders, not wanting to leave her, not even if she were going to be within her sight. Carrie understood. 'I'll stay with Melanie,' she said.

Alice swallowed, and with her hand trailing down Melanie's arm, she walked over to Willow.

Carrie watched them go before turning to Melanie. 'Did Willow set up the trap?'

'My dad made it,' said Melanie, and then, 'who're you?'

'I'm Detective Sergeant Carrie Flynn, that's Detective Constable Paul Harper.' She nodded towards Paul, crouched in the grass, checking the pulse of the man whom Melanie had lured into a trap and whom Willow had smashed on the head.

'Are you okay?' she asked anxiously of the girl who stood silently in front of her, never taking her eyes off the people who clustered around the man who had taken her.

Melanie shrugged. 'I'm all right,' she said.

'Come, sit here for a moment. Is it okay if I check you over?' Carrie asked as she drew the girl to sit on a fallen trunk out of the long grass.

She checked Melanie's vitals quickly, satisfied with her pulse, happy there were no injuries that had befallen her. *Not external ones, anyway*, she thought sadly.

'Melanie, that's such a pretty name,' Carrie said, for something to say.

Melanie smiled slightly. 'I'm named after Melanie Hamilton, from the book *Gone with the Wind*.' She paused, narrowed her eyes. 'Do you know the book?'

It was like being punched. Carrie managed not to double up with the physical pain. She forced herself to nod, made her mouth smile in acknowledgement.

Melanie tilted her head to one side, her eyes big and round. 'What's wrong?' she asked.

Carrie cleared her throat, mentally checked herself. She hadn't moved, hadn't changed her position or her expression at all. How did the kid know her reference to that particular book was like being bashed with a metal pipe? Curiosity got the better of her.

'Why do you ask that?'

Melanie dropped her gaze. She scuffed at the dusty ground with her trainers. 'Your colours changed,' she said softly.

'What?' Carrie blinked as the sun came out from behind a cloud. 'What do you mean?'

Melanie was hesitant, and, mindful of her people-skills training, Carrie faced away from her, bent over to tie her lace even though it hadn't come undone.

'I see people's colours, they tell me what the person is feeling, what mood they're in. When I first saw you, when you came into the field, I saw the prettiest colours I'd ever seen, that told me you were a really strong person, and capable, and… just wonderful.' Out of the corner of her eye Carrie saw Melanie's face blush to a deep red.

'Wow, that's… awesome,' said Carrie, at a loss how to actually respond. 'What colours was I?'

'A deep blue, flashes of silver. It was wonderful,' repeated Melanie. She glanced over at Carrie, emboldened suddenly. 'Then I mentioned that book, and my name, and your colours kind of… died.'

Despite the sunshine, Carrie shivered.

For a few moments they sat in silence.

'Do you know the film, too?' Carrie asked eventually.

Melanie nodded solemnly.

'My sister was named Hattie, after the woman who played Mammy in *Gone with the Wind*. She was the first African American to win an Oscar.' Carrie swallowed, realising she had never, ever told the history of her sister's name to anyone before.

'Is your sister black?'

The question, asked in an innocent, straightforward manner that only a child can pull off, brought a genuine smile to Carrie's face. It stayed there, on her lips, for just a moment before fading, apparently just like her colours had.

'She was black, yes.'

Carrie braced herself for more questions from the deliberate past tense use.

Eventually, Melanie said, 'So who were you named after?'

'Carrie Fisher.' Carrie smiled over to Melanie. 'Do you know who she is?'

Melanie nodded, a serious look on her face. 'She died too,' she said.

An unexpected lump in her throat made Carrie cough. 'Yep,' she said. It was all suddenly too much, the indirect talk about Hattie, about Carrie's past, subjects she usually buried deep.

'I always wondered why my parents didn't call me Scarlett, because she was the best, right?' Melanie looked up at Carrie, a frown knitting her forehead. 'Melanie was…' she trailed off before coming back stronger. 'Melanie let everyone walk all over her.'

Carrie detected the undertone in the girl's voice, along with the 'second-best' name her parents had given her.

'Melanie Hamilton was *kind*,' she said. 'She was loyal and very determined. There's a lot to be said for that.'

Melanie tilted her head and looked up at Carrie. Her eyes shone as though she'd never considered that possibility.

Carrie cleared her throat. 'We should get back to the cottages, back to your father, okay?'

Melanie nodded, pushed herself up. 'What about him?' she asked.

Carrie followed her gaze to the form of the man who still lay motionless. 'We'll deal with him,' she said.

Carrie walked towards Paul, and in tune with her as always, he led her a few feet away from the others.

'We need to get them back to Harry and Lenon, and hope to God that Ben has come back with the boat,' she said.

Paul nodded in agreement, jerked a thumb over his shoulder. 'And him?'

Carrie looked around Paul. 'We've got no way of restraining him ourselves. How secure is that trap?'

'Very secure,' replied Paul. 'But his leg could be in a bad way.'

'Did you get a look at it?' she asked, concealing a shudder.

'No, not with them so close.'

'I'll do it,' she said. 'And then we'll get them back to the cottage, I don't want them seeing any more than they have to, don't want those kids any more traumatised than they are already.'

Willow spoke up, her eyes not leaving Gabe as he lay in the grass, until she turned to face Carrie, her eyes flashing suddenly dark. 'I told you I would do this. If you'd have listened, when I first called you…' Her lips pinched together and she glared meaningfully at the blood-spattered rock by her feet.

'It's all right, we're here now, we can deal with this,' Carrie said.

Thank God they had come to the island. She felt a burst of relief mixed with pride. What if she hadn't insisted on tracking the mystery calls? It would have been so easy to dismiss them, to not take it seriously. And if she had shrugged them off, a man would soon be dead, and a girl would be taken through the messy courtrooms with the stigma of murderer attached to her for the rest of her life.

It wasn't too late. She breathed out.

Paul spoke up. 'Everyone needs to go back to the cottage, we'll deal with him,' he nodded to the inert man. 'Ben will come back, and we'll get the river police over.'

Carrie raised her eyebrows at Paul's confidence that their river taxi would return. She wished she shared his optimism. But Paul was right; Ben was their only hope and she needed for the rest of the group to stay together and be ready to board.

She clapped her hands together. 'Guys, start heading back to the cottage, don't separate from each other. We'll soon be home.'

She grimaced, hoped it was true, offered up a prayer to a God she didn't believe in that Ben would return. Next to her, Paul herded the others together, opening his arms wide, looking just the way he did when he was at a crime scene, cordoning it off, keeping everyone in check. When the cluster of people had moved back to stand at the edge of the field Carrie took a deep breath and bent down over the man.

'Mr Hadley?' she said, brisk and business-like. 'Gabe Hadley?'

He moved, slightly, at the sound of his name. Slowly he turned his head to face her. She took in the mess of him first, the smear of blood near his eye, the skin on his temple, grey with a fresh bruise. His forehead, red and white, the skin pink and tender…

Red and white and pink.

She lifted her gaze back to rest on his face. He met her stare head on.

This time she couldn't conceal the feeling of the punch. There was no covering it up. It broke her and she leaned over, one hand on her stomach, the other seeking the ground. Her fingertips grazed the dirt and she sank to her knees.

Look at him, she screamed at herself. *Look at him!*

She swallowed back the bile in her mouth and with great effort she looked up at him again.

'You,' she said, her words ragged and ruined. 'It's you; you're the man who took my sister.'

36

She didn't go far. She'd been running for less than a minute before the guilt set in.

Carrie smacked the heel of her hand against her forehead. What was she thinking? You didn't leave little girls alone in the woods. Carrie hung her head in shame as she turned back. She would collect Hattie, they would go home, and Carrie would take a few quid out of her mother's money jar and they would go to the little shop on the corner and get ice-creams.

Carrie nodded, a smile twitching her lips. Hattie would forgive her then. Hattie would forgive her anyway, without ice-cream, Carrie realised. The thought made her feel even worse, and at that moment she swore that for the rest of her life she would treat Hattie like the princess their mother believed her to be.

'Hat!' she called. 'Come on, we're going home.'

The sun beat down, Carrie stopped. Ahead, a hundred yards away, stood Hattie.

'Hattie!' Carrie laughed, relieved to see her sister. She raised a hand. 'Come on, I'll get you an ice-cream.'

Carrie put her hands in her pocket, walked towards her sister. Stopped again, a frown knitting her brows. Why was Hattie so still and silent? So *not Hattie*.

Carrie's heart beat a little faster. Was Hattie moving further away? And where were Hattie's shorts? Carrie blinked. Kermit the Frog stared out at Carrie from Hattie's shirt, his mouth open, his frog hands on his head, an image which always made Hattie laugh, but to Carrie, suddenly it seemed like a scream. Carrie raised her gaze to her sister's face. Brown skin, shiny, with tears or sweat? There was something else, something... *wrong*.

Her sister's shorts were missing!

Panicked, Carrie broke into a run. A tree root reared up out of nowhere, clawing at Carrie's ankle, bringing her down, her face landing in the undergrowth of leaves, twigs and dirt. Carrie pushed herself up, blinked, her hand going up to her face to scrub the dirt away from her eyes. She blinked again, closed her eyes, opened them.

A man was there now, behind Hattie, one hand on her shoulder, his fingers large and white, digging into her sister's skin, pulling the T-shirt with his grip. Hattie was motionless, the whites of her eyes large, staring, chest heaving, shuddering sobs wracking her small body.

'HATTIE!'

Carrie's feet spun in the dirt, the man's eyes, hooded, lazy and sleepy, widened a little, and a smirk pulled at his mouth. *He's young*, thought Carrie, *not old and creepy like Mr Lacey, not scary like some of the tough, leather-clad kids who hung around the town hall, revving their motorcycles and glaring and spitting at the world.*

This man was just that. A man, who looked decent, young-ish, smartly dressed, *normal. Charming*, her mother would have said.

But he had his hand on her sister's shoulder, and Hattie was missing some of her clothes, and Hattie was frightened and scared and crying and this man was not normal or charming.

A fallen tree blocked her way, and Carrie plunged at it, tried to climb over its enormous girth. Slipping back, she shrieked in pure frustration, slapped at the tree trunk, pushing off it to circle it.

Panting, her breathing sounding like a scream, she shouted for her sister. It came out a whisper.

The man smiled, once, briefly, a genial grin.

Hattie opened her mouth, a silent plea for help.

The world circled Carrie, the sky and the trees spun. Dizzy, she fell to her knees, face down, once again in the now empty woods.

Later, the dog and the police and her mother found her. She thought they woke her, pulled her out of a state of unconsciousness, but it hadn't been a sleep, or a coma or a fugue. It had been everything and nothing, and Hattie was gone, and the memory of a man who looked quite young, and rather charming, and very normal, was gone too.

37

At first, there was a sense of euphoria. *I remember!* Carrie almost crowed at the breakthrough, all these years later.

As soon as the elation arrived it vanished, like smoke, like the mist that hung over the canal back home, dissipating as soon as the sun caught at it.

Agony, as searing as a knife wound. Twenty years had passed, how many other little girls had suffered, had vanished, had lost their lives?

On her hands and knees Carrie shuffled a little further away from him. Not through fear, that was long gone, but if she got too close, she knew she wouldn't be able to stop herself from picking up Willow's rock that nestled in the grass by her feet. She saw herself raising it, bringing it down on his head, his face, the tender, fleshy parts of him.

She blinked, trying for self-control.

'W-what did you do to her?' she uttered the words too soon, covered her mouth with her hands to try and push them back. Did she want to know?

'Willow?' Gabe raised his eyes, heaved a sigh, wincing as he tried to move the leg snared in the trap. 'The girl is very dramatic—'

'NOT HER!' shouted Carrie. She scooted towards him, an inch at a time, animal-like. 'I'm not talking about her,' she added, quieter now.

He frowned, looked closer at her, and she wondered if he remembered her at all, the little blonde girl who left her tiny sister alone to be found by a monster. Had he even looked at Carrie? Had he, for a single second, thought about changing his mind, shoving Hattie aside and taking Carrie instead?

She would have let him, Carrie realised, if it would have saved Hattie's life.

A strange thread held them together. Gabe, staring, wondering, remembering. Carrie unable to break her gaze, thinking about the rock on his skin, using the sharp edge to slice, and the blunt edge to hit.

'Carrie!'

She leapt to the side, toppled, pushed herself unsteadily to her feet.

'Paul,' she said, dully.

She had forgotten about him. Had forgotten about all the others.

'He stays here, right here, just the way he is.' She snapped the words, clicking her fingers, back to who she was; Detective Sergeant Carrie Flynn, little Carrie gone for the moment.

Paul cocked his head to one side. For the first time he touched her, his fingers closing vice-like round her upper arm, pulling her to one side. 'Carrie?' He said her name, a question on his face.

She swallowed, looked back at Gabe Hadley. She said the words in her head, to herself, wondered if she could manage to say them out loud. Decided she could, she *had* to.

'He's the man who took Hattie all those years ago, I remember him. I can see him so clearly. We have to get him into custody, charge him not just with assault or abduction, but with murder.'

She hardly dared to look at Paul, but she forced herself, made herself stare into his deep brown eyes.

His nostrils flared, his mouth a straight line, his jaw clenched. He nodded, just once.

Carrie almost fell against him with thanks for his belief, but instead she pulled herself free of his grasp.

'Take the others back to the cottages, make sure they stay there. Send Harry or Alice to the dock to wait for Ben. Check Liz and the boy, they might need medical help. I'll wait here, I don't want to risk moving him, we'll leave him here until back up arrives.'

Suddenly it was easier to breathe, issuing instruction, doing what she was good at, flipping commands the way she did. She wasn't the victim's sister, she was the police officer, doing the actual job she'd promised. Keeping people safe; catching the bad guy.

Paul glanced once at the trapped man. 'You should take them back, stay with them, I'll wait with—'

'No.' She made herself look at Gabe once more, knowing that although she trusted her partner with her very life, she had to do this. 'No,' she repeated, quieter now, 'I'll stay. You get help.'

*

'Did I hear that correctly?' Alice twisted to face Paul as she stumbled along at his urging, marching back to the cottages now, back to Harry, starting the journey home, back to Ben. Blindly she reached for Melanie, pulled her close to her, the only thing that mattered now. Not Ben, not Harry, just Melanie. Melanie let herself be held in the vice-like grip for a moment before squirming free of her mother's hold.

Detective Constable Harper didn't answer. She pushed on, falling into step beside him. 'He hurt her sister? That policewoman's sister?'

'She's a Detective Sergeant, and… that was private,' replied Paul finally.

'But that woman, that *Detective Sergeant*,' Alice corrected herself, 'said murder. I heard her, she said the word *murder!*'

She stared at him, but he faced resolutely forward, marching along, his face set, his mouth firmly closed.

'I can't believe this,' Alice said, and tears sprang to her eyes. Angrily she dashed them away. 'Why was he free, not already locked up, if his daughter reported this?'

Alice saw Willow, ahead of her, stiffen at her remark. Alice shouted to the girl.

'Willow, what's this all about, did the police ever speak to you after you reported him?'

Willow stopped and turned to face them, stony-eyed. 'No,' she said shortly.

A fury rose in Alice, and she put her hands on her hips. 'Why? How has this been allowed to happen?'

'They don't care!' cried Willow. 'That's why I was taking matters into my own hands. The police don't care.' The young girl staggered before sinking to the ground, as though everything she had carried on her shoulders was suddenly too much.

'That's not true,' said Paul, and for the first time, he looked to Alice like he was out of control. He swallowed, shook his head, crouched down beside Willow. 'When you kept ringing Carrie, she didn't let it go, she insisted we go back over old files. You didn't give us your name yet still she tracked you to the phone box you called from, she wouldn't quit even when it seemed like an impossible task. She believed you, Willow, that's why we're here, because Carrie cares, and I do too. And I'm so sorry you were let down before.'

Alice turned back to Willow. 'Did you know Gabe had hurt that police officer's sister?' Not waiting for a reply, she turned to Paul. 'How long ago did that happen? How old was her sister?'

Paul, cornered, held up his hands. 'A long time ago, twenty years, I think.'

Alice felt her throat constrict, anger flowed through her, filling her body with a white-hot heat. 'He's been doing this for twenty years?' she asked through gritted teeth.

Melanie slipped her hand into Alice's. Alice jumped at the sudden contact.

'Carrie's sister is dead,' she said. At her mother's blank expression Melanie gave an exasperated sigh. 'That lady officer, her name is Carrie, her sister was called Hattie, and she's dead.'

The heat vanished, a chill settling over Alice instead. 'Did *he* kill her sister?'

Paul cleared his throat, glanced behind him at where he'd left Carrie and Gabe. 'It's not my business, but I don't want to leave Carrie too long, and I need to speak with your husband. We're alone here, and we need to stick together and find a way off this island. Please, can we get to your husband?'

Alice spun around, her skirt swishing as she upped her pace. 'Come on, kids,' she said. She stretched out a hand and gently pulled Willow to her feet, keeping her close as they began to walk.

As she walked along, she glowered. What did this police officer expect from Harry? Did he envisage him as some sort of superhero; did he want to recruit him? Did he not remember the way he was before, prone in his chair, dribbling and drooling and tanked up on medication that didn't even belong to him?

'I'm not sure how much help he'll be, but come on,' she said, 'I want to get these kids off this island too.'

*

'Are we actually certain of this?' Harry asked, holding onto Melanie. He would never let her go again.

Alice stepped into his view, her face red and angry, still so angry at him. 'He took Melanie, he forced her to go with him, have you not listened to anything we've told you, Harry?'

He lowered his eyes. *Yes*, he had been listening, but he wanted desperately for it to be untrue. He looked at each of them in turn, at pale, sick Lenon, at Willow, who returned his stare coldly. His angry wife, his hurt daughter.

The policeman in his running gear, official and professional and… haunted.

'But, that's why we came here, so she would be safe, away from all the danger.' His voice broke in a sob and he turned away, the realisation catching up fast now.

By removing Melanie from the city, he had led her here, straight into Gabe's trap. His thoughts tumbled over themselves, bursting free no matter how hard he tried to keep them at bay. *I did this, I took my daughter away from everything she knew for her own safety. Instead I invited a monster to come with us. I pressed him to join us, I* convinced *him to come here.*

Harry stared at what looked like a puddle of vomit near to where Lenon sat with Willow. He looked away, wondering whose it was. Any of them, he guessed. This revelation was enough to make anyone hurl.

He shook his head a little, realising he was suddenly alert, suddenly clear-minded. He bit down hard on his lip, hating himself for thinking only about himself and how he had been feeling when these kids, his own wife and his daughter were facing horrors beyond imagination.

'I'm so sorry,' he gasped at last, shuddering, and covered his mouth with his hand.

'You weren't to know,' Paul said.

Harry hung his head. No, he wasn't to know. Gabe Hadley was clever and skilled and that had been all Harry had needed. But would he have seen something else, had he not been loaded first on the Fluoxetine and then on Liz's damn pills? He shivered. The pills Gabe had been feeding Liz to keep her complicit and unaware.

Another thought hit him, a sudden realisation why everyone was just standing around and *not doing anything.*

'Oh, God,' he said, the blood draining from his face. 'We're trapped, that's why you're all still here, because there's no mobile signal, and we're cut off from the city.' He looked at Paul. 'That's right, isn't it?'

'Yes, we're trapped.' It was Alice who answered, her voice controlled but with an underlying coat of steel. 'You wanted to live without all that, no phones, no internet, no way of getting off this island.' She smiled, but it was bitter and cold. 'You got your wish, Harry. We're stuck here.'

'But we'll get help soon, right?' Melanie stood up, leaned the length of her body against Harry's. 'Ben will be coming back soon. He can take us all home.'

It pained Harry to hear her refer to Manchester as home, even now, after everything that had happened, was still happening. She still thought of the city as home. His great plan had failed. *He* had failed.

He gave her ponytail a gentle tug. 'I don't think Ben will be coming, we haven't made any arrangements.' It was harsh, telling the truth so bluntly, but what other choice did he have? The severity of the situation sat on his chest like a dead weight. He cast his eyes over the others, his cold, livid wife, the sickly Lenon, the stoic Willow, and the police officer who seemed to have stumbled across someone else's living nightmare.

Harry blinked. Detective Sergeant Harper, and another one, also a detective, both of them here. He stood up, keeping his hand on Melanie's shoulder to steady himself. They must have got here somehow, they hadn't swum.

As he rose to his feet, Melanie spoke up.

'Ben's been coming to the island every week,' she said. 'He's been coming to see Mum.'

Harry's first response was to laugh, and it bubbled up, a snort of mirth, and he looked at Alice, ready to share the moment with her, the hilarity that their daughter could get it so wrong. That creative, daydreaming mind of hers that he was so proud of. His laughter faded at the sight of Alice, her cheeks, neck and chest crimson. Not rage this time, but shame.

And the dead weight crashed down again, the realisation heavy, the truth on his wife's face, bare and naked for all to see. Harry lowered himself unsteadily back to the bench.

38

The silence was deafening. Carrie walked backwards and forwards, stopping only to pick up the rock that Willow had smashed his head with, turning it over and over in her hands. In front of her, Gabe watched her.

'Do you remember my sister?'

He regarded her with lazy, hooded eyes.

'Mandale,' he said.

Carrie swallowed back the bile that filled her mouth. It *was* him. It was HIM!

'Where – what did you do with her?' Carrie managed, wishing Paul was here, but knowing if he was, Gabe Hadley might well not talk.

Gabe remained silent, shifting slightly, uncomfortable, clearly in pain with his leg in the steel jaws.

'I could show you,' he said slyly, almost shyly. 'I can draw a map for you, if you like.' He lowered his eyes, and she noticed his lashes were wet. 'I'd do that for you if you take my leg out of this thing. I can't think with it cutting me. I wouldn't do anything.' He drew in a jagged breath. 'I'd–I'd like to try and put some things right.'

'How about you tell me instead?' Carrie said roughly.

His shoulders lifted before falling into a slump. 'I can't explain, not with this on me. The pain…' he said hoarsely. 'I'm sorry.'

Carrie turned her back on him and walked the hundred yards to the edge of the cliff. She stared down at the water. It was still angry, wind-blown. Ben wouldn't be coming any time soon. She passed her hand across her face. Her head, along with all her years of training, told her not to free him, that he was lying, that she needed to wait for Paul, get Gabe back to the mainland and into custody and then try to prise the information out of him.

Her heart fluttered in her chest. It told her to trust him. Her head screamed at her not to be stupid. Her heart beat a gentle rhythm. In her pocket her fingers touched the crumpled paper that Ganju had given her, the point of the stubby pencil she always carried. He could tell her where Hattie was, put an end to the twenty years of suffering that she and her mother had endured. Because the not knowing was the hardest part, and the temptation to believe that Gabe would give her what she needed won out.

With a deep shuddering breath, Carrie turned to face him.

She walked back to him, moving behind him, his eyes following her, his body twisting to watch her. Behind him she spotted a large branch, bleached pale by years of sun, a dirty, bleak brown at the end. She stooped to pick it up.

'I'm going to get this off you, if you try anything…' she trailed off. Words of warning were pointless. He would either do as he had said or he would run, or attack her.

He twisted his head in her direction. 'I want to help,' he said. 'I want to put things right.'

Her breathing was heavy, thick as though she'd run ten miles as she inserted the stick into the heavy jaws of the trap. She leaned on it with all her weight, praying the branch wouldn't snap, praying he wouldn't attack her. Not fear for her own safety, just a blinding anxiety that if he escaped, if he did anything to her, then the truth of Hattie's fate would be forever unknown.

Her face was wet. *Sweat*, she thought, though she knew by her blurry vision it was tears. Tears that fell as her fingers touched the body of the man that had touched her sister. Her sleeve grazed his hand. The hand that had taken her sister's life.

With a final yank she pulled his leg free. He didn't stand, but shuffled round to face her, rubbing at the place the jaws had held him captive. She watched as his fingers came away, red with his own blood.

'Thank you,' he said.

And as he pushed himself to a standing position he smiled. And with that single, charming smile, even before he had turned to run, Carrie knew she should have followed her head instead of her heart.

She reached for the branch as his arm came up, ducked as it arced down towards her, not moving quick enough as the blow landed painfully on her neck, pushing the air from her lungs.

Winded, she scrambled to follow him, pushing off on her hands and knees as he moved towards the cliff edge.

He turned to face her once more and his meaning became suddenly, horribly clear. He was going to jump. She knew she should be thinking of Hattie, and justice for the little girl who never got beyond six years old, but something switched deep inside Carrie.

He shouldn't be the one to choose to end his life. He shouldn't get to make that decision. She barrelled towards him, wanting now for it to be her that made that choice, to knock him over the edge of the cliff, and if he took her with him then so be it.

Because she had left Hattie too, she had let her sister down, and perhaps Carrie needed the punishment just as much as Gabriel Hadley.

She sprang at him, primal, feral, twisting her arms and legs around him, staring through a red haze at his shoulder, animal, as she lowered her face to it and closed her teeth around the pale, bony skin.

*

'Willow, you keep an eye on everyone. DC Harper and I will be back as quickly as we can,' Alice instructed.

Willow nodded, her grey eyes serious as she sat between Harry and Lenon on the bench.

Alice turned away, furious that out of four adults on the island she had to resort to leaving a fifteen-year-old girl in charge. Harry put out his hand, she brushed it away, unable to speak to him, unable to even look at him.

'Come on,' she said to Paul. 'Let's get this over with.'

'Be careful!' Harry called, his words still slightly slurred.

She ignored him. And even as she walked away with Paul she realised she should feel shame, guilt. All she had was distaste for the man she had loved for so long. She had cheated on him, been unfaithful, and still he told her to be careful.

I should hate myself, but it's all aimed at him, she thought, and it was a bitter taste the thought left in her mind.

'How are you holding up?' Paul asked, as they made their way across the field towards the cliff top.

'Okay,' said Alice. She heard the bitterness in her voice, and wondered if she would ever feel anything other than anger again.

'What are you going to do when you get back to Manchester?'

Alice stared down at her feet as she walked. Bare feet, she noticed still. Absolutely filthy now, and there was a good chance her second toe was broken. She pressed her weight on it and felt nothing.

'You sold your house, right? Are you going to be okay renting for a while, the three of you?'

It was a simple question, but it set off little fissures of light in Alice's mind. An epiphany, she thought, and suddenly all the white hot fury melted away. She turned to Paul, offered him a little smile.

'I know exactly what I'm going to do.'

He nodded. 'Good,' he said.

They walked through the underpass in silence, the only sound Paul's trainers creating an echo around the dank, graffitied space.

Alice moved silently, relishing the feel of the damp concrete on the soles of her feet. She looked at the spray-painted art as she passed, allowed herself to smile at the thought that soon she wouldn't have to see this ever again, or face the deadly, unearthly silence of the island any more. Soon there would be sirens, the sound of the bottle banks being emptied at an ungodly hour, the noise of the residents complaining about it.

Her smile faded. All that would be hers if Ben came back for them.

She turned to Paul. 'Hey, Ben's not in trouble is he, for coming here? I mean, you two didn't scare him off, did you? He will come back, right?'

Paul summoned a smile, but to Alice it looked forced. 'We know where he lives,' he joked. 'If he knows what's good for him, he'll come and get us.' He hesitated, words ready on his lips, and she nodded at him to let him know whatever he was going to say was okay. 'He seems to care a great deal for you,' he said. 'I'm sure—'

A yell pierced the air, travelling down the concrete underpass, bouncing off the walls. The echo hadn't even faded and Paul was off, pounding the ground now, leaving Alice in his wake.

Alice paused, let the chill of the inhuman noise pass through her, before picking up her skirt and racing after him.

*

They were on the ground now, Carrie trying to ignore the pain in her cheek from Gabe's blows, her only purpose to keep hold of him, no longer trying to push him, no longer trying to pull him back from the edge. Just holding, just keeping her fingers, arms, legs wrapped around him.

Finally, after a lifetime, she heard pounding feet.

Her body went slack with relief. She knew that sound, she knew those feet.

Paul.

Beneath her Gabe felt her body weaken. He bucked and writhed, shaking her legs loose, and his shirt slipped through her fingers until she was holding onto nothing but air.

She let out a ragged shout of anger, clawed her way after him, seeing the blood that sprang from her ripped nails, ignoring it, calling for Paul to catch him, to get him. And the feet pounded closer, and out of the corner of her eye she saw the billowing sails of Alice's skirt and she lifted her head, tried to find Gabe in her sights, and she saw him for a second, free of her, running loose limbed, arms raised, his body as straight and poised as an arrow as he skidded off the side of the cliff, and then she was looking at nothing but blue sky, an empty space where he had been.

They watched for a while, all three of them, lying on their fronts, peering over the edge.

The current washed over the rocks below, but Carrie knew they were there, deathly, just beneath the surface. There was no sighting of Gabe Hadley's body. Had the current taken him?

'Can you sit up?' Paul asked eventually, and Carrie started at his voice, half-forgetting he was there.

She did as he asked, rolling onto her back, using her elbows to push herself up. The area around her kidney hurt, but she didn't show it. Paul came to crouch beside her. Carrie looked at him, wondered why he was such a strange colour before realising it wasn't him, it was her eye, something on it, or in it. She scrubbed at it and peered at her fingers which came away red.

'Need to clean you up a bit,' said Paul, leaning close, inspecting the cuts and scrapes and bruises.

'Here.' Alice yanked at the seam on her skirt, ripped a length of it, using her teeth to cut away the loose threads and passing it to Paul.

Carrie stiffened as Paul came at her, dipping the material in the rainwater puddles beside them, brushing it gently across her face. But the stiff posture hurt her already beaten joints and muscles, and she forced herself to relax. Alice pulled more ragged strips from her clothes, and moved up to sit beside Paul.

Together they tended her, patched her up, cared for her, and Carrie let them.

*

There was no rush any longer, none of them spoke, until Alice broke the spell.

'Look,' she said, her voice a whisper, as though if she spoke any louder she might frighten whatever it was away.

Carrie twisted her body around to stare in the direction Alice was pointing. It hurt too much, and she gave up, leaned back on the rocky boulder against which Paul had propped her while he soaked her cuts. She looked at Paul, and he nodded, put down the last piece of cloth and stood up.

Carrie waited, closing her eyes against the bright sunshine. She tilted her head back, welcoming the warmth on her face. When she opened her eyes again Paul was close to her, putting his hands underneath her arms, heaving her to stand upright.

'Ben's here,' he said, and the relief was evident in his voice. 'Ben has come back for us.'

EPILOGUE

Six Weeks Later

Carrie raised her hand and knocked sharply on the door. She looked around while she waited for someone to answer it, appraising the area.

It was nice, not flashy or showy, just a standard but spacious terraced house, with views over the Heaton Park Reservoir. Peaceful, Carrie noticed, but residential at the same time.

The sound of multiple locks scraped on the other side of the door and Carrie turned, expectant. Finally, the door opened. Carrie smiled.

'Hi, Melanie, how are you doing?'

Melanie grinned, opened her arms and ran at Carrie. Carrie let out an *oomph* of surprise, her hands hovering in mid-air before settling on the young girl's back.

'Melanie, let the detective in!' Alice appeared behind her daughter, a loaf of bread in one hand, the other resting on the door frame. She gave a little wave. 'Come in!' she said.

Carrie allowed herself to be led over the threshold, Melanie's hand pulling her along. Alice came down the hall.

'Mel, get your shoes on, nearly time to go.' She regarded Carrie, head tilted to one side. 'Come in, excuse the mess, it's a madhouse in the mornings.'

Carrie blinked at Alice's choice of words. *Madhouse*. But it had been said so easily, so breezy, that Carrie smiled and nodded and followed Alice into the kitchen.

Carrie stood in the doorway, looked around, impressed by the interior. Open-plan kitchen diner, the counters covered in juice cartons, milk, and now the bread that Alice had been holding which she tossed onto a board at the side of the sink. At the breakfast bar sat Lenon, his head bent over his phone, right hand clicking and swiping the screen, his left hand moving spoonfuls of cereal to his mouth. He glanced up; a smile as he recognised the visitor.

'Hello,' he said.

Carrie grinned back at him, in awe at the change in the boy. No longer was he reed-thin, he was thicker, fleshier, his skin had tanned as the summer went on. He looked… normal, probably for the first time since Gabe Hadley had entered his life.

'Uh, Lenon.' Alice raised her eyebrows, tapped at her watch.

He flashed her a grin, pushed the empty bowl and spoon over to her, dragged the back of his hand across his mouth and climbed down from the stool.

'See you later,' he said, and moments afterwards his feet pounded up the stairs.

Carrie sat in Lenon's chair, wincing slightly as she hoisted herself up.

'You feeling better?' asked Alice.

'Getting there,' said Carrie, reminded of her fractured cheek bone every time she smiled, which, she realised soberly, wasn't that often.

Alice held up the coffee percolator, a silent question, and Carrie accepted gratefully. Coffee poured, Alice gestured to the dining table and Carrie followed her over. Alice sat down, beaming, and Carrie raised her eyebrows questioningly.

'What?' she asked.

Alice leaned across the table and gripped Carrie's hand. 'I got special guardianship of them, I just heard yesterday,' she said. 'Hopefully in a few months it will become permanent.'

Carrie sighed, it was impossible not to match Alice's own smile, no matter how much it hurt her fractured cheek. She squeezed Alice's fingers.

'I'm so glad,' she said. 'I can't think of anyone better.'

Memories, clearer these days, and a specific one caught at Carrie. Karen, her old next-door neighbour, her confession to Carrie that she'd asked to foster her. The kindness of strangers, she realised now, outnumbered those awful crimes. They were there, if you looked hard enough, people like Karen, people like Alice, who instead of concentrating on herself and her own recovery from a horrific ordeal, had taken on two more teenage children, and built a home for them. More than a home; a place of safety, of warmth, of love. A sanctuary.

'You're amazing,' said Carrie, and she meant her words.

The woman whom she had met on the island, seemingly self-involved, aloof, panicky, had vanished. A mother was in her place.

'Ha, not sure about that.' Alice withdrew her hand, topped up both their coffee cups. 'I was never maternal, not really. It came so naturally to Harry, caring for someone, looking after their every need.' She sighed, a deep breath that came from her very core. 'But this, with the three of them, it just feels… right. It feels like this is the way it should be.'

'And Harry?' Carrie asked, now that Alice had mentioned him.

Alice shrugged, and for a moment her eyes dulled. 'He's working on himself, he's in an apartment in Pendleton. Melanie sees him a lot, but I always see him before I leave her with him, make sure he's not had a setback.' She raised her eyes to Carrie, defiance evident in them now. 'But I don't look after him, I'm not looking after him.'

At that moment Lenon and Melanie came through to the kitchen. Alice blinked Harry away and stood up. Reaching over the counter, she handed them a package each.

'Sandwiches. Melanie, eat the crusts. Lenon, make sure she gets to school, and I mean in school, not just the gates, okay?'

He nodded dutifully, raised a hand in a farewell wave at Carrie. Melanie wrapped her arms around Alice, kissed her cheek, and hurried to the front door to catch up with Lenon.

'And be back straight after school,' Alice called as the front door opened. 'Ben's taking us out for an early dinner, so no dawdling.'

The children called a reply, and Carrie smiled as the door closed on their voices.

'Ben,' she said, eyebrows raised.

Alice shrugged, began mopping up the table even though there were no crumbs or spills that Carrie could see. 'He's good with them, I like his company. It's good for Lenon to spend time with a man who treats women *normally*.' Alice stilled. 'Did they find him yet?' she asked, quietly.

There was no need to ask who *him* was. Gabe Hadley. Or rather, his body.

She shook her head.

'He won't come here, he won't come near us,' said Alice, though to Carrie her confidence seemed like a front.

Carrie nodded in agreement, but even as she did so, she thought of the multiple locks on the door of this house.

'He's not alive,' she said. 'That fall, that distance, the rocks and the current. He's not alive.'

She told herself this every day, though a part of her wished dearly she could have saved him. He was the only person in the world who had information on Hattie, on her resting place. For Alice's sake, and Willow and Lenon and all the girls before and all the ones that would have been she was grateful he had gone.

And he had gone, it was near on impossible to survive that fall. Gabe was dead.

A shiver ran through her. He *had* to be dead.

She opened her mouth to speak some more, closed it as soft footsteps sounded above their heads.

'You're here for her?' Alice asked, resuming her cleaning.

'Yeah, if that's okay?' Carrie said, pushing herself up from the chair.

'Of course, it's good for her.' Alice let out a little laugh. 'I think it's good for you, too.'

Carrie bobbed her head. 'Maybe,' she said.

Just then, Willow walked in to the kitchen, not so much a walk, as a ghostly, silent movement. Carrie swallowed and forced a smile. She wasn't as far along the healing process as her brother, that would take time, a long time. Carrie rubbed uneasily at her chest. It had taken her, Carrie, twenty long years, and she was only just starting the road to recovery.

'Morning, Willow. Are you ready?' said Carrie.

Willow nodded, offered her a tight-lipped smile.

'You'll drop her at school after?' Alice asked. 'Her first lesson is at ten.'

Carrie nodded. 'No problem,' she said. 'I'll see you soon, Alice.'

*

Melanie, halfway down the road with Lenon, looked back towards her house as the door closed. She watched as the two figures walked down the driveway to Carrie's car. Carrie's original colours were back, that lovely blue, with the healing strips of silver. Melanie looked at Willow, at her dull colours, more often than not grey, like old dishwater. Sometimes, like now, there would be a flash of pink, a rosy glow. Melanie nodded to herself before turning to catch up with Lenon.

The pink would continue to grow and spread throughout Willow, Melanie was sure. One day, all that grey would be nudged out, and Willow would be happy again.

'I'll meet you after, at the gates and we'll wait for Willow too, okay?' Lenon asked, anxiety in his voice, eagerness to take care of her and his sister, trying to prove himself now he was man of the house.

Melanie didn't mind. She nodded, smiled openly at him.

His school was next to hers, and in September she would be in the same building as him. They would walk to school, all three of them together, and Melanie actually looked forward to it, to walking through those gates and down the corridors alongside Lenon and Willow. She thought of Tanisha and Kelly, how they had been the first day she had gone back to school, the twins bidding her goodbye at the school gates. Tanisha's eyes, round with surprise, Kelly impressed.

They fawned over her now, because she had an honorary brother and sister who were cooler than Tanisha and Kelly would ever be. In return Melanie was polite to them, but she no longer chased after them or their company. She had no need to now.

*

Willow was silent on the drive back to the city. Carrie didn't mind, she enjoyed spending time with a person who only talked when she had something to say. Carrie glanced sideways at the young girl, wondering not for the first time exactly what Gabe had done to her.

Nothing physical, Willow had admitted to the specialist officers who had interviewed her upon her return from the island. Not to her; but he had hinted over the years, whispered to Willow what he had done to other girls, so she was in no doubt of his plans for her.

'But he never did anything.' Carrie remembered Willow's voice on the tape, confused, troubled, worried. 'I waited every night for him to make a move, and he never did.'

It was all part of his game, the professionals had said. It was enough for him to know the impact his not-so-subtle threats had on his stepdaughter. It was the anticipation, the waiting. The knowledge that he had to be clever and cunning was almost as much of a rush for Gabe as the actual act. Just like the mask he sometimes wore in front of her; it was all part of the game.

Kelly Prout had been questioned further, and away from the watchful gaze of her mother they had come someway to understanding what had really happened in the house of horrors that day.

He had sensed an opportunity, a chance to do whatever he wanted with the freedom he desired. A girl who had suddenly appeared in a home that wasn't his, providing him with just a minimal risk of exposure. He hadn't realised Kelly wasn't alone. Hadn't counted on the young girl who would gamble with her own safety to save a friend.

And Kelly, Melanie and Willow had come out of their encounter with Gabriel Hadley unscathed. Melanie had managed to escape twice.

Hattie had been the unlucky one.

After twenty minutes, Carrie pulled off the road into a large, looping driveway. She eased the car into her usual parking space and switched off the engine.

'All right?' she said.

Willow nodded.

'Come on then.'

Together they walked up to the main house, had almost reached it when Willow stopped.

'How long have you been coming here?'

'Eighteen years,' replied Carrie.

She watched the girl's face, making no further comment, offering nothing. Instead she looked at the building that housed her mother. The same building that was now home to Willow's mum too. She imagined what the girl was thinking, wondering whether she could cope with coming here for the next twenty years. Substance-induced dementia. That was what they'd diagnosed Liz Hadley with. And Gabe had been feeding Liz the meds for so long, in such a dosage, who knew if she would ever get back to the woman she once was?

Carrie felt a flare of fury at the man. Thank God Lenon's poisoning had been so slight, and so infrequent, he'd recovered fully.

In the reception area they parted, Carrie walking down the corridor towards her mother's room, Willow heading left.

'Meet you here in an hour,' Carrie called.

Willow turned. A real smile aimed at Carrie, and one that changed the young woman's face altogether. Carrie smiled back, watched Willow as she loped off.

'You'll be fine,' Carrie whispered.

Two hours later, with Willow dutifully dropped off at the school, Carrie checked her phone. A text from Paul.

I'm here, they're ready to start.

Carrie shivered despite the warm summer day. Putting the car into gear she sped down the A58 towards Rochdale.

He was waiting for her at the entrance, a serious look on his face as he raised a hand in greeting.

'How're the kids doing?' he asked. 'They all getting on all right?'

She nodded. 'Really well. Lenon looks great, Willow is more fragile, but she's got a good home with Alice and Melanie.' She nodded, thinking back to her brief visit. 'I really think they'll be okay.'

'Good,' he said. His voice was heavy with relief, and she knew he felt the same sense of having let Willow down as she did. She thought back to their return to the city, once everyone was safe and medically cared for. The only question left on everyone's lips was why no action had been taken in response to Willow beforehand.

'You were right, it was Willow calling all along, and it was Willow who reported Gabe to the police two years ago,' he'd announced grimly.

She was still in the hospital, and she recalled glaring at him, as though it were his fault. 'What happened when we followed up on Willow's initial accusation?'

Paul had taken a deep breath. 'They sent out a couple of uniforms to interview him, but they sent them to a man called Gabriel Hanshaw.' Paul had slapped his hand on a file. 'The uniforms were sent to the wrong address, the wrong man.'

'Shit,' hissed Carrie, and inexplicable tears sprang to her eyes. She clenched her fists as she sank back against her pillows. '*Shit!*'

'Take it easy,' murmured Paul.

Take it easy. Carrie's nostrils flared. This was exactly the reason she had joined the police force, after what had happened to her, after she and her mother had fallen through the official cracks, she had vowed that it wouldn't happen to any other child. Not only had it happened to someone else, it had been on Carrie's watch, in her own police station.

'It wasn't too late,' Paul said now, mildly, as though he knew what she were thinking.

'This time,' she retorted. She softened, it wasn't Paul's fault, not hers, not really. It was better to see it as a lesson, one to learn from in the future.

'And you,' he said as they began to walk, 'how're you doing?'

It was on the tip of her tongue to reassure him that she was fine, prepared for whatever might come, that she was okay and she was strong. But he had been a good friend, a good listening ear – when she let him – and she owed him the truth.

'I'm not sure. Some days I think I'm ready, some days I wonder if it's better not to know.' She cast her gaze around

Mandale Park as they strode through the entrance. 'But it's too late to back out now.'

She thought back to six weeks ago, as she lay in the hospital, the Detective Chief Superintendent by her hospital bed, Carrie lowering her face, not wanting him to see her fractured cheek, the black eye, the cut to her brow. Ashamed that she had failed in her role, that she had willingly released a dangerous man, let him getaway.

There would be no consequence for Carrie, not in the way of verbal or written warnings, though it was clear those higher up had disapproved of her actions. But in any case, Carrie didn't care about reprimands from work; she would punish herself more than they ever could.

'He said she was in the park, somewhere in the park, he was going to draw me a map, he said it was too hard to explain.' The words, Gabe's words, tumbled from her lips, tripping over themselves in her need to be heard. She swallowed hard past the lump in her throat. 'She never had a funeral, or a resting place, it's, it's…'

He had patted her hand. A fatherly gesture. 'It's important to you, I understand,' he replied. 'But you know he may not have been speaking the truth. People like that, they enjoy playing with people's minds, it's part of their sickness.'

She nodded mutely. Knowing what she was asking of him, knowing the funding and the red tape and the bureaucracy that went with this sort of request.

He patted her hand again, nodded at Paul on his way out.

Three weeks later the call came through. Plans had been made to dig up Mandale Park.

Now, it was happening. Police tape cut the park in half, the east section being prepared first. It was a big job, diggers, forensics, dogs. The diggers couldn't work as though they were simply laying gas pipes. They had to be careful, gentle, and the park was closed to the public for as long as it took.

'I can't believe the Chief Super arranged this,' she said, staring around in awe. 'I can't believe this is actually happening.'

Paul gave her shoulder a friendly punch. 'What you did on the island, risking yourself to save the others, the kids, all that work in tracking them down.' He stopped, looked around and shook his head. 'You earned this, *you* did this.'

The police tape flapped in the slight breeze. Carrie moved a step closer to Paul, nudged him with her arm.

'*We* did this,' she said, softly. 'I couldn't have done any of it without you.'

The first machine rumbled into life, the mechanical shovel raised high in the air. As it came down to tear through the first piece of earth Carrie closed her eyes.

The weight, the heavy, crushing burden of failure which she had carried through childhood, adolescence and through all of her career was still there. It would always be there.

But maybe, she thought, just maybe, as time went on, she could try to forgive herself a little.

AUTHOR'S NOTE

It may surprise some readers when I say the setting for this novel – Pomona Island – actually exists in real life.

A narrow strip of land nestled between Salford and Trafford, Pomona has a rich and exciting history. During the Industrial Revolution, Pomona Island was home to the Royal Pomona Palace, a venue bigger than the Albert Hall, with a capacity to hold 30,000 people. Sadly the palace was damaged beyond repair in 1887, as a consequence of an explosion in a nearby chemical factory. Originally known as Cornbrook Strawberry Gardens, in the 1800s it also housed an impressive Botanical Garden. The island was renamed Pomona after the Roman Goddess of fruit.

In 1974, a nightclub was opened on Pomona, aboard a decommissioned passenger ferry, brought up from the Isle of Wight and moored dockside. It proved so popular the owners brought in an old RAF aircraft to act as an overflow restaurant and dance floor. As part of the network of Manchester canals, it has also been a thriving dockland site.

I have used creative licence with the Pomona in my book. In *The Quiet Girls*, access to Pomona is near impossible; the only way of getting on the island is by an experienced boatman, battling against the currents. In real life, there is a footbridge from Pomona Tram Stop, and by Cornbrook Tram Stop you can go through a gap in a fence to access the island. Pomona is also not set as far back from the bright lights of Manchester city as this book leads you to believe.

Today, the real Pomona is a wasteland of flora, fauna and concrete. The bridges and brick walls are a canvas for street artists. It is the shadow of industry, overtaken by nature and wilderness. Used needles and discarded sleeping bags lie side by side with the various species of wildlife, such as the Brimstone butterfly, kestrels, lapwing, skylark. Fifty pairs of sand martins have been recorded, nesting in the dock walls; pochard ducks are listed, a species now on the globally vulnerable list. Ospreys, sparrowhawks, indeed over one hundred separate birds make their home here, and over one hundred and fifty types of plant life have also been recorded.

Proposals for several hundred new flats to be built on Pomona Island have been approved, construction has started. Soon, this hidden gem, this little oasis in the midst of urban city life will be gone, replaced by nineteen-storey high-rises, retail, leisure and commercials units, and Pomona will be no more.

Manchester Waters – Pomona's new name – will be there instead. But the history, the stories, the graffiti and the photographs will remain, as will my own version of Pomona, within the pages in this book.

A LETTER FROM
J.M. HEWITT

I want to say a huge thank you for choosing to read *The Quiet Girls*. While writing this book, I became very interested in the increasingly popular survivalist lifestyle. People around the world are planning for the apocalypse, for war, or simply wanting to go off-grid. It intrigues me greatly, as does choosing to live in a self-sufficient manner. As most novels usually are, this one was born from a question; what would it take for you to give up everything and live off the land? For Harry, it was his beloved daughter, Melanie, and the narrow escape she experienced with the near-abduction. He figured if they lived a solitary life this wouldn't be an issue. Little did he realise that he was only propelling her straight into an even more intense danger.

If you did enjoy it, and want to keep up to date with all my latest releases, just sign up at the following link. Your email address will never be shared and you can unsubscribe at any time.

www.bookouture.com/jm-hewitt

I hope you enjoyed *The Quiet Girls* and if you did I would be very grateful if you could write a review. I'd love to hear what you think, and it makes such a difference helping new readers to discover one of my books for the first time.

I love hearing from my readers – you can get in touch on my Facebook page, through Twitter, Goodreads or my website.

Thanks,
J.M. Hewitt

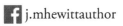 j.mhewittauthor

@jmhewitt

www.jmhewitt.com

ACKNOWLEDGEMENTS

Writing a novel is a team effort, and I've most certainly got a great team with me. Huge thanks as always to Maisie, my fantastic editor, without whom this book wouldn't be in half the shape that it is. Also thanks to Noelle Holten and Kim Nash who work so hard on publicising the brilliant novels that Bookouture put out there. The whole Bookouture team are an absolute joy and I'm so grateful to be a part of it.

My agent, Laetitia, of Watson Little, who works tirelessly alongside me and is always there at the end of the phone or email. Your advice and knowledge are amazing, I count my lucky stars constantly to be a part of your fantastic collection of authors.

My girls; Vic, Lou, Lisa, Kim, Heidi, Ruth, Susi, Jane, Vicky – I'm so lucky to have a friendship circle made up of such strong, brilliant, resilient women.

My family; my parents, Janet and Keith and my brother, Darren. Jordan, Eloise, Emily and little Dawson – you're all fabulously supportive and I'm eternally thankful to be one of the 'Hewitt' clan! And my little Marley, my constant friend and writing companion.

Thank you to Professor Stuart J. Marsden of Manchester Metropolitan University for his valuable information on the wildlife on Pomona Island.

The crime fiction community; the writers and the bloggers and the publishers –is such a wonderful place to be and I may not see you all the time but when we do meet up it's simply fabulous.

Finally, a huge thank you to the readers, it's thrilling that you enjoy my books. As long as you keep reading, I'll keep writing!

Printed in Great
Britain
by Amazon